INTO THE CRONESPHERE

TIMOTHY LACHIN

Venom Milk Press, Paris, France
Published in the USA
Fourth printing

Printed in 11-point Georgia
ISBN: 978-0-9895074-0-0

For Adam Wesley Outlaw

PART ONE: THE BOOT

"Or, in order that there may yet be something in the void – which, though it first came about as devoid of objective Things must, however, as empty in itself, be taken as also void of all spiritual relationships and distinctions of consciousness qua consciousness – in order, then, that in this complete void, which is even called the holy of holies, there may yet be something, we must fill it up with reveries, appearances, produced by consciousness itself. It would have to be content with being treated so badly for it would not deserve anything better, since even reveries are better than its own emptiness."

G.W.F. Hegel

1

Trey was a wigger and a baller. He lived in Lacombe, Louisiana, a sleepy ghetto community outside of New Orleans. Although Trey owned a Glock, he had never split anyone's wig with it. He'd bought his Glock from a black named Pee-Wee for a hundred dollars. On his way home from Pee-Wee's trailer, Trey saw a white dog on the side of the road. The dog was eating feces. Trey stopped the car and split the dog's wig. That was the first and last time he had fired his Glock.

Trey always wore the same thing: a backwards LSU baseball cap, knee-length Tommy Hilfiger jean shorts and an oversized striped Polo shirt with a white Hanes undershirt underneath. He had thick country wrists and a muscular neck. His hair was blond and shaved. Both of his eyebrows were notched. Girls told Trey that he looked like Brad Pitt. Trey thought Brad Pitt was a homo. He lived in a trailer and sold drugs.

Trey owned a purple 1999 Ford Taurus with tinted windows, chrome Sprewells, and 15's in the trunk. At home he sat on white leather. When the weather was fine, he drove his Taurus to Lake Road and went crabbing. He used raw chicken as bait.

Trey was a dogman. His Pits never failed to scratch. When Trey scrapped, he channeled the gameness of the Pit.

Rhonda Jefferson parked her rust-pocked 1984 Chevrolet Celebrity next to the purple Taurus, turned off the engine, and lit a Kool cigarette. Her oldest daughter Shemeta silently ate a Big Mac in the passenger seat. Rhonda was a user. Her coarse, cruel, ugly features could have appeared as an illustration of degenerescence in a nineteenth-century medical textbook on eugenics or phrenology. Her pinprick eyes looked both calculating and barren of intelligence. Although only twenty-six, she had four illegitimate children already. Rhonda liked watching

TV, taking X pills, smoking that Oscar the Grouch green, eating Big Macs from McDonald's, and getting freaky. She especially liked it when the man had a big D and hit it from the back.

She wore a pair of small hot pink shorts that had cost ninety-nine cents at Family Dollar and an oversized airbrushed T-shirt bearing a silkscreened photograph of a smiling black man in a prison uniform with the caption “Free My Husband – Free Danky”. Her daughter wore a dirty striped tank top with no bra. Rhonda had never bothered getting her one. The puffy black circles of her nipples could be discerned through the thin fabric of the tank top. Big Mac Sauce had dripped on her breasts and her hair was tied into braids with plastic colored ball twisties.

The battery of tests administered to Shemeta in the fourth grade after her first seizure revealed her to have an IQ of 76. Every few months she collapsed on the floor in spasms and urinated on herself. The doctor gave her a prescription for epilepsy medicine. Rhonda gobbled a handful of Shemeta’s Gabapentin pills on the way home from Walgreen’s to see if they would get her high. When nothing happened, she discarded them on the floor. A few weeks later, blackout drunk, she found the bottle under the sofa and swallowed the rest of the yellow pills hoping they were Xanax. She never bothered refilling her daughter’s prescription after that.

Shemeta’s body was half girl and half woman. Although her buttocks and breasts already projected like bookshelves, her hips had yet to spread. From the side she resembled a mature Hottentot Venus and from the front, a disturbed preadolescent. Her thin legs were long for her compressed torso and they came together too close to each other at the pelvis. The layer of baby fat around her stomach accentuated the ghetto lordosis she had inherited from her mother.

Shemeta liked listening to the radio. Her favorite musician was R. Kelly. When a song that Shemeta liked came on, she would jump up with her trademark big smile, put her hands against the wall or a railing, and bounce her hindquarters up and down. This dance was called *pussy popping,* or P-popping for short. Shemeta's mother had taught her how to P-pop.

"Finish your Big Mac...why you eat so slow," said Rhonda to Shemeta in an annoyed voice. Shemeta moved her eyes to meet her mother's without moving her head or taking the Big Mac away from her mouth. She looked like a squirrel nibbling a motherfucking nut. Rhonda hated the stupid way Shemeta had of staring at her all the time. Shemeta shifted her gaze back to her Big Mac and crammed the rest of it into her mouth with her hands. Rhonda smacked her.

"You stay right here in this motherfucking car til I get back, ya heard me?"

The doorbell rang. Trey took a last hit from his blunt and pulled the fitted yellow LSU baseball cap down tight across his eyebrows. Time to grind. He opened the door. Rhonda grunted and pushed in without looking at him. Trey snorted. Already he wanted to pop a cap in her monkey ass. All fiends were animals, but Rhonda had a special gift for making his blood boil. He had been her pill man ever since setting up shop on the low in Lacombe two months earlier.

"Stay here," he said. He went into his bedroom and unscrewed one of the air vents on the trailer's floor. This was his stash spot. He took out a Skittles bag and with a steady hand shook five Oxycontins into a plastic baggie. He rolled the rest of his stash up, put it back in the air vent, and screwed the cover back on. His gestures were methodical and professional.

When he came back out, Rhonda was standing with her arms crossed and her eyes glued to the Maury Povich program on his flat-screen plasma TV. The remote control dangled from her hand. Trey couldn't believe the cheek on this clucker. She turned to him.

"You got them 20's for me, white boy?"

"You know I need my money first, baby." Trey's voice was smooth and silky.

"Man, fuck you, I got money, nigga." She reached into her bra and tossed a wad of crumpled bills onto the coffee table.

Trey counted the money. One of the wrinkled ones had *Happy Birthday Shamita!!!* written on it.

"Even with your little girl's birthday money you only got seventy-one dollars here. You missing twenty-nine dollars. You ain't even got enough for four."

"What you mean? The money all there, nigga...count it again."

Trey sighed. Always the same bullshit. Triflers all day. He took out the baggie and removed two of the five pills. Rhonda's eyes bugged out.

"You know I'ma get my check from them people," she said in a wheedling voice. Her eyes stayed glued to the Oxy's. "You know I'ma come over here when I get my money."

Trey smiled. His baby blues went down to Rhonda's chunky, mottled thighs. Trey was high and Trey was horny.

"Come here." He rolled over to his couch, sprawled back, and unbuttoned his shorts. "Let me think about it." Rhonda dropped to her knees, unzipped Trey's Hilfigers, and commenced sucking.

"Yeah, suck it, ho," said Trey, half to himself. Her head bobbed up and down on his dick like a bird pecking bread. With no warning she deep throated him. Trey still couldn't believe Rhonda could take the whole thing. Most bitches couldn't even get half of it down. She came up gagging.

"Donkey dick motherfucker..." She slapped it against her face, spat on it, and gulped it down a second time. Trey groaned. His eyes went to the television. Rhonda was slurping so loud he couldn't hear what Maury Povich was saying. With his free hand he picked up the remote and turned the volume up. There was a teenage girl on Maury's sofa telling her fat mother that she was a slut and proud of it. She claimed that she had already slept with over a hundred men at the age of sixteen. She was wearing a tube top and looked like a chubbier Britney Spears. Trey wondered how hard it would be to turn the teenage slut out. There were a lot of stacks to be mined from that ass. He closed his eyes and imagined that the teenage slut was sucking his dick and not Rhonda.

"Yeah, bitch, there it is." He grabbed Rhonda's cheap weave, pushed her head down, and exploded into her esophagus. She swallowed his load without flinching and came up with a nasty smile.

"That all you got for me, baby?" She turned around to see the TV.

"Fuck, you got a fucking mouth on you!" Trey rolled his head from side to side to stretch his neck muscles.

"That's the best brain in the *boot* right there, motherfucker."

Trey pulled his shorts back up and reached into his pocket. He put only one of the two pills back into the baggie. Rhonda's bloodshot eyes flared in anger.

"What the fuck, nigga! Gimme my fucking pills...fuck you, nigga!"

If Trey had been in a bad mood, he would have punched Rhonda in the nose, but he was high as a motherfucker and feeling right, so he picked up the half-finished blunt from the ashtray, hit it, and held it out to her.

"Yeah, you better gimme some, motherfucker." She glared at him as she sucked the dank into her lungs.

"We ain't done yet. Take off those shorts."

"Man, fuck you. You too fucking horny, cracka." She turned around and pulled them off. Her ass rippled when he slapped it.

"Wobble it for me."

Rhonda leaned forward and put her palms on the floor. Trey sprawled back and watched her splotchy ass roll back and forth. He imagined that it was made of Gyro meat. The way it moved was fascinating.

Rhonda's voice snapped him out of his dolja trance.

"Nigga, you gonna fuck this pussy, or you gonna take a motherfucking nap?"

Trey got up and slid his jimmy into the pink spot in the middle of her wet, hairy, purple-black pussy. He wouldn't have admitted it to his homies, but he loved nasty, gamy, gutter pussy like Rhonda's.

"You like that chocolate pussy, huh white boy?" teased Rhonda, pulling forward before sliding back towards him hard. "All *day*...them white girls don't know how to fuck...don't know how dirty you white boys really be...ain't that right, pinky?"

Trey looked over at the TV. There was a Morris Bart commercial on. Morris Bart was a personal injury lawyer in New Orleans. He made a serious face and pointed at the camera. "Before you take a quick check...check with me!". Trey laughed. Morris Bart had a neck like a chicken and a voice like a faggot. Trey was fucking high. He thrusted with renewed vigor.

"Shit...oh shit...fuck!" gasped Rhonda when he pushed in to the hilt.

Trey groaned and blasted a nut into her.

Rhonda pulled her shorts back up with a twist of her hips, took out another Kool, and lit it.

"Now give me my fucking pills...motherfucker...and give a bitch some lagniappe while you at it, ya heard me?"

Trey put the fifth pill in the baggie and held it out for her.

"Here you go, ma'am. Enjoy yourself."

"Fuck you." Rhonda swiped for the baggie. Trey pulled it back again with a stupid grin.

"Man, fuck you, nigga, what the fuck!" exclaimed Rhonda. Her face twisted into a mask of rage. "Give me my fucking pills, motherfucker!" Trey laughed and tossed them at her. They hit her saggy breasts and fell to the floor. She snatched them up and gobbled two right away.

"Now give me a kiss, sweetheart," he said, puckering up like in a cartoon.

"Fuck you...you fucking crazy, motherfucker." Rhonda was all smiles now that she had her pills. "I ain't giving you no motherfucking kiss."

A sound outside caused Trey's ears to prick up. Someone was running towards the trailer.

Had the Cutt Boyz found him in Lacombe already?

He dropped to the ground, pulled the Glock from his pants and leveled it at the door just in time to see Shemeta barrel in.

"Momma! Momma!"

She stopped dead in her tracks when she saw the Glock.

Trey shoved his gun back in his pants and sent Rhonda sprawling to the floor with an open palm slap from one of his thick hands.

"Fucking whore! Fuck!" he shouted. "No one ever opens my fucking door except me! You got that?" He lifted up his leg to stomp her in the head, then stopped himself. An old prison reflex. In any case, his attention was already elsewhere. Shemeta's tits had just about doubled in size since the last time he had seen her. Girl was looking tight.

Rhonda jumped to her feet and began pummeling Shemeta with the heel of her hand.

"I told you to stay in the motherfucking car...you so stupid...stupid lil' bitch...look what you done did!" Shemeta balled up to protect herself from the rain of blows. One of her thumbs went to her mouth.

"I had to pee, momma! I tried to hold it in but I couldn't!"

Rhonda punched her in the neck. Trey bear hugged her from behind.

"You done made your point...now lay the fuck off."

"Nigga, fuck you laying hands on me! Who the fuck you think you is? Let me go, motherfucker!" She struggled without real conviction. Trey turned to Shemeta. She continued to suck her thumb in the fetal position.

"Get up," said Trey. "The bathroom's down the hall." Shemeta looked at Trey. Her eyes were round with fright.

"You said you had to fucking pee...well fucking go!" Trey barked. Shemeta bolted to the bathroom. Trey pushed Rhonda onto the sofa.

"Cute kid."

"Yeah?"

"Maybe you could leave us alone for a little while."

She crossed her arms. The corner of her mouth turned up into a knowing smirk.

"Gimme five more."

"Wait here." Trey went back into his bedroom and got four more pills from his stash. He would have given Rhonda as many as ten OxyContins for a crack at Shemeta, but he refused on principle to let a clucker dictate the terms of the bargain. He walked back out. Shemeta had returned from the bathroom and was looking at him. *Damn*, he thought, *look at those fucking tits!* The nipples pointed straight up, in contrast to Rhonda's nasty, saggy titties that felt like zip-loc bags full of watery oatmeal. Trey tossed the baggie with the four pills at Rhonda.

"Get the fuck out of here."

"Nigga, I said five!"

Trey opened the door. Rhonda gave him an icy glare and turned to Shemeta.

"You gonna stay by this man for a lil' while. I got to go take care a some business but I be back in a lil' while." Rhonda gave one last look at Trey and smirked before hurrying out the door.

Trey shut the door behind her and turned to Shemeta.

"Come here," he said in a nice voice. "You got nothing to be afraid of, girl."

Shemeta hesitated. Trey walked over to her with his hands in a pacifying gesture.

"Your momma's a pain in the fucking ass, ain't she?"

"Uh-huh."

"How old are you, girl?"

"Twaylve."

Damn, Trey said to himself. Twelve! He had lost has virginity at the age of thirteen to a fat twenty-four-year-old who lived in a trailer ten miles from his in Bogalusa. He and his friend Terry had heard she liked to fuck boys their age and would do it for twenty dollars. One day after school they rode their BMX bikes over there. It took them two hours. She answered the door smoking a cigarette and waved them in without saying anything.

"Forty bucks."

Trey and Terry paid the fat girl. They had stolen the money from a teacher's purse at school.

"You first," she said to Trey. She brought him into her room, laid on her back, and pulled off her acid-washed jeans. Trey took off his Girbauds but not his "Poison" T-shirt and climbed on top of her. As soon as he slid inside, she began moaning and her face turned red. Within thirty seconds, her thinning hair was moist with sweat and her eyes had rolled back into her head. Her body jerked up and down with pleasure. Trey busted.

"You fucking came already?" gasped the breathless fat girl. Trey dismounted, put his pants back on and swaggered out of the room.

"Faggot!" she snarled as he shut the door behind him.

Trey still remembered the fat girl's name: Brandy Blackwood.

"Twelve, huh? Well, fuck it, you a woman now. Take off your shirt."

Shemeta peeled off her tank top. Her breasts were as firm and round as watermelons.

"Shemeta, you got the nicest fucking titties I ever seen."

Shemeta looked up at him with her big calf eyes.

"For real?"

"Yeah. Now take off your shorts."

Shemeta's pubic hair formed a vast thatch that extended almost up to her bellybutton and spread onto the tops of her thighs. *Fuck it*, thought Trey. He turned Shemeta around, pulled his dick out of his pants, and penetrated her.

Shemeta's pussy was wet as hell. He noticed with satisfaction that she was in the same position that her mother had been in only a quarter of an hour earlier. *Some straight alpha male shit*, thought Trey. Shemeta whimpered in pleasure.

"Damn, you a little ho already," chuckled Trey. He moved his head to the left so he could see her titties from the side. They were so firm that they didn't swing around at all, just stayed bolted onto her chest. Shemeta's face looked simultaneously childish and slutty. Some element of this tableau stirred Trey's libido on a deep level.

He busted.

2

Rhonda smiled as she drove off in her Celebrity. That stupid-ass white boy Trey was so high that he hadn't even noticed when she took his gold watch and slipped it into her bra.

Now that she had the watch, she had to dump the bitch. She scrunched to a stop in the clamshell parking lot in front of Mr. Cousin's pawn shop on Highway 190 and waddled to the burglar-bar protected door. It made a beeping noise as she walked in. She marched straight to the counter where Mr. Cousin's Creole ass was watching TV, fished the watch out of her bra, and dropped it down in front of him. She leaned way over the counter in a pose that was halfway between aggressive and seductive.

"How much you give me for that?" Ashes fell from her Kool cigarette onto the counter.

Mr. Cousin picked up the watch with velvet hands. It was made of solid eighteen-karat gold and had an oversized gold face with platinum hands. It was very heavy. The inscription on the back plate read *BALLIN'*.

He pushed it back towards her with a frown of judgment.

"This watch is hotter than a can of Sterno. Take it somewhere else."

Rhonda's face twisted into a snarl. "Fuck you, nigga...this mine...I bought it with my own motherfucking money...that watch mine, nigga, I bought it for eight hundred dollars."

"No sale, and that's final!"

Rhonda looked away from Mr. Cousin in frustration. Who the fuck did this nigga think he was? Accusing her of stealing...fuck this yellow nigga. Rhonda scooped up the watch and walked back outside into the broiling, moist heat. What the fuck was she supposed to do with the watch now? She stuck it back in her bra and got into the car. She would think about that later. Right now she just wanted to go home and get right.

Shemeta downed her first Coke in three gulps and was now working on her second. Trey took a sip of Budweiser and grunted. His face bore an expression of annoyance. Shemeta sat on the sofa and kicked her legs back and forth. Trey stood up and paced.

"Where ya mama at?"

"I dunno," said Shemeta without breaking her gaze from the Jenny Jones show. Trey lifted his left hand to look at his watch.

It wasn't on his wrist.

Before he even looked at the table where he knew it ought to have been sitting, his hustler's instinct told him that Rhonda had taken it.

Trey closed his eyes and took a deep breath. He refused to allow himself to blow his top. He imagined a meadow with a perfect, fluffy rabbit jumping through the flowers. Trey observed the rabbit through the scope of a rifle. At any moment, all he had to do was pull the trigger and the rabbit's head would explode. Instead of murking the rabbit, Trey forced himself to concentrate on every detail of the scene: the white fur, the green rye grass, the sound of the birds chirping. After a few moments the rage melted away. He had learned this trick in jail.

Trey prided himself on his intelligence and cool head. Anger wouldn't help him find his watch. He would put the fury on ice and thaw it out later. Rhonda was stupid enough to try sell it to the first person she saw on the street for a hit of dope. By the same logic, she was also stupid enough *not* to get rid of the watch right away, especially if she was high.

"Get up," said Trey to Shemeta. "We gonna go find ya mama. You want another Coke?"

3

Shemeta smiled and smiled. She felt like the Little Mermaid. Every time the cracker squealed around a corner in his purple Taurus, she imagined the sun glinting off his chrome Sprewell spinner rims...imagined how jealous everyone must be of her...Shemeta...rolling with her white man!

"*They hating*," she mouthed. Shemeta imagined herself holding a perfect little white baby in her arms. The baby was smiling at her! She put a bottle in its perfect little mouth and rocked it back and forth

Trey thought in silence as he drove. The blunts were beginning to wear off. Although part of him felt violent and aggressive, ready to crack skulls and drink blood, another part of him realized that it was all play-acting. *That's why they call it Tha Game*, thought Trey with philosophy. He looked over at Shemeta again. *I just fucked that*, he thought. He reached over and roughly pulled her shirt up. She smiled. He grabbed her left breast and waggled it.

"What the fuck you smiling about?"

"Nothing."

Trey put on a CD and advanced to track eight, a remix of "Down Here" by the white Baton Rouge rap group South Coast Coalition. The throb from his thousand-dollar woofers sent energy from his toes to his fingertips. This song always got Trey's adrenaline pumping. Although Mista Matt and B-Rock weren't the best rappers, the beat was fire and the track featured three of Trey's favorite spitters: T-Bo, white and from Baton Rouge, Lil' Boosie, black and from Baton Rouge, and the legendary Soulja Slim, black and from the Magnolia Projects in New Orleans. Trey felt T-Bo in particular. Although he was white, he was a gangster, as grimy and shady as any other goon in the game. He had a unique gruff flow that was half Tupac and half Eminem. Boosie held it down after Bo. Soulja Slim's verse was last because he was the biggest star. Even when his lyrics were low-key, they communicated icy menace. A certified hustler could hear right away that he was no studio gangsta but a cold-blooded killer.

Trey freestyled a few rhymes over the syncopated beat as he drove.

Bitch, you know that down here we killin' and rapin'
Snatch yo ass out the Cutlass then we steady duct tapin'

Shemeta bopped her head. It took them less than ten minutes to get to Rhonda's mildewed orange-and-white trailer. It was situated in the middle of a large, treeless, grassless lot on a little promontory surrounded by trash. There was no trash pick-up in Lacombe and the only way to get rid of household garbage was by driving it to the dump yourself. Trey felt a wave of disgust as he scanned the avalanche of Styrofoam food containers, aluminum cans, and used disposable diapers that covered the ground.

Fucking animals, thought Trey. *Like monkeys in a zoo. No, worse! Even monkeys are cleaner than these people.*

He cut the engine and coasted in slow and quiet next to Rhonda's Celebrity. The aluminum screen door gaped open like the mouth of a fiend gone on that gak.

"Stay in the car," said Trey.

"Okay," said Shemeta.

Trey took a quick look in the mirror, grimacing so he could see his gold teeth. "Boot up, cracka," he growled, then jumped out of the car.

Trey swaggered in with his game face on. Rhonda's mother Dolores sat in a plaid easy chair with wooden arm rests and a doily across the back. She was watching the end of Jenny Jones. The dark black crone held a withered-looking newborn in her arms: Rhonda's last baby. She was smoking a Kool cigarette. With her yellow eyes and stringy crackhead neck, she resembled a mummified version of Rhonda. Trey had always wondered what it would be like to fuck her. Two more babies crawled around on the same ratty brown built-in carpet that Trey had in his trailer. They wore nothing but disposable diapers: soiled ones.

"Afternoon, ma'am, I'm looking for Rhonda."

After a long pause, and without breaking her gaze from the television, the aging rockhead extended one bony index finger towards the hallway.

"She in there."

When Dolores opened her mouth, Trey could see that she only had two teeth left, one on the top and one on the bottom.

Trey pimp-rolled over to the door of Rhonda's room. It was ajar. He looked in and saw Rhonda laid out on her back with her eyes half closed, high out of her mind on his kickers. Trey closed the door behind him and straddled her on the bed.

4

"Wake up!" Trey slapped Rhonda across the face. "Wake the fuck up!" He slapped her again. Rhonda responded with a weak spasm. Her red eyes rolled open.

"What the fuck...nigga...fuck..." she slurred.

"Where...is...my...watch?" Trey spoke slowly and firmly but did not shout. Rhonda's eyes rolled closed again.

Her room was disgusting. The floor was covered in crushed Styrofoam cups, rotting French fries, and cigarette butts. The carpet underneath was so stained that it no longer had any discernible color. The only furniture was a plastic crate next to the mattress. A Styrofoam gumbo plate sat on the crate next to a crusty crack pipe. The walls were gray and greasy with Jheri curl in the corner where the mattress lay on the floor. The mattress itself looked like it had been soaked in medical waste.

Trey began his search with a patdown of Rhonda's unconscious body. He found his watch in her bra within ten seconds. *Jesus, how could someone be so stupid?*

Trey reached into his pocket and pulled out the razor-sharp Buck knife that he used to gut and dress deer. Gripping her face with his left hand, Trey cut a straight line an inch and a half long down her left cheek. It twitched when the knife went in, but she did not wake up. A small trickle of blood ran down her cheek. The incision was not deep. His goal was not to injure but to leave a souvenir. With the concentration of an artisan, Trey shifted the knife in his hand and made a second incision, horizontal this time. Wiping away the blood with a T-shirt he found on Rhonda's floor, he admired his handiwork: a perfect motherfucking T.

Dolores' ears were as good as her eyes were bad. As soon as she heard Trey slapping Rhonda, she leapt out of her chair with the agility of a hood goat and ran next door to Duke's trailer.

Duke lived alone and did odd jobs: hauling, construction, repairs, plumbing. Like Dolores, he liked to smoke rock. He was a big man with the physique of a nose guard gone to seed. He must have been about forty-five years old. Whenever there was a problem, Dolores or Rhonda went to Duke first. In exchange for his protection, he got an hour with Rhonda every Sunday night. Duke was considered slow and lazy by his neighbors. If he had any ambition, they said, he would have seized the opportunity to pimp Rhonda out for real instead of settling for a measly hour a week of ass and no cash. But that wasn't Duke's style.

Dolores and Rhonda made fun of Duke for the funny faces he made when he ejaculated inside them. His eyes would close and he would get a serious look on his face as if he were doing something important.

Most of all Duke loved to eat pussy. He could do it for two hours at a stretch. Rhonda and Dolores appreciated this. To them he was a big, stupid bloodhound.

Duke was a peaceful man...that is, until he needed a smoke and couldn't get one. In such a situation he didn't hesitate to put the Tec-9 and black ski mask that he kept in the glove box of his pickup truck to work. Duke didn't get off on robbery and violence but he didn't mind them, either. He had spent four years in Winn State for attempted murder after pistol-whipping a minor into a coma during a botched mugging. Duke had pulled his gun on the skinny white teenager as he walked back to his car from the "Cinema Eight" movie theater in Slidell. The white teenager had just seen *Twister,* starring Helen Hunt and Bill Paxton. The images of Helen Hunt in a storm-soaked and transparent white undershirt had not left the white pussy indifferent. He was on his way home to masturbate to the clinamen between her large breasts and plain face when Duke crossed his path. Unfortunately for the white teenager, Duke was high on PCP.

"Give me your money, bitch!"

The compliant teenager only had four dollars in his pocket. Duke flew into a rage when he saw the four moist, worn bills.

"Four dollars? Four dollars? Bitch, I can't even get a hot sausage po-boy for four dollars!" Duke smashed the teenager on the head with the butt of his Tec-9. In a stroke of bad luck, a police patrol car drove by at this precise moment. Duke was tazed, clubbed unconscious by the police, and arrested.

Duke was watching television and smoking a Kool cigarette when Dolores ran in. He wasn't wearing a shirt and Dolores could see his powerful shoulders and thick gut.

"Duke...we got trouble!"

He knew the drill. It was not unusual for a john to start causing problems next door. Usually Duke's size was enough to scare them into coughing up the stacks and leaving. He picked up his Tec-9 just in case, jammed it in his waistband, and jog-walked over to Dolores' trailer.

Shemeta was still dreaming of her white baby, whom she had named LaShawn, when she saw Mr. Duke run out of his trailer. She liked Mr. Duke. One day when her mother and grandmother were gone he invited her into his trailer, where he made her take off her clothes and then licked her kitty. Afterwards, he said he would buy her a Wedding Cake sno-ball if she promised not to mention anything to her mother. He said that it had to be a Wedding Cake snowball because it was like they were married to each other, only it was a secret.

The door flew open as Trey was sheathing his buck knife. Duke's eyes went straight to Rhonda's cheek.

"Motherfucker..."

He lunged. Trey twisted just in time. Duke crashed to the ground between the bed and the wall. By the time the big man had righted himself, Trey had backed towards the door and drawn his Glock.

"Don't move, motherfucker."

Duke held his hands up. His face bore an expression of confusion.

"I ain't moving. Man, I ain't moving."

The two men stared at each other with bulging eyeballs for a moment.

An agitation behind Trey broke the silence.

"Motherfucker!"

Dolores screamed and stabbed Trey in the back with a steak knife. Trey howled and twisted backwards. Duke drew his Tec-9 from his waistband and let off three quick shots. The first bullet hit Dolores in the forehead and she dropped. The other two bullets hit the wall.

Trey ducked and riposted immediately. His first bullet hit Rhonda in the stomach. The hot lead ripping through her soft abdominal tissue awakened her. She screamed. His second shot hit Duke in the chest. The big man spasmed and collapsed like a puppet with its strings cut. Trey knew immediately that he had killed him. He spun around. The top of Dolores' dome had been blown off. Her brain glistened in the artificial light.

"Fuck," said Trey. He blinked and turned around.

Rhonda shrieked and clutched at her stomach. A bunch of blood leaked out of her.

"Fuck you...motherfucker..." she blubbered. Trey stared as her blood pooled around the mattress. His ears rang from the gunshots. The surface of the advancing puddle was so shiny that he could see a reflection of the window in it. It bulged as the blood spread. Rhonda continued to insult him. Tears ran down her hideous face.

"Motherfucker..."

The puddle of blood was now only inches away from Trey's Nikes. He cursed and jumped back. His polo shirt was splattered. He peeled it off and used it to wipe off his face and arms. He dropped it to the floor, paused, then picked it back up.

It was evidence!

What about fingerprints? He stepped over Dolores' body and used his polo shirt to wipe off the doorknob. Was that all he had touched? He couldn't focus. His heart was hammering against his ribs. As the ringing in his ears subsided and Rhonda's sniveling grew weaker, he became aware of a baby crying in the living room.

Then Trey had a very wicked idea.

5

Shemeta looked down at the baby she held in her arms. There was a smear of blood on her Pampers. She knew that her momma was dead the moment she saw the white man running out of the trailer holding her little sister Tamica. Shemeta hated her momma and she was glad that the fire white man had murked her. She looked over at him. He was driving like insane in the membrane. She imagined him popping her mother in the head with his gat and her mother's head exploding. She trembled with excitement. Now she had a baby and the cracker was her baby daddy. They would live together in the white man's trailer and she would have six babies, three boys and three girls.

Shemeta looked down at Tamica and frowned. She didn't want Tamica. She wanted a white baby, a fat one with blue eyes.

"Why you so ugly." She gave Tamica a shake.

The limp infant began to cry. Shemeta felt compassion for her new baby and rocked it.

"Baby, baby," she whispered.

6

Tyrone Washington pushed open the door to his grandmother's trailer. His earnest, juvenile face bore a troubled expression.

"Is that you, Tyrone?" called his grandmother from the kitchen.

"Hi, Grandma."

Tyrone slunk into his bedroom, opened his backpack and took out his European History exam. He shook his head. How had he gotten a C? He deserved an A+! What Mr. Raleigh had told him after class made no sense.

"Tyrone...this was an essay test. I asked you to tell me the *story* of the French Revolution."

"But I put all the dates!"

"I see that. That's why you got a C instead of an F. You're very good with dates, even if a few of those are wrong too. But all you did was list them. The goal of this class is to get you to *weave* those dates into a narrative.

History is more than just discrete bits of information. History is a *story*. And half of the facts you included have nothing to do with the French Revolution. Look, here you put '1732: birth of George Washington.'"

"But Lafayette helped George Washington in the American Revolution!"

"Yes, but that isn't relevant to the *French* Revolution."

No matter how hard Tyrone tried to explain himself, Mr. Raleigh refused to understand. He had been wrong to trust him. Ultimately, he was no better than Coach MacGregor. Tyrone looked up at his bookshelf. It was lined with every edition of the *Almanac* as well as every edition of the *Guinness Book of World Records* from the year of his birth, 1989, to the current year, 2007. He owned all three versions of the *Book of Lists*, none of which were still in print. Tyrone snorted. He knew more about history than Mr. Raleigh ever would. He knew that St. Peter was the first pope. He knew that President McKinley was assassinated by Leon Czolgosz on September 14, 1901. He knew that Thomas Jefferson wore size 12 shoes. He knew that Joseph Conrad's Polish name was Joszef Korzeniowski. He was practically a historian already.

He jammed the test back in his overstuffed backpack and turned on his Sony PlayStation. A smile came to his face as soon as the theme music to Final Fantasy VII began. It was his favorite video game of all time. For some inane reason, his friend Victor liked Final Fantasy VIII better. Victor could be obtuse sometimes. Onscreen, Tyrone's avatar Cloud slashed at a Guard with the badass-looking Buster Sword. Dramatic battle music played in the background. Tyrone chortled when the Guard's counterattack inflicted a pathetic eight hit points of damage.

Cloud was a stylized adolescent hero with a spiky blond hair, a slight physique, a giant blade, and a tortured psyche. Japanese dorks identified with him. Sometimes, as Tyrone lay drifting off to sleep, he imagined himself as

Cloud in the Final Fantasy universe, slashing his way towards a final showdown with the wicked Sephiroth.

Outside of the fact that they were both short and skinny, Tyrone bore no physical affinity to Cloud. His broad, flat nose, globular eyes, thick lips, and receding chin caused him to resemble a frog. Two prematurely droopy periorbital pouches gave his face a phlegmatic, melancholic aspect. His dark black skin made the heavy acne that he spent hours squeezing and picking harder to notice. His unkempt hair occupied the intermediary zone between nappy corona and small Afro. He smelled like dandruff. The cheap-looking light blue plastic eyeglasses he wore were one of only four models available at the welfare ophthalmologist's. One of the retarded boys in Tyrone's homeroom had the same frames.

Tyrone was equipping Tifa with new Materia when he heard tires screeching to a stop outside. He felt immediately nauseated and twisted on his bed. Every few months his mother showed up to ask his grandmother for money. She was only fourteen years older than Tyrone. Every time she came over she forced her way into his room and told him she loved him. She had yellow, psychotic eyes and smelled like crack. On the rare occasions when she came by sober, she didn't bother to say hello to him.

"Stay here!" shouted a man's voice from outside.

Tyrone breathed a sigh of relief. It wasn't his mother. A car door slammed.

Tyrone paused the game and craned his neck to the window just in time to see his next door neighbor running into his trailer. There was a deep red blotch on his back.

What was going on?

Trey frightened Tyrone. The two of them had never spoken. Tyrone avoided all contact with him. Scummy people came and went from his trailer at all hours. Every square inch of his appearance advertised his capacity for violence.

There was a black girl in the passenger seat of Trey's purple car but he couldn't discern her face. Trey made a lot of noise banging around in the trailer. Something was up. Tyrone got up to his knees and pressed his face to the window to get a better view.

Trey shot out of the trailer with a laundry basket full of stuff that he threw in the trunk. He had changed his shirt. He ran back into his trailer and emerged again holding a set of deer antlers. He scanned his surroundings one last time and jog-walked back to the car.

Trey stopped dead in his tracks. Tyrone felt the blood drain from his face as well as a strange tingling in his crotch.

Trey was looking at *him.*

A cruel smile spread across his neighbor's face. His gold teeth sparkled in the bright sunlight.

Time stopped. Tyrone couldn't move. Trey's reptilian gaze nailed him to the spot.

Slowly Trey lifted a finger to his mouth. Tyrone felt Trey's warm breath on his neck as he whispered.

Shhhh...be quiet...bitch...

Then, with the same finger, Trey made a gun with his hand and extended it towards Tyrone in a horizontal grip.

He left the gun pointed at Tyrone for an agonizing few seconds, then pulled the trigger. Tyrone felt a cold, stabbing pain as the bullets pierced his body. A sound like the crackling of radio static filled his ears.

Trey put his finger to his mouth one more time and tapped his temple. Even though his lips didn't move Tyrone could once again hear Trey's voice as clearly as if they were together in the same room.

Use your head...bitch...

Trey winked, jumped back into his car, started it up, and peeled out.

Tyrone lowered his frozen body back onto his bed. He didn't feel like playing Final Fantasy VII anymore.

7

Trey relaxed once he got on I-12 going east. The danger was behind him. *If only that little fucker hadn't seen me leaving town*...but Trey had a feeling that the kid wouldn't talk. He could just tell. He had a sixth sense for these things. He was like Neo in *The Matrix*. There was a reason that big buck's bullets had all missed. He imagined himself as Keanu Reeves dodging bullets in slow motion. Trey was different...special...the Chosen One...whatever the fuck you wanted to call it. Always had been. Looking at his speedometer, Trey saw that the car was cruising at a steady seventy miles an hour.

The situation was on lock.

By the time they hit the Mississippi state line, he was feeling straight enthusiastic.

Trey reflected on the fact that he was now a killer. He was glad that he had made his bones. As he had always suspected, taking a life had been about as difficult as putting a gallon of milk back in the refrigerator.

He looked over at the baby Shemeta was cradling in her arms. He still wasn't sure if taking it had been a mistake or not. A few days earlier he had seen a Geraldo Rivera investigative report about human trafficking on television. Newborn babies were worth plenty of cheddar on the black market – twenty G's or more. There were thousands of cluckers out there ready to pay top dollar for the chance to be parents. Anyone else would have panicked, run out of the trailer and ended up in jail within twelve hours. He had kept his cool, thought fast, and flipped a bad situation into a money-making opportunity. It was some Kung Fu shit. Twenty thousand dollars! Why would anyone on earth pay that kind of money for a *baby?* He looked down at Tamica. This one didn't look like it was worth more than fifty bucks, he thought with a snort. So...shriveled and unhealthy-looking. Right now he would have paid someone fifty dollars just to shut the fucking thing up. Tamica had been crying for the last thirty minutes.

"Shut it up!" he exploded.

"She hungry," said Shemeta.

Trey imagined palming the baby and tossing her out the window like a Styrofoam cup. He focused on the yellow line in the road and took a deep breath. *Stay frosty. Babies need that milk. Breathe, homeboy.* A big payday like this was worth some static.

"Well we just gonna have to get her some food then."

Trey spotted a Wal-Mart sign and veered off the interstate, nearly hitting a mini-van. The driver blasted his horn and gave him the finger. Trey ignored him. He chose a parking space way out by the edge, away from any other cars.

"Remember," he said to Shemeta, "if anyone asks, you waiting on ya mama." Shemeta gave a lazy nod. He grabbed her face with his hand and twisted it so that she was facing him.

Tamica shrieked.

"You look at me when I talk to you! Don't even think about leaving this car! You understand? Don't even think about it!" Trey punctuated his speech with a petite slap across the face from his free hand. Shemeta nodded as best she could given Trey's iron grip. Trey stared at her with his icy eyes for a moment, then relaxed into a testy smile and let go of her face.

"Smart girl." He stretched his head left and right to crack the vertebrae and lit a cigarette. His hands and cheek muscles twitched as he sucked down lungful after lungful of smoke in tense silence. After a long moment, he flicked his cigarette out the window and spoke.

"Fuck it...you want anything for the road? Some sweets? What kind of candy you like?"

"Twizzlers," said Shemeta in a timid little-girl voice.

"Yeeaah...Twizzlers...you got good taste for a little kid...I love me some Twizzlers...I been eating Twizzlers since motherfucking day one, ya heard me? Twizzle my

Nizzle...fo shizzle..." Shemeta laughed. Trey's imitation of Snoop Dogg had broken the tension. He got out of the car.

Walking into Wal-Mart, Trey felt positive. This was it: life. Them dawgs were on his tail. That made him a fox, and foxes were smart. He was in total control of the situation. A rheumy-eyed geezer with a mesh-back KOREAN WAR VETERAN baseball cap covered in pins greeted him at the entrance.

"Welcome to Wal-Mart, young man."

Trey wondered how many dink wigs the old pimp had split. He shook the greeter's hand, scored a shopping cart, and rolled over to the baby supply section. There were Mexicans everywhere. He grabbed a crate-sized jumbo pack of Huggies and tossed it into the cart. Further down the aisle he grabbed a baby bottle and stared at the wall of baby formula. When he moved to take one from the shelf, a fat white woman with a puffy-paint Teddy bear on her oversized T-shirt who was shopping behind him piped up.

"That formula's no good...gives mine diarrhea. *Parent's Choice* is better." Trey put the cheap stuff back on the shelf and thanked the woman, calling her ma'am.

"Just trying to save you a surprise," she said in a tired voice as she rolled away.

What else did babies need? Trey couldn't think of anything else. He pushed his cart to the clothes section. It wouldn't hurt to change his style, given his situation. He scored a pair of dark blue Pioneer brand pleated slacks, a dress belt, a pack of white button-up shirts, and a pair of brown dress boots with a puffy rim around the top. On an impulse he grabbed a clip-on tie with a Tabasco pattern on it. He might as well go full businessman. In the girls' section he picked up a new tank top for Shemeta for ninety-nine cents and a new pair of shorts with Tweety Bird on the butt. A couple of fat Mexican women gave him a dirty look when he grabbed a three-pack of cotton girls' underwear. He turned and gave them an eighteen-karat gangster smile. They looked away and rolled off.

Last stop was the snack section. What the fuck did she say she liked...Goobers...no...Twizzlers. A trucker-sized bag of Jack Link beef jerky caught his eye. The package read: 28 GRAMS OF PROTEIN! He tossed it into the cart along with a big Gatorade. On his way to the checkout counter he made an impulse stop at the jewelry island. There was a whole wall of little gold pendants and lockets for girls. As a drug dealer and ex-convict, Trey had an intuitive sense of the proportions in which to mix seduction and cruelty to hijack someone's will. Without looking, he grabbed a locket in the shape of a heart that cost $6.99 and put it in his shopping cart.

"Thata be $125.65," said the cashier, a fat black girl whose name tag read *Nikkel*.

"A hundred and twenty-five dollars! Damn...your boss Mr. Wal-Mart be on his hustle today fo shizzle...you *slanging*, girl."

Nikkel laughed, exposing two gold-capped canines. "That man be straight stacking all *day*, ya heard me?"

Trey casually took the banana bankroll out of his pocket and peeled off three fifties. Nikkel stole an admiring look at it. When she handed him his change, she scratched the inside of his palm with one of her hot pink fake fingernails and gave him a raunchy smile.

"My name's Nikkel. Come holla at a bitch next time you in Wally World buying your Huggies."

"I'm out of town, baby. Stay gangster, boo."

Trey leaned way over his cart and pimp-wheeled it out into the blinding sunlight without looking back.

When he got back to the car, he went straight to the trunk, shook an OxyContin out of the Skittles bag, crushed it into powder, put it in the bottle he had just bought, and filled it with formula. He tossed the cardboard and plastic packaging on the ground.

"Lot of folks in there...Sunday shopping," said Trey to Shemeta as he dropped into the driver's seat. "Here you go." He tossed the Twizzlers on Shemeta's lap. "And this is for Taleeka...Takeela...whateverthefuck." He handed her the bottle.

"Tamica," said Shemeta.

"Whatever."

When the rubber nipple went to Tamica's mouth it was as if she had been touched with a live wire. Her tiny body shivered and jerked.

Legs loose, Trey ripped open the bag of beef jerky, stuffed a big piece into his mouth, and rolled his head back so he was looking up. He closed his eyes as he chewed.

He turned to Shemeta as if he had just remembered something.

"I almost forgot. This is for you. I got a little steamed up back there. This is my way of saying that...we gonna be cool soon as you get the wax out your fucking ears and learn the rules." Shemeta's eyes widened when she saw the jewelry box come out of Trey's shirt pocket. She made to open it but Trey stopped her. "Naw, let me." He held the heart pendant up so that Shemeta could get a good look at it before putting it over her head himself and even...giving her a little kiss on the mouth.

8

After finishing her formula, Tamica fell fast asleep. Shemeta made a little clothes nest for her in the back seat. Night fell as they crossed into Florida. Trey had decided that Daytona Beach would be a good place to hide out for a little while. He had been there once a few years before on vacation with some of his homies and had a real good time. In the daytime they set up camp on the beach, drinking rum and Coke and conversating with all the fine-ass bitches getting their tan on. At night they cruised the beach in Trey's Taurus, throwing their sets up, stunting, and just generally wilding out before hitting the club. One of Trey's boys brought back a freak one night, a fat bitch with big, floppy titties, and they went family-style on her, slapping her ass and titties around and cumming on her face. She sucked them all dry and when they woke her up to kick her out the next morning she still had dried cum all over her face and hair.

Good times.

Daytona it would be. But this time he was in town on business. Trey had matured since that last trip and now he had only one thing on his mind: getting his paper right. He had been thinking it over. This shit back home was the sign he had been waiting for. It was time to stop fucking around with the small-time bullshit and take a step up to the big leagues. No more $71 drug deals. No more counting wrinkled ones. No more dope fiends. Trey felt like a tiger or a Pit that had just been let out of its cage: lean, mean, and ready to rip into some buttery, innocent flesh.

But first things first. Right now, he had to find a motel, something cheap where no one would ask him any questions.

After driving around the strip for a little while, Trey saw a place that looked perfect. It was a squat, fifties-style dive motel with a pool surrounded by a low brick wall called the "Sun Tan Motel." The sign out front said "Free HBO". The units in the back were set off from the street. He parked in a dark corner of the lot and loped over to the office.

The man at the desk was a fat, middle-aged Mexican with a mustache. He watched *Cops* on TV. He straightened up in his chair when Trey walked in.

"I'm looking for a room," said Trey. "You got any vacancies? Something in the back, away from the street. My girl's sick and don't want to be disturbed."

"Just the two of you?" replied the Mexican with a heavy accent.

"That's right," said Trey.

"How long will you be staying, sir?"

"We on vacation...just chilling. Be here at least a week. Swimming, getting a tan. That's why we came here. *Sun Tan Motel*. How's the water?" said Trey with a big smile.

"Oh, it's alright, still a little cold. But it's OK. People be out there all day, getting tans, having fun in the water."

"I hear that, bruh."

"Will you be paying by cash or credit card?"

"Cash, dog...one week. How much that come to?"

The Mexican showed his calculator to Trey. It read $413. Trey peeled nine fifty-dollar bills off of his roll and dropped them on the counter. He made a point of always keeping fifties instead of hundreds. Benjamins were played out, so Trey flipped the script and carried Grants instead. The Mexican took the bills and gave him thirty-seven dollars. Trey pushed the bills back towards the Mexican.

"Naw, bruh...that's for you. Just make sure we get some privacy, ya heard me? I don't want no one coming in...no maids, no room service, no fucking tax man, nobody, ya heard me? Me and my girl want some privacy...if I need anything I'll come by and ask for it my own damn self. You can do that for me?" Trey now leaned across the counter.

The Mexican shrunk back and smiled queasily. "Of course, sir, no problem at all. Take this and leave it on your door just in case." He handed Trey a "Do Not Disturb" door sign.

"I'ma put it on there, bruh, but I don't want no just in case, ya heard me? You go ahead and tell your people to just forget about room number" – Trey looked at the key – "room number eighteen for a lil' while." Pulling even closer, Trey added, "I'll be honest with you, homie, me and my girl gonna be straight freaking all week...she wild but she shy too, you see what I'm saying? So just tell them people we good, we set, we don't need *nothing* in there." Trey was almost whispering, leaning way in and looking straight into the Mexican's eyes.

"Yes sir, absolutely sir, I understand," stammered the Mexican.

Trey nodded and signaled that the conversation was over by holding out his fist for dap.

Once in the squat room, Trey cracked open a beer, sprawled back on one of the beds with a loud groan of relaxation, and turned on the TV.

"Shit," he said, "I'm fucking bushed." Shemeta set Tamica on the floor next to her bed and lay down on her stomach. Trey gulped down his beer in three minutes, cracked open a second, and rolled a blunt with a Swisher Sweet. The situation was still critical but he was too tired to do anything more for the day. He would wake up early with the chickens and start straight hustling...tomorrow.

Trey extended the blunt across the particle-board night table to Shemeta without breaking his gaze from the TV. She took it nervously and put it to her mouth. He was surprised to see that she didn't know what to do with it.

"You mean your mama ain't never smoked you out before? With all the dope she burns? Damn." His eyes had already turned red and swollen shut a little bit. "Just put it in your mouth and suck on it. Shit...that shouldn't be a problem for you." Trey chortled at his joke. "Breathe it in deep. Get all that good stuff way down in your lungs." Shemeta took a big hit and started coughing.

"There you go," he said. "Keep it down as long as you can. That's good shit you smoking."

"It taste *sweet*," said Shemeta as she handed the blunt back to Trey.

"Why you think they called Swisher Sweets, dummy? Have you some more, put you right to sleep."

Trey got up and found the big bag of Chili Cheese Fritos that he had salvaged from his trailer in Lacombe. He ripped it open and chowed down. After eating half of them, he abandoned the bag on the nightstand. Shemeta snatched it up and began eating the Fritos by the fistful as Trey flipped through the channels. It only took her a few minutes to finish the fried corn snack.

"You got the munch too, huh?" said Trey. "Shit...your first time...I bet you high as a motherfucker!"

Shemeta stared at her hands. They were full of Chili Cheese powder. Her face bore an expression of perplexed fascination. She licked her fingers down to the webbing. It felt freaky. After sucking off most of the flavor, her hands were wet and sticky with saliva and patches of Chili Cheese spice that her tongue had missed.

Shemeta dropped the bag on the floor next to her bed where Tamica slept. Some of the Chili Cheese bottom debris spilled on Tamica's face. She gave a jerk and began to gurgle. Shemeta hoisted the infant up to the bed and began to wipe her face with her sticky, spicy hands.

"You dirty," said Shemeta. She wiped Tamica's eyes. The baby turned red and began crying.

"What the fuck are you doing?" shouted Trey. "You woke her up!"

"She lonely," said Shemeta. She rocked Tamica. "She miss her momma." Tamica fought against Shemeta's painful, suffocating embrace.

Shemeta squeezed her sister and stared with bloodshot eyes at ESPN's SportsCenter. Within a few minutes Tamica was asleep again.

Trey got up to get another beer. Instead of calming him down, the blunt had made him anxious and paranoid. He began to pace.

"We gonna get something straight here," he said. "Here's how this shit works. That baby is your business. You gonna feed it, you gonna change it, you gonna fucking burp it." He scratched his cleft chin. "Here's what we gonna do." He went out to the car and came back with the toaster-sized ninety-six ounce mug of Sprite that he had bought at a gas station in Tallahassee. He dumped the pop into the sink. One by one he opened the seven remaining formula cans and flung them into the oversized plastic cup, which he hadn't bothered washing out. He walked into the kitchenette, rummaged around in the drawers, and came back out with a turkey baster, which he dropped into the formula mug. From the Skittles bag he extracted six Oxy pills and crushed them up. He dumped the powder into the formula and stirred it with the turkey baster. It clumped up.

"What that is?" asked Shemeta.

"That's to help her go to sleep...make sure she behaves herself. Give her nice dreams...bout bunnies and shit. Now, watch me carefully. I'ma put this shit in the fridge – baby likes her milk nice and cold, right? Specially when it's hot outside like this. Now, whenever she get hungry, you just roll over to the fridge, suck some of that good stuff up into this bitch, and then squirt it in the bottle. You and Tamica rocking and rolling." Trey paused for a second and looked around. Spotting the diapers, he lunged towards them and held them up.

"You know how to change a diaper?" Shemeta nodded. She had changed plenty of diapers. "Good, cause I sure the fuck don't. I'ma put them right here. Baby Tamica takes a dump, you take the old one off and pop one of these clean motherfuckers on there. I don't want to smell no fucking baby shit so keep your nostrils open."

"Where the wipey box at?"

"The what?"

"The wipey box."

"I ain't got no fucking wipey box...this ain't the fucking Hilton. Toilet paper's good enough for my white ass...it's good enough for hers. Speaking of which...I gotta take a shit."

Trey went into the bathroom and closed the door. Thirty seconds later, the toilet flushed and he came back out gesticulating. He was getting manic.

"Another thing. We got to get the rules straight. Rule number one, we laying low, and that means you ain't leaving this hotel room, ever, for any reason. You understand? You gonna stay in here and take care of the baby. They got HBO here so you straight. But if I catch you even looking out the door"– Trey stopped pacing and jabbed his finger in her direction– "you gonna regret it. Just fucking forget about the sun for a little while. You understand? You don't need no motherfucking tan anyway." Trey nodded in assent to some inner imperative, paced around the apartment for a few more minutes, then abruptly turned off the TV.

"Bedtime. We waking up early tomorrow."

9

"Tyrone! Come on outta there, baby! I just made some chili dogs and they good!"

For the past hour Tyrone had been lying immobile in bed. He did not feel good. Something strange was happening. His mind was racing so fast that he didn't even know what he was thinking about. How was it possible that he had heard Trey whispering to him from outside the trailer? He knew it was impossible but the facts were there: he had heard him. And then the way Trey had looked at him...looked *through* him...and then *killed* him...must have rattled him because he really didn't feel very good at all. He couldn't shake the thought that maybe he really *was* dead...that maybe Trey really *had* just killed him. Crazy...but he couldn't get this thought out of his head.

"Tyrone! Come get you one while they still hot!"

"I'm not hungry, grandma," he shouted through the door.

He unpaused Final Fantasy 7 and tried to play but it was impossible. His head hurt. He found a save spot, turned the game off, and settled into a heavy, sickly late-afternoon nap with all of his clothes on.

When he woke up it was after eight P.M. His cheek was wet with drool and his muscles ached. His head still hurt but not so much as before. The late spring sun had not quite set yet and it took him a moment to realize that it was Sunday night and not Monday morning.

He had a painful erection and needed to pee. He dissimulated his hot, hard, small penis under the band of his sweatpants and pulled his T-shirt over the bump so his grandmother wouldn't see the telltale bulge. He snuck out of his room like a little mouse.

Tyrone's grandmother was humming a gospel song and making a big bowl of potato salad in the kitchen. He slunk past her and locked himself in the bathroom. He had to bend over almost double in order to orient his still-erect penis in such a way that the urine would go into the toilet and not on the wall.

He began to stroke his wand. If ever he needed to masturbate, now was that moment. He barely had time to imagine his fat Gothic friend Jessica's huge breasts spilling out of one of the frilly black lace shirts she liked to wear before he had ejaculated into the toilet bowl.

He was seized with a sudden feeling of guilt and self-disgust. He wiped down the inside of the weak-flushing bowl in order that his grandmother would not see his sperm. He fashioned a piece of toilet paper into a little cap for his penis so that the drops of semen that would slowly drip out over the next fifteen minutes wouldn't leave telltale sperm stains in his underwear. He looked at himself in the mirror. Tyrone had seen movie characters splash their faces with water and scrutinize their dripping visages in such situations so he did it too. He looked away when his mirror image began to expand and rotate, which always happened when he stared at his reflection for too long.

"Tyrone, help me open this jar of mayonnaise...you young and strong, not like your old grandma," asked his smiling grandmother when he emerged from the bathroom.

"Sure, grandma." He opened it.

"It sure is nice to have a man around the house." She dumped half of the sixteen-ounce jar of mayonnaise into the bowl with the potatoes, celery, and onions. The sight of so much mayonnaise made Tyrone queasy. "We gonna have pork chops tonight while we watch your program. I made them just how you like them, too."

Three years earlier, Tyrone had gone through a Japan phase after seeing the Tom Cruise movie *The Last Samurai*. Imagining himself a novice samurai, he asked his grandmother to make Teriyaki pork chops instead of the pork chops in barbecue sauce she usually cooked. She bought a bottle of Kraft brand Teriyaki sauce, dumped it over a bowl full of Wal-Mart pork chops, and stuck them in the microwave for ten minutes. Ever since then she cooked them all the time. Tyrone had never actually liked Teriyaki pork chops and now he no longer even liked the idea of Teriyaki pork chops. He would have preferred to eat nothing but vegetables but his grandmother was incapable of preparing a meal without pork. She considered vegetarianism to be Satanic.

"Thanks, grandma," he mumbled as he sat down on the sofa. He and his grandmother watched "Star Trek: The Next Generation" together every night at nine P.M. His favorite characters were Lieutenant Commander Data, Jean-Luc Picard and Geordi LaForge. He didn't like Riker or Worf and hated the putative boy genius Wesley Crusher, who looked and talked like any of the preppy nomads Tyrone went to high school with. "Nomad" was a nickname that he and Victor had come up with during gym class one day for the wealthy suburban jocks that ranged from one end of the basketball court to the other. It didn't make much sense but it stuck. Sometimes Tyrone masturbated while thinking of Marina Sirtis as Lieutenant Deanna Troi even though he didn't like her character. Empathy was lame. He hoped that tonight's episode would be one he hadn't seen before. He especially hoped it wasn't an episode from one of the earlier seasons with the useless Tasha Yar, a glabrous Will Riker, and the form-fitting V-neck uniforms that bothered him for some reason.

"I heard you snoring in there," said his grandmother. "I don't know what you been doing to make you so tired...must be that big brain of yours!"

"Grandma..." said Tyrone, rolling his eyes. "Brain size has nothing to do with intelligence. Everyone's brain weighs the same: about forty-eight ounces. What really matters is the brain-to-spinal cord ratio. For humans it's fifty-five to one. What do you think the dumbest vertebrates are? I bet you can't guess!" Tyrone's high-pitched, squeaky voice bore no trace of Ebonics.

His grandmother shook her head from side to side and clucked her tongue in admiration. Such a smart boy!

"Cows?" she guessed. Tyrone closed his eyes and shook his head with a patronizing smile.

"Grandma...cows are mammals and mammals are already at the top of the evolutionary ziggurat. I estimate them to have a brain-to-spinal cord ratio of at least thirty-five or forty." Tyrone made this figure up on the spot. "No...think lower...slimier...smaller..."

"Tyrone, baby, I don't know what the stupidest verteba or whatever you talking bout is...why don't you just tell your grandma and stop wearing her out with all these questions?" She was still smiling and chuckling.

"Well...OK...you like them fried with ketchup on them...give up? Fish! Their brain-to-spinal cord ratio is one-to-one...that means that their spinal cords are the same size as their brains! Just a miserable snarl of electrified organic material. They're so dumb they have no memory. They're fully capable of biting the same hook they bit ten seconds before!"

By the time Star Trek came on, Tyrone was feeling better. He had taken the smallest pork chop in the pan along with a tiny portion of potato salad. His grandmother had taken four pork chops and a serving of potato salad as big as a baby's diaper.

"Get you some more, boy, you too skinny," she entreated her grandson at each commercial break. Tyrone gave her his standard response, that he had to watch his "caloric intake" because he was "on Sugar Busters". This joke never failed to cause ripples of hilarity to shudder through his grandmother's enormous, gelatinous body.

He went to bed feeling better.

10

"Duke, where you at?" called Willy Johnson, a big smile on his face. He pushed open the screen door and looked around the empty living room of Duke's trailer. The TV was on but Duke was not in his rocking chair.

Maybe he was in the bathroom.

"You on the shitter? Man, you gotta eat more vegetables, cousin!" shouted Willy as he walked through the trailer. But Duke wasn't in the bathroom either.

"Where you hiding, bruh? Come help me smoke this blunt." Duke wasn't in the bedroom.

Must be next door, thought Willy.

"Duke, you in here?" called Willy as he pushed open the door to Dolores' trailer.

Inspector Batiste, a tall, shabby Creole with a pencil-thin Duke Ellington dandy mustache, surveyed the scene. There was blood everywhere. All three victims were well known to the police force. Duke had done time in Winn State for armed robbery and Dolores and Rhonda had been in and out of trouble with the law all their lives for countless petty offenses: drugs, prostitution, robbery, domestic violence.

Fred Batiste was the top homicide detective in St. Tammany Parish. What other detectives thought of in awe as his near-psychic powers of intuition were a product of a degree in philosophy with a concentration in epistemology. Nights spent reading Canguilhem and Popper had honed his conception of causality to a razor sharpness.

Looking at Duke's crumpled, bloody body, Batiste was once again reminded of the fact that there was an irredeemable class of people who could only be described as *criminals*. Rather than being one predicate among others, this word, *criminal*, corresponded to some more fundamental existential position, one that overdetermined all of that person's other characteristics. This was the depressing conclusion that he had settled on after more than twenty years of police work.

Ballistic analysis would reveal a stolen, unregistered weapon. No one had seen anything and if they had they wouldn't talk about it.

Inspector Batiste liked to watch CSI on television. As a David Caruso fan he preferred the Miami version. Of course, there was no state of the art crime lab back at Slidell police HQ and none of that kind of forensic evidence was admissible in court in real life anyway. In real life crime wasn't interesting like it was on television. Crimes were committed by criminals and the motive was never complicated. Drugs were always involved. Evidence never put anyone away. Snitches did. Even if there were enough time and money to gather and analyze evidence, the average harness bull was too dumb not to fuck it up for the DA. And if, by some miracle, the case made it to court, the jury would acquit, because juries were composed of idiots.

There was no point in checking fingerprints. Half the men in Lacombe had passed through Rhonda's bedroom at some point. He would check anyway.

One detail caught Inspector Batiste's attention: the fresh knife wound on one of Rhonda's cheeks. What could the T shape of the incision possible signify? Some sort of sexual perversion? Many criminals were perverts and sadists. The murder weapon was nowhere to be found, which indicated that the killer had escaped. Inspector Batiste went over a few possible scenarios. Maybe Duke got his snout into some bad PCP and got rough with Rhonda. Hearing her screams, Dolores comes in with backup of some sort. A gunfight ensues, and everyone gets hit but Dolores' friend, who then sneaks out. Maybe. But then what about the bloody knife in Dolores' hand? Maybe Dolores and a friend were cutting up Rhonda for some sick reason – the woman was a rockhead after all – and then Duke came in and tried to stop them. But then how did Duke end up on the other side of the bed? Maybe there was no fourth man. Maybe Duke shot the two women and then shot himself in the chest. No, there were no powder burns. There were at least ten equally valid scenarios. Inspector Batiste felt his head growing cottony at the idea of all the possibilities. The fact was, without a witness or some providential piece of evidence that Inspector Batiste sensed would not be found, this case would go cold and die, like 56% of the other murder cases in Louisiana.

11

Tyrone scuttled to his seat as the bell rang. The ragged purple backpack stuffed with heavy reference books slung over his shoulder caused him to resemble a hunched medieval tinker. It was seven-thirty A.M. World Geography class on Monday morning never failed to agitate him. The teacher, Coach MacGregor, was one of the baseball coaches. He had a strong Southern accent and wore the same thing every day: blue athletic shorts and a white "Mandeville High" T-shirt tucked into the shorts.

As soon as the bell finished ringing, Coach MacGregor handed everyone a piece of paper with an unmarked world map Xeroxed onto it. At the bottom of the paper were the names of twenty-three world capitals: Tokyo, Hong Kong, New York, Mexico City, Cairo, etc. Looking closer, Tyrone could see that there were twenty-three dots on the map. Obviously, they were supposed to match the names of the cities to the dots. Tyrone snorted to himself. Too easy!

As soon as the students saw the test, hands began to go up.

"Is this for a grade?"

"You didn't tell us there was going to be a quiz!"

"This isn't fair!"

"Is this for a grade?"

Coach MacGregor stood in front of the class with his hands up in the pacifying stance of a harried politician addressing an angry electorate.

"This is not for a grade...I repeat...*not* for a grade...this is just an exercise...I want to get an idea how aware you are of basic geography after six months of this class. Match the names of the cities to the dots. It should only take you five minutes."

Tyrone was done within two. Looking up, he saw with satisfaction that he was the first one done and that most of the other students seemed lost.

After twenty minutes, Coach MacGregor put down the copy of *Sports Illustrated* he was reading, stood up and told everyone to exchange their sheets with their neighbors. Tyrone gave his sheet to Jennifer Dupré, a pale white girl with freckles and a tight ponytail whose Daisy Dukes were so short that the bottoms of her ass cheeks hung out. Jennifer was also from Lacombe.

Coach MacGregor labored through the list, holding a copy of the map up to the class and pointing at the cities with a pen. Tyrone gloated as he put X after red X through Jennifer's wrong answers. When it was over she only got one city right out of all twenty-three: Miami. She even got New York and Los Angeles wrong. When Jennifer gave Tyrone his paper back, he was annoyed to see that he had missed four cities.

"Wow," said Jennifer. She spoke with a strong Southern accent. "How did you know all that?"

"I follow world affairs very closely," he snapped. To no one in particular but in a theatrical voice that was a little too loud, Tyrone added that he "always confused Manila and Phnomh Penh." He was even more upset to see that he had not received the highest mark in the class: a quiet boy named Bill who was in the gifted program and never talked to anyone had received a perfect score.

Tyrone raised his hand as if it were an emergency. Coach MacGregor called on him with a little sigh of exasperation.

"Yes, Tyrone?"

"Coach MacGregor, I would like to formally challenge my score. The dot that you claim represents Tokyo is actually located somewhere in the middle of the Tokyo-Sapporo conurbation."

Coach MacGregor paused. "Well, Tyrone, I believe you're thinking of the Tokyo-*Osaka* uh...agglomeration..."

"*Conurbation.*"

Coach MacGregor winced.

"...yes, well, class, Tyrone has made an interesting point here, that Japan is so crowded that the whole east coast is essentially one big endless city. Does anyone know what the most popular sport in Japan is?"

"Karate?" said Jennifer in a chirpy, flirtatious voice. The class laughed. She pushed her breasts in Coach MacGregor's direction. His eyes flicked down for a split second.

"No, Jennifer, although karate *is* very popular in Japan. The most popular sport in Japan is actually baseball. Does anyone here know Ichiro Suzuki? He plays right field for the Seattle Mariners..."

Tyrone drifted off. He was annoyed and agitated for the rest of class because of the four missed questions and had a hard time sitting still in his seat. His penis tingled.

When the bell rang, Tyrone shouldered his heavy knapsack and bolted out into the hall where he met Victor, who was in all the rest of his classes.

Victor Sanders was a husky boy with a pasty complexion and doughy, unlovable features. His red hair was already beginning to thin at the temples. He loved weapons and wore a black trench coat to school every day, even when it was hot outside. At home he kept a gigantic fantasy Rambo knife with H.R. Giger-inspired blade detailing in the place of honor on his well-kept desk. Behind the knife was a composite image of his own face morphing into the face of a dog. Victor had made it using PhotoShop and refused to explain the story behind it to anyone.

Tyrone considered Victor his best friend. Today Victor was wearing a large silver medallion with what looked like

Druidic runes inscribed into it. It was as big as an Olympic medal.

"What's with the bling?" asked Tyrone, assuming the crabbed lackey's position next to Victor, which gave him a stutter-step as they walked to gym class.

"This isn't *bling*," snorted Victor. "This is a genuine Baphomet medallion...and let's just say I had a pretty badass weekend in the French Quarter."

Victor looked into the distance and shook his head a little bit. The gesture signified that he would have liked to tell him what happened but couldn't, either because it was too crazy or because Tyrone just wouldn't understand. The implication, of course, was that *sex* was involved. Tyrone took the bait.

"Well, what happened? Come on, tell me!"

"Let's just say my cousin Chip knows how to have a good time."

Chip was twenty-eight years old and lived across Lake Pontchartrain in New Orleans. The two boys looked like twins. From Boris Vallejo fantasy comics to the Unabomber manifesto, Victor's entire culture came from Chip. Every few months he spent the weekend with his idol in the city. Chip worked at the big-box Barnes and Noble bookstore on Veterans Boulevard in the suburb of Metairie and lived in a dark, dingy apartment on Adams Street in Uptown New Orleans. The neighborhood was home to a mix of Tulane students, middle-class whites and poor blacks. It was segregated into black blocks and white blocks. Chip lived on a black block. Most of the houses were elegant turn-of-the-century wooden homes with high ceilings and original plaster moldings. Chip's four-unit apartment complex was neither elegant nor poetic. It was a cheaply built, dimly lit brick bloc with low ceilings, rusting fixtures, and peeling, yellow seventies wallpaper.

At that precise moment in New Orleans, Chip was sitting outside on his balcony smoking a cigarette before leaving for work. His red, thinning hair looked even thinner than usual because he had just taken a shower. It was humid in New Orleans and Chip's naturally greasy hair stayed wet-looking all day. Chip had just lit his cigarette. His neighbor Latrell emerged from his unit smoking a cigarette of his own. Latrell wasn't wearing a shirt and Chip could see a couple of scars that looked like bullet wounds on his muscular, tattooed torso.

"What up," said Chip, offering his fist in a weak dap gesture. Latrell sat down on the broken folding chair next to his door without saying anything or offering reciprocal dap. He looked nervous and agitated. He was tweaking on crack cocaine.

After a few minutes of uncomfortable silence in which both Chip and Latrell smoked, Chip stood up, crushed out his cigarette, and tossed it in the wastebasket between the two of them.

"Get your fucking cigarette out of my trash can."

Chip stopped in his tracks and looked at Latrell. The gangbanger sat dead still and stared straight ahead.

"Uh...what's that?" said Chip, a tremor in his voice.

"You heard me, motherfucker."

"Hey man, it's just a cigarette butt...and that's the uh...that's the whole building's trash can," said Chip in a faltering voice. "It's cool."

Latrell took a deep breath and walked into his apartment. Chip wasn't sure if their conversation was over or not. He was still standing there deciding whether or not to walk away when Latrell came back out of his apartment holding a pistol. He lifted it to Chip's temple.

"Bitch, you can either bend your ass down and get your shit out of my motherfucking trash can or I can split your wig right here, your choice!" Latrell's eyes were bulging and bloodshot. A little squirt of urine left Chip's penis. He put his hands up in a pacifying gesture and croaked, "Hey man, it's cool, it's cool, I'm getting it...look, no need for violence, man, I get it." Chip bent down and rummaged in the trash can. His hands were trembling so much that he had a hard time holding onto the cigarette butt. "Look, here it is, I got it," said Chip, attempting a smile. Latrell kept the gun pointed at Chip for a second before sticking it in his waistband and sitting back down.

"Come on, man, you have to tell me what happened!" squealed Tyrone as they walked into the gym.

"Wait until we sit down." The two of them walked into the locker room and undressed. Victor's bluff posture and arrogant smirk disappeared. His face and body now displayed fear and submission. A deaf Cajun named Brandon Comeaux changed next to them. He had usurped Victor as top locker room bait animal when his chalky penis trembled to erection in the shower earlier in the year. The three boys pulled on their P.E. uniforms and took their place in the calisthenics formation just before the bell rang.

Coach Roberts sat on the bottom rung of the bleachers holding a clipboard. His hard, fat stomach forced him to adopt an obscene splay-legged position that molded his tight nylon athletic shorts to his testicles. A squinty smirk played across his red, fleshy face. The St. Tammany Parish public school system was run by an unofficial football coach cartel and Coach Roberts was on the fast track to become the next principal of Mandeville High.

Marnee McDonald walked into the gym. Her blue cheerleader's uniform broke the school dress code by two inches. She had a small nose, a ponytail, and a blue Mandeville Skippers anchor painted on her cheek. It was Spirit Week at MHS. Coach Roberts grinned and patted one of his thighs.

"Well, look who it is! Come here, girl."

Marnee smiled and sat down. He put his arm around her shoulder. Mandy Akers emerged from the locker room. Marnee smiled and waved her over. Mandy had a blue ship's wheel painted on her cheek. Coach Roberts patted his other thigh. Mandy took the hot proffered seat. He put his other arm around her.

The calisthenics formation began to disintegrate. Coach Roberts whispered something to Mandy. She giggled. A couple of students got up and walked off. Coach Roberts put a plug of chewing tobacco into his mouth and strutted out of the gym with Mandy and Marnee. He had not even called roll. Victor and Tyrone scuttled into the bleachers.

Victor relaxed back into his Young Nietzsche persona and continued his story.

"Chip had to go to work on Friday night, which was cool with me. I mean, you know me, I'm a lone wolf at heart. So I decided to grab a beer and reconnoiter the hood, solo style. Not without my blade, of course. Any little wannabe hoodrat tries to step, he gets a poke in the gut. It's the ghetto down there, man. No joke. Shit's real Uptown. So I start walking..."

"Hey! Children of the Clover!" called a female voice from the gym floor. Both boys turned to see Jessica lumbering up the bleachers towards them. "Children of the Clover" was her nickname for the three of them. She had come up with it in junior high school.

Jessica's shoulder-length hair had been bleached a sickly yellow the last time they had seen her. Today it was maroon. Jessica changed hair color all the time. Her small, porcine eyes were surrounded by heavy black eyeliner. The new eyebrow piercing above her right eye was infected and the skin around it was red and swollen. She wore red Doc Martens boots, a *Nightmare Before Christmas* hoodie, and a black choker necklace with a chrome ring hanging from it. Jessica was a big-boned girl with wide, solid shoulders, heavy, pendulous breasts, and pasty white skin.

"Hi, boys," she said with a flirtatious smile as she wedged herself into the little space on the bleachers between them. Tyrone anxiously scooted away a few inches.

"Cool medallion," said Jessica to Victor, grabbing it and holding it up so she could see it. The cord bit into Victor's neck as she pulled him off-balance.

"Hey, watch it! Are you trying to break my neck or what? That medallion is no joke! I got it from Mystic Curio in the French Quarter. The guy that runs the place is, like, this real dark priest with a long white beard. You can just tell that some real occult shit goes on in there behind closed doors. I mean, the tourists are, like, *afraid* to go in there. My cousin Chip knows the dude and said he might be able to get us invited to a black mass sometime."

"Cool, maybe you'll bring me there with you." Jessica let the medallion fall back against Victor's chest. "So, how do y'all like my hair? The color is *burgundy plum*." She shook her head from side to side in a studied attempt at Riot Grrrl insouciance.

Before Victor or Tyrone could respond, Jessica stood right back up. "Okay boys, this was just a cameo appearance. I've got to go play basketball with the *nomads* or else Coach Bitch will chew me out!" She turned back towards Tyrone and tousled his nappy hair. "See you Tyrone!"

The two boys stared at her as she clomped back down the bleachers. Victor shook his head in admiration.

"Wow...that choker..."

He snapped his fingers and rummaged through his bag as if he had just remembered something.

"Hey man, check *this* out. I drew it over the weekend at Barnes and Noble's." It annoyed Tyrone that Victor called it *Barnes and Noble's* instead of *Barnes and Noble Bookseller,* which was its proper name. Victor and Tyrone always spent P.E. class making funny drawings, which they called *drawrings* with a fake British accent. The drawring that Victor pulled out was in ballpoint ink on a sheet of loose leaf paper. It was a superhero-style rendition of a muscular black man wearing nothing but combat boots, a military beret, and mirrored aviator glasses. In one hand he held a bloody machete and in the other hand he held what looked like a human heart. A lit crack pipe protruded from his mouth. Victor had also made a point of giving him an enormous, semi-erect penis with intricate vein detailing. Behind him could be seen an "African" landscape of burning straw huts and hacked-up bodies. The block-letter comic book-style caption read GENERAL BUTT NAKED.

"Pretty badass, huh?" said Victor.

"Sweet! Let me see that!"

"Chip told me all about this guy. General Butt Naked is *real.* During the civil war in Liberia, there were all these different warlords that just, like, assembled mercenary armies and then went from village to village killing everybody. General Butt Naked was the baddest of them all. They say he killed twenty thousand people. The night before a raid, he and his colonels would find a baby somewhere that they would cut up and eat raw to give them strength before the attack. See, that's why he's holding a human heart. Then they would get wasted on crystal meth, take off all their clothes, and roll out with machetes and AK-47's. These days he's, like, reformed and turned into a preacher or something. Unbelievable, huh? No offense, dude, but your people are fucked!"

"Ha! As if yours are any better," chortled Tyrone. "Do the names Jeffrey Dahmer and John Wayne Gacy ring a bell? Dahmer used to *trepan* his victims to turn them into sex zombies!" Victor and Tyrone had spent most of the first semester drawing serial killers. The handsome cipher Ted Bundy was Tyrone's favorite murderer. Victor preferred Gacy, fat and full of sexual rage just like him. "Oh, and by the way, my passion for verisimilitude obliges me to draw your attention to a certain factual inaccuracy in your *drawring,* namely the high unlikelihood of the real General Butt Naked being circumcised."

"Shit, you're right!" exclaimed Victor with an exaggerated laugh. "Well, I guess it doesn't really matter. Still, it's pretty badass, huh? Check out the veins on his dick. It took me like half an hour to draw them right."

Tyrone's face clouded. "You might be more right than you realize with that tasteless 'your people' comment. The Liberian population is composed of descendants of former American slaves sent back to Africa at the beginning of the nineteenth century. For all I know, General Butt Naked is my uncle."

"That would be pretty fucking sweet, man! My dad says we might be distantly related to Goebbels, but this dude would be even more badass than that!"

Tyrone's mind raced. Although he couldn't explain how or why, he was suddenly certain of it: he was related to General Butt Naked. Not only was he sure that he was related to General Butt Naked, he knew that the whole thing had something to do with what had happened to him the previous day. These thoughts were accompanied by a tingling in his stomach.

Victor resumed his story where he had left off. He and Chip went to some coffee shop in the Ninth Ward and saw a guy walking a baby goat on a leash. Chip got into a fistfight in the Barnes and Noble parking lot with a coworker over a girl or something. Victor and Chip got drunk on absinthe one night in his apartment and recorded some music.

Tyrone drifted off.

Victor snapped his fingers again.

"Hey man...I meant to ask you...did you hear about the murder in your 'hood? Three dead! A real bloodbath, man. It wasn't too far from your house, either! Did you hear the gunshots?"

Tyrone felt a sudden chill.

"No...what happened?"

"They found all these people blown away in some trailer off of Lake Road. Two women and a man. They haven't caught the guy yet."

"What time did it happen?"

"I don't know. Why?"

"Just wondering." Tyrone looked away and closed his eyes. His head hurt.

"What's up, man? You OK?"

"It's uh...it's nothing," said Tyrone. "I have a headache. I think I'm going to lie down and try to take a nap."

"OK," said Victor. "Shit, maybe you have a brain tumor, man! That would suck!"

Tyrone went to the top of the bleachers and lay down.

His grandmother was frying chicken when he got home from school. He went straight to his room and took out the African history book he had checked out from the school library at lunchtime. There had been a slow but steady trickle of immigration from the US to Liberia all throughout the nineteenth century. Today the descendants of freed American slaves formed five percent of the Liberian population. They had ruled the country for almost two hundred years until Samuel Doe, a member of the indigenous Krahn tribe, seized power in 1980. Tyrone slammed the volume shut, took the 2007 *Almanac* from his bookshelf, and flipped to the entry on Liberia. He shivered with excitement when he found what he was looking for.

Augustus Washington, a sugarcane planter and daguerreotypist from New York, served as Liberia's Speaker of the House from 1854 to 1858.

Tyrone slammed the book shut. He felt elated. Everything was coming together. He held his hand in front of his face and waved it from left to right as if he were conducting an orchestra. His gesture participated in some greater universal unity. He walked into the living room where his grandmother sat eating fried chicken and watching television.

"Get you some fried chicken, boy, it's good," said his grandmother.

"Sure, grandma," said Tyrone. He grabbed a wing, took a bite and began speaking.

"Grandma, did you know we have relatives in Africa?"

"Sure I do, boy," chuckled his grandmother.

"No, not like that! I mean *real* relatives. The Washington family is a very important family in Liberia. Augustus Washington was one of the founders of the country. He owned the largest sugar plantation in Monrovia. Their most famous general is a cousin of ours. I've been doing some research." Tyrone gesticulated energetically with his chicken wing. "It's an established fact. And that's just the tip of the iceberg."

"You sure about that, Tyrone?" She looked at her grandson with compassion. His eyes were bloodshot and he was speaking in his motormouth voice. It was happening again. Over the last six months the devil had been visiting her grandson more and more frequently. She clutched the large wooden cross that hung across her floppy bosom.

"Our family never been outside of Louisiana. We been here since slavery, Lord help us. You been reading too many books, Tyrone. You too smart for your own good. Why don't you find yourself a nice girl and some nice friends? You know I love Victor, but why don't you go out and find yourself some black friends? Put down those books and them Chinese video games and go play ball or something. And you need to eat more, you too skinny."

"Grandma, don't start with that again!" said Tyrone, rolling his eyes. "You know I'm on Sugar Busters..." Tyrone's grandmother didn't laugh like she usually did. She stared at him with concern for a few seconds, then smiled again.

"Sit down next to your old grandma, boy. It's time for our program. I wonder what kind of foolishness that Data going to be getting hisself into this week."

12

Trey woke up at seven A.M. with some kind of appetite. Shemeta slept in the fetal position on the bed next to his. He threw on a polo and walked outside. The sun was shining bright and the air smelled nice and fresh. Seagulls cawed around him. He dropped to the ground, blasted out forty rapid-fire pushups, and walked to the office for his free continental breakfast.

Trey nodded at the new Mexican behind the counter as he approached the buffet table. There was an air pot of coffee, green apples, bananas, a pitcher of orange juice from concentrate, bagels with cream cheese, and donuts.

Trey chugged a glass of orange juice and threw the empty Styrofoam cup into the trash. He opened up a banana and ate it in three big bites. The Mexican typed at his terminal. Trey tossed the peel in the trash and filled a second styrofoam cup with coffee. He poured in six packets of sugar and tasted it. Sweet as hell but still not sweet enough. He creamered up and grabbed three donuts. He sat on the cheap sofa in the reception area and chowed down, alternating gulps of coffee and mouthfuls of donut. Within two minutes he had finished.

Time to grind.

He walked back to the room and turned on his laptop. The first site he visited was the Times-Picayune. He wanted to see if the cops had discovered the crime scene yet.

The headline read THREE DEAD IN LACOMBE SHOOTING. Rhonda had died. Trey didn't give a fuck. There was nothing in the article about Tamica or Shemeta being missing. The rollers hadn't figured that part out yet.

The next step was going to be tricky as a motherfucker. He had to find Tamica a new mommy and daddy. The bitch on Geraldo had broken it down on a pabulum level. Couples had to wait years for a baby, especially a white baby. When demand exceeded supply, prices went up. There were bookoo rules about who could adopt and who couldn't. Fags and pedos were out. Ex-cons and 5150 were out. When supply was artificially restricted, prices went way up. Every drug dealer knew that. America was full of marks. He just had to find one. The way Geraldo flipped it, the internet was crawling with sick fucks looking for babies. Trey shook his head. What kind of pervert would want to adopt a baby?

Trey found his way to a website called Fertilethoughts.com where people who couldn't adopt legally exchanged information about other ways to get a baby.

You could buy a plane ticket to some shithole country in Africa and score an AIDS baby, but it was dangerous and you had to stay there for a long time. You could make a private arrangement with someone to get pregnant and give you the baby, but it was illegal and the mothers often changed their minds once they had their babies.

Whatever.

Trey isolated three freaks leaving comments who might be potential buyers: EarthLove46, GreggDogg, and RayOfLight. EarthLove46 lived in California and couldn't adopt a baby with her "life partner" because they were dykes and both on SSI for being bipolar. What the fuck was a life partner? What the fuck was bipolar? GreggDogg was straight fruit. There was picture of him and his "husband" holding rainbow flags at some penis puffer parade. They had identical tank tops, beards, and dick-sucking smiles. Pedos for sure. They also lived in California. What a fucked-up place.

RayOfLight was another story. He lived in Atlanta and was some sort of wacked-out hippie biker. He and his wife couldn't adopt a baby because he had done time protesting for civil rights in Georgia in the sixties. His paranoid, capitalized rants against the government told Trey he was 5150 all day. The kind of foolio who might actually break bread for black baby. Trey created a new e-mail account under a fake name and signed up to Fertile Thoughts.

He leaned back and lit a cigarette. He would have to think carefully before posting. Who was he? What was his story? Why did he have Tamica? His eyes hurt from staring at the little screen for so long. Tamica and Shemeta were still sleeping.

Trey opened a new tab and navigated to YouJizz.com. He clicked on the first video. A banging brunette with little perky tits and a tattoo of an eagle on her hand was getting fucked by the MILF Blaster. Trey smiled. He loved the Blaster. He was a short, pumped middle-aged guy with a goatee who looked like a horny pool supply salesman. He never stopped cracking jokes and mugging for the camera even as he was pounding ass.

In this video the MILF Blaster wore nothing but a camouflage hunting cap. The brunette told him to *fuck that pussy*. Trey unzipped his pants and pulled his dick out. This brunette was smoking hot. Trey liked her skinny waist and her round, apple-shaped ass.

He advanced the video. The MILF Blaster was fucking her in the ass now. Trey nodded in approval.

The MILF Blaster accelerated. The bitch moaned. He pulled out, turned her around, and blasted a load of cum all over her face. The Blaster grinned from ear to ear and gave a double thumbs-up. The camera panned down to the brunette. She opened her mouth and showed the cum to the camera. She reminded Trey of a sac-au-lait fish gasping for air. He stopped the video and walked over to Shemeta. Tamica stirred next to her. Trey began slapping Shemeta's face with his erection. After a few taps around her lips, she gave a start and opened her eyes.

"Morning," said Trey.

Shemeta blinked in confusion.

"Time to go to work," said Trey. "Breakfast of champions. You need you some high-quality protein." He forced his penis into her mouth.

She flubbed the insert.

"Watch the fucking teeth!"

He tried again. This time she gagged on it.

Shemeta had not inherited the dick-sucking gene from her mother.

"Fuck it." He pulled out of her mouth, jerked himself off with a flourish, and let out a major groan as he blasted a few ropes of sticky cum all over Shemeta's face. The pearly white cum gleamed in the lamplight against her dark black skin.

"Damn," he said, "look at you...fucking splashed! You look good like that, girl...got your war paint on." He grabbed a couple of paper towels and brought them over to Shemeta. "Good girl," he said, patting her on the head.

Shemeta got up and walked to the bathroom. Before wiping herself off, she took a good look at her reflection. What she saw in the mirror was *a real woman*. She arched her back and admired her breasts in the mirror. The white man had told her she had the nicest titties he had ever seen.

She sashayed over to Tamica's bottle and squirted some cold formula in with the turkey baster. Tamica was sleeping. Shemeta wanted to feed her. She made sure the white man wasn't watching, then grabbed Tamica and shook her. Her sister's neck wobbled like a bobblehead. She immediately began crying.

"Shh, shh, baby, baby," said Shemeta as she rocked Tamica. "You hungry." She forced the bottle into Tamica's mouth. Tamica squirmed away and wailed.

"Why you so stupid...that's breakfast you sucking on, dummy." Shemeta forced the nipple into Tamica's mouth.

"Shut it up!" barked Trey from behind his computer. "And change her fucking diaper...it fucking stinks in here!"

Within ten minutes Tamica was out cold again. Shemeta carried her into the bathroom and took off her diaper. She didn't even try to wipe all the smeared poo off her bottom before putting on a new one. What could she do with no wipey box?

Trey fired up a blunt to get his brain working and sat back down. There was no way he could front as anything but the goon he was. He wouldn't even try. His story would be straight ghetto.

I have a baby and I want to sell it. Family died in a drive-by. Stray bullet. Fourteen years old. That hood life, bruh. Me and my girlfriend snuck into the trailer and took the baby before the government could put it in an orphanage.

RayOfLight would like that part.

A week later my bitch girlfriend runs out on me in the middle of the night and takes all my money too. I can't take care of the baby myself so I'm looking for a responsible couple to raise her right. Promise made to her dying momma.

Trey was tempted to send RayOfLight an e-mail right away. First he had to pimp the backstory. Everything had to be straight in his mind from the first e-mail. He hit the blunt again. What was the mother's name? Tammy, like his stepsister? No, too white. Something blacker. LaNigra? Trey chuckled and then stopped himself. *Get serious, bruh. Play around later once your paper's right*. He would say the mother's name was...Lanita. Who was the father? No father. What would the baby's name be? It would be smarter to give her a fake name. What was the little girl's name on the Cosby Show? He couldn't remember. Raven Simone? No, that was the actress. He was wasting time. Fuck it, call her...LaTasha. Good enough. Where did all this happen? RayOfLight didn't need to know that. What if RayOfLight got spooked and tried to call the cops? That was a risk Trey had to take. There was no way for them to trace the e-mail address. He would have to be careful when he set up the rendezvous. If there was one thing Trey knew how to do, it was sell dope and not get caught. That's what Tamica was: dope. Looking over at her sleeping on a pile of clothes on the floor, Trey imagined that the withered preemie was filled with cocaine.

What else did he need? A photo of Tamica.

Shemeta was eating a big bag of cheese puffs on the bed and watching TV.

"What the fuck are you watching?" asked Trey.

"Highway to Heaven."

He stopped and watched the television set for a few moments. Some guy with a beard and a baseball cap was talking to an old lady while sappy music played in the background. Shemeta was absorbed.

"Looks boring as shit." Trey walked over to Tamica. *That is one ratchet-ass baby,* he thought. She looked more like a skinny grocery store chicken than a newborn human. How could he make her look cute? What the fuck did he know about making babies cute?

"Hey!" barked Trey. "Turn that shit off. I got a job for you."

Shemeta didn't respond. Trey walked over to the TV and slammed it off. "Hey! When I say move, you move, you heard me?"

"That white man mean," whispered Shemeta to Tamica in a baby's voice.

"What the fuck did you just say?"

"Nothin."

He slapped her. "Don't you ever talk back to me like that! I'm the fucking boss around here, you heard me? When are you going to get that through your fucking skull?"

Shemeta glared at him. He slapped her again, harder this time. Two fat tears rolled down her cheeks and her thumb went to her mouth.

Trey pretended to look contrite.

"Come here, girl." He dropped his head and made an apologetic gesture with his hands. "Look...I'm sorry about that. It's just that we're in this shit together, ya heard me? I need you right here by my side. I need you up in the cut with me. Now, I see you paying more attention to fucking Highway Angel than me and I get a little burned, that's all. Cause I need your help."

Shemeta's lower lip trembled.

"Come here," said Trey. Shemeta hesitated, then buried her head against his chest. "There you go. It's all good, girl." He stroked her hair. "Now, we got a little job to do. Baby Tamica ain't looking so hot. We want her looking cute cause I want to take some family photos, ya heard me? Now, I'm a man, I don't know shit about making babies cute. So I need you to take care of that for me while I go take a little walk. Wash her up, get her fresh, whatever. You can do that?"

Shemeta wiggled with excitement.

"She gonna need barrettes, and a lil' blanket, and a bracelet with pink and yellow hearts, and lil' booties, and..." Trey was amazed at the speed and enthusiasm with which Shemeta enumerated everything Tamica would need to look cute. He hadn't planned on going back to the store but a ride would do him good. He needed more beer anyway.

The bright midday sun hurt his eyes. All of a sudden he felt exposed and paranoid. There were ears and eyes everywhere. It wouldn't take much for the situation to flip on him. All the girl had to do was walk three hundred feet from the motel room to the lobby and tell the Mexican behind the counter everything. *Go straight to jail, do not pass Go, do not collect two hundred dollars*.

He cursed, grabbed the nylon rope he used to truss bucks, and marched back into the room.

Shemeta was gobbling Jalapeno Cheddar Cheetos and watching TV with a big smile on her face. She hummed and bopped her head left to right in time with the M.A.S.H. theme song.

Trey walked back out to the car shaking his head. He stowed the rope and took a deep breath. *Slow your roll, homeboy* he thought as he pulled out of the parking lot. His eyes went down to the license plate of the car in front of him. It read DIC 666. He chuckled. Then he froze.

"Fuck!" He punched the steering wheel in rage. How could he be so stupid? His identity was billboarded on the back of his car for every last cop in the world to see! He pulled into the first big beachfront hotel parking tower he saw and drove straight to the empty top floor. He found what he was looking for against the far wall: an abandoned car. Parking garages were full of them. It was like *Where's Waldo*. You just had to keep your eyes open for the telltale layer of dust.

Trey chuckled as he thought of stupid-ass Waldo with his faggot puffball cap and stripy shirt. When he was a kid he had stolen a "Where's Waldo" book from his second-grade classroom. After finding and circling Waldo on every page he threw the book in a ditch.

Good memories.

It took Trey less than five minutes to unscrew the license plates from the silver Lincoln Town Car and make the exchange. He slipped his own plates under the backseat rug.

At Wal-Mart, he bought a package of plastic barrettes, a fuzzy baby jumpsuit with pastel cartoon birds on it, a case of Budweiser, a gallon of milk, a loaf of white bread, a prepaid cell phone with a new phone number, a thirty-two slice pack of American cheese, a pack of Hormel brand salami, two bags of Chester's Flamin' Hot Fries and three King-sized Snickers bars.

On the way home, Trey put on Master P's 1996 single *Bout It Bout It* and cranked the bass on his 15's. He bopped his head as P shouted out every damn state in the South over one of the grimiest beats ever laid on wax.

Niggas in Florida...Down in that water...

Trey looked out the window at the ocean. White boys fucked with water too. He pulled over. The beach was nearly empty. He stripped down to his shorts and plowed straight into the still-cold early summer Atlantic. With powerful strokes he propelled himself away from the shore. He did not stop swimming until his lungs burned and his thick arms were as limp as Funnoodles. When he turned around, the shore was so far away that his car looked like a Hot Wheels. A porpoise crested ten feet in front of him. Trey wondered if a flush punch to the dome would kill it. He swam back.

He walked out to the end of one of the narrow concrete piers that jutted into the water and sat down cross-legged. The yellow ball of the sun hovered overhead. He had a lot of thinking to do. In the distance was a yacht. Trey thought he could see a fat man in a captain's hat surrounded by women in bikinis. He wondered if they were shooting a porno.

Nodding, Trey reminded himself of first principles. *Remember the big picture. Don't get lost in the details. Stay focused. Plan your moves. Always go for the throat. Never give up.*

When he stood up to walk back, his features were once again calm and composed. His flat, taut muscles rippled in the sun.

13

Trey found Shemeta holding Tamica and watching "Perfect Strangers" on television. As usual, the baby was asleep. Shemeta squealed when she saw the Wal-Mart bag.

"Lemme see!" She grabbed the bag and dug through it. "Where the booties at?"

"Don't need no booties. Her little suit got booties built-in. They sewed on there."

Shemeta frowned.

"What about the bracelet?"

"I forgot the fucking bracelet. That ain't important. She got her little suit and her barrettes. A baby cute as Baby Tamica don't need no bracelet."

Shemeta pouted.

"She need booties."

Trey fired up a blunt and watched Shemeta put the barrettes in Tamica's hair. The baby protested every time Shemeta pulled her hair tight to get the barrettes on.

The hydroponic hit fast and hard. Trey took a closer look at Tamica. There was something wrong with her goddamn face. Her eyes were too far apart and the openings were too small. Her nasal bridge was totally flat. The area between the bottom of her upturned nose and the top of her mouth was too wide and too smooth. Her head looked suspiciously small and her ears had a weird extra ridge near the top.

What the fuck?

Tamica was as tricked out as she was going to get. Trey took her from Shemeta and laid her on the bed as he would have laid a ten-pound redfish across the top of his ice chest to fillet it. Tamica stirred. Trey stood on the bed next to her and aimed the camera downwards to get the framing right. He took a few photos with and without flash.

"Lemme see! Lemme see!" cried Shemeta.

Trey showed her the pictures.

"She look *Chinese.*"

Trey laughed. "Shit, you're right."

"Now take one of me holding Tamica!" Shemeta held Tamica up next to her and smiled so hard her eyes almost closed. Trey smiled and took their picture.

"I got an idea!" said Shemeta. "I'ma do my hair just like Tamica!" She ran into the bathroom. Trey was amazed by the speed with which Shemeta duplicated the exact same complicated-looking barrette arrangement in her own hair. She held Tamica up to her face and smiled extra wide. He snapped a few more photos, then grunted.

"That's enough."

"One more! Please!"

"Put her down." Shemeta pouted and put Tamica down on the bed. "Me and you are gonna take some pictures *without* Tamica. Take off your shirt. Lemme see them big ol' titties." He walked over to the bed, picked up Tamica with one hand, and set her carelessly on the night table. She began crying. "Come on, chop-chop." Trey snapped his fingers. Shemeta stuck out her bottom lip and crossed her arms. She wanted to take more pictures with her sister.

Trey didn't give a fuck what she wanted. He grabbed the bottom of her tank top and yanked it up so that she had no choice but to lift her arms and let him peel it off. With his left hand he roughly palpated her breasts and with his right hand he held the camera, which he had switched to video mode.

Trey reached down and pulled down his shorts. His erect penis sprang out of the elastic waistband like a cobra preparing to strike. It bobbed just inches from Shemeta's face. She gazed at it, mesmerized. It looked gigantic and frightening. All of a sudden she felt hot in between her legs

Shemeta shivered and giggled with each passage of the clippers. Thirty seconds later, it was finished. "Now go look in the mirror," he said. Shemeta ran over to the mirror.

Her kitty looked funny but she liked it. She reached down and scratched between her legs.

"It feel like...*cold.*"

"Now come here!" Trey couldn't hold it any longer. The sight of Shemeta's meaty, engorged lips had turned him into a bull in rut. He threw her over his shoulder like a sack of corn and carried her back into the bedroom.

Trey then once again committed statutory rape on Shemeta with great vigor and enthusiasm, slapping her face and calling her a whore. Shemeta did not try to hide her enjoyment. When he ejaculated on her lower belly, she gasped with pleasure. Outside, the sun disappeared over the rooftops of Daytona Beach.

14

Trey woke up from his post-nut snooze disoriented. Shemeta was still sleeping and the TV was on. He looked at his watch. It was nine P.M. Had it really only been thirty-six hours since was sitting back in his trailer in Lacombe watching TV and firing up a blunt? He rubbed the sleep out of his eyes, dropped to the ground, and did fifty quick pushups to clear out the cobwebs.

The air in the motel room was dank. Tamica must have taken another shit. Trey considered waking Shemeta up so she could change the diaper but decided that peace and quiet were more important. He transferred Tamica to the bathroom floor and shut the door to reduce the smell.

Trey walked outside and lit a cigarette. The still-warm asphalt felt good on his bare feet. He sat down on the back of his Taurus and stared at the beach across the highway. He could hear the sounds of screeching tires, ringing bells and rock music emanating from the Go-Kart track down the road. After a few seconds, he recognized the song,

Cherry Pie by Warrant. Trey wouldn't have minded going Karting himself.

He flicked his cigarette onto the pavement and walked back into the cold, squat, dungeon-like motel room. His stomach rumbled. He walked over to the fridge and made himself two salami and cheese sandwiches and a glass of milk, which he set on a paper towel next to his computer. Time to put his plan into action. He cracked his knuckles, then rolled his head from left to right to crack the vertebrae in his neck as well.

First he uploaded the photos of Tamica to his computer. Next, he navigated back to FertileThoughts.com and found RayOfLIght's email address. He opened up his own e-mail inbox and began composing a message with his two index fingers. After twenty-five minutes, he sat back and reread what he had written.

RayOfLight,

I believe your looking for a baby to adopt. I found your e-mail address on the adoption website. I sympathize with your situation and have a proposition that might interest you. I am looking for the right person to adopt my baby. She is a black baby named LaTasha. If your interested I can tell you the whole story. She is looking for a good family. Please respond as soon as possible as my situation is urgent. LaTasha may be the "ray of light" that your waiting for. I'm in a similar situation to you with the goverment so I know how it is. You sound like the kind of person who know's how to do business. So lets do business together.

Sincerely,
Trey Green

It looked pretty good to Trey. Rereading it a second time, he had an idea. Chuckling, he deleted "black" and replaced it with "African American". He was now sure that RayOfLight would eat it up. He hit the *send* button and sat back in his chair. All he could do now was wait. He would give RayOfLight twenty-four hours to respond before sending the message to GreggDogg and EarthLove46.

Trey got up and grabbed a beer from the fridge. He downed it in three swigs, then grabbed another. He felt antsy and started to pace. Every few seconds he glanced at the computer screen.

Halfway through his third beer, a chime indicated that he had just received a new e-mail. A jolt of electricity shot through his body. RayOfLight had not wasted any time. Trey guessed that he was the kind of pathetic freak who spent sixteen hours a day on the internet. RayOfLight's message was short and to the point.

Dear Mr. Green,

Please send me some proof that your proposition is legitimate.

Sincerely,

Ray Jackson

Game on. A month earlier, Trey had caught a monster five-foot alligator gar in Bayou Lacombe. It looked like a fucking dinosaur. It took him thirty minutes to land the fish. He had hooked RayOfLight but he hadn't landed him yet. He would have to handle the line carefully, knowing when to pull back and when to give out slack. Now was the time to reel RayOfLight in. Within two minutes, Trey had sent an e-mail with the "Chinese" photo of Tamica.

RayOfLight's next message surprised Trey.

Dear Mr. Green,

She certainly is a beautiful little angel. But how do I know that you didn't just get that photo off the internet somewhere? If you are serious about your offer, please take a photo of LaTasha holding a piece of paper with my name written on it. Then we can talk.

Sincerely,

Ray Jackson

You want to play tha Game...well, let's play the motherfucking Game then, bruh. Trey grabbed the Wal-Mart receipt and wrote "RayOfLight" on the back with the free pen the Sun Tan Motel had left on the nightstand. He placed the receipt across Tamica's chest and snapped a photo. Within two minutes Trey had uploaded the picture and sent it to RayOfLight along with the following message:

RayOfLight,

I mean business. If your interested, call me at this number in the next ten minutes. No more emails.

Trey

This was the big moment. Trey wanted to keep RayOfLight disoriented and on the defensive. By forcing him to call right away, he would keep the initiative. More importantly, Trey didn't want to give RayOfLight the time to talk to anyone, record the phone call, or get the police involved. If RayOfLight called, the deal was sealed.

Trey grabbed his brand-new untraceable phone and walked out to his car to wait for the call. He put the phone in the cup holder of his Taurus and lit a cigarette with steady hands. The parking lot was empty. He could make out the Mexican from the night before sitting behind the desk in the brightly lit lobby of the Sun Tan Motel. It looked like he was watching TV.

Trey checked his watch. Four minutes. This was the crucial moment in the deal, the moment when the lines of authority were being drawn.

Trey scratched his balls. Thirty seconds before the ten minutes were up, the phone rang. Trey didn't say "Hello?" like a chump when he answered the phone.

He assaulted through the objective.

"Just in time, RayOfLight."

"Start talking," said RayOfLight. He had a deep, gravelly voice. He didn't sound intimidated at all. "Who is she, why do you have her, why are you offering her to me. The whole story. Start."

"Alright, bruh. Be cool. Here's how it is. LaTasha's momma is dead. Died two weeks ago. Got shot. Stray bullet. She was sitting at home watching TV. Died just like that, holding her baby. No family, no baby daddy, no money, no *nothing*. Me and my girl heard the shots and ran over there. LaTasha's momma was *all* banged up. Gruesome sight, bruh. LaTasha didn't even know what happened and she just had a big old smile on her face even though she had her momma's brains all over her. Like a little angel from Heaven, bruh, I ain't lying. That's how sweet she is. We took her before the social services could get her. We good people, bruh, we didn't want her growing up in no orphanage. We was tight with her momma. A week later, my girl runs out on me. Middle of the night. Took all my fucking money. Now, I ain't too happy about that and neither is LaTasha. Fact is, I'm broke. I don't know shit about taking care of babies. I can't even take care of myself. I just learned how to fry a egg yesterday, bruh, no joke. How the fuck am I supposed to raise a baby? So I'm trying to find a family for LaTasha without giving her to the fucking government. There it is."

"And do you have any proof for that extravagant story? Where will I be able to find a newspaper article corroborating what you've just told me?"

"No article, bruh. Let's get this straight. I'm helping LaTasha find a new family. Don't you worry about proof. I'll be straight with you. This whole situation is fucked up. You don't need to know any more than what I just told you. In fact, the less you know, the better. You get LaTasha and ain't no one going to be asking you no questions after that, ya heard me? That's a promise. You just going to have to believe me. You can take LaTasha as is – and she cute, bruh – or we can stop doing business right now. Your choice."

RayOfLight went silent. Trey had scored a point. This turkey really wanted Tamica.

"How do I know this isn't a scam?"

"Ray, you know this ain't a scam cause I just told you it ain't a scam. Now, I understand you got no reason to trust me. But you just gonna have to trust me. I'ma level with you. This some shady shit we doing, bruh. Now, you know and I know that we just trying to do right here. Problem is, the government don't see it that way. They don't care about LaTasha. They don't care about shit. That's why you can't adopt a baby, and that's why I got LaTasha to begin with. That's why you talking to me right now. Fact is, you don't like what you hear, you can just hang up that phone and go back to watching TV. Grab yourself another beer from the fridge and change the channel. What time is it, ten-fifteen? You still got time to catch the sports on the news. But if you hang up, don't try calling me back, bruh, cause I won't answer. Opportunity knocks once, Ray, and you got to know when to open that door."

Trey was in the zone. With his left hand he idly massaged his semi-erect penis. He could hear defeat in RayOfLight's voice when he responded.

"How much do you want?"

"Like I told you, bruh, I'm broke, my girl left, I'm sick. I won't lie to you, Ray. I'm in a fucking jam. Now, we ain't talking bout a plasma TV. We ain't talking bout a flatboat. We talking about a baby. You can't bargain shop on that one, bruh. You can't just grab a News On Wheels and pick out the one you want. You can't drive over to Wal-Mart. Now, how much does a new car cost? Fifteen, twenty grand? You ask me, a family's worth more than a pickup. Now, I ain't greedy, bruh. I just want to get my life back on track. Fix my car, buy my medicine, pay off them people. You know how it is."

"How much?"

Trey dusted his voice with gangster frost.

"Given my situation, I can let you have her in exchange for thirty G's."

"Thirty thousand dollars! That's a fortune!"

"It ain't cheap, bruh. But like I said, you ain't buying

toothpaste at the Time Saver. You ain't buying Doritos. You buying a human life. You buying grandchildren, bruh. You buying a family. You buying happiness for you and for Baby LaTasha. You ask me, thirty grand sounds like a deal."

There was a long pause.

"I...I can't give you an answer right now. I have to talk with my wife first."

"Sure thing. You talk it over with the missus. You think about it. Give me a call tomorrow night on this number at ten P.M. sharp. I'll be waiting for you. One more thing. You sound like a reasonable dude, Ray. Like I said, this shit ain't exactly legal. Don't get any funny ideas about talking to anyone besides your wife, ya heard me? I done my research, I know who you are, I know where you live. We'll just leave that train of thought right there, alright bruh? You play straight with me and everyone going to be happy, you, me, the missus, LaTasha, her dead momma up in Heaven. We can leave it right there, ya heard me? It's been good talking with you, Ray."

Trey hung up the phone before Ray could respond.

"Fuckin' A!" he exclaimed. He pumped his fist and raised two middle fingers to the haterz. He had stayed in control from beginning to end. RayOfLight was going to say yes. He had read RayOfLight like an old Batman comic. Highballing the price had been a gamble but it was clear that RayOfLight was willing to break a hustler off. Fuck, he should have asked for more! He jumped out of the car, lit a cigarette, and started panther pacing.

Thirty G's, motherfucker!

Trey punched the air, did a back flip, and walked back into the motel room.

15

Ray Jackson hung up the phone and lit an American Spirit brand cigarette with trembling hands. His wife would be home from the bio-dynamic gardening class she taught at the local Anthroposophy Institute in half an hour. Bio-Dynamic gardening was an agricultural method invented by the turn-of-the-century Austrian guru and esotericist Rudolf Steiner that involved talking to plants and fertilization by gnomes. Ray and Wanda Jackson were Steiner people. Wanda taught kindergarten at the local Waldorf school. The educational methods practiced in Waldorf had been revealed to Steiner in moments of divine clairvoyance. The gods that spoke to him had told him that humans learned in seven-year cycles. For this reason, many Waldorf parents did not cut their children's hair until they reached their seventh birthday. Instead of learning to read, Waldorf kindergarteners learned to move their bodies in a calisthenic dance known as "eurythmy." The gods had revealed to Steiner the movements that made up eurythmy. Wanda also taught eurythmy.

Ray shifted his bulk in his wooden desk chair. He was a fat man with a long white beard and long white hair that he wore in a ponytail. He had lost his left leg below the knee in a motorcycle accident twenty years before and wore a prosthesis. He was naked. Ray valued his comfort and felt more free and natural when he was nude. The table was stacked high with papers, plastic knick-knacks, prescription bottles, and bills. Ray and Wanda's house was a mess. They were hoarders and they never cleaned. To the right of Ray's laptop sat an ashtray overflowing with butts. Next to the ashtray was Ray's penis-stretching device. One of Ray's websites was Thunder's Place. He had taken up penis enlargement two years before in the hopes of being able to give Wanda more pleasure when they made love. Wanda had a very large vagina. Ray's gains had been modest but palpable: he had gone from having a penis that was 4.75 inches long by 4.5 inches around to having a penis that was 5.5 inches long by 4.75 inches around. His penis was now on the small side of average. Of course, he fudged the length a little bit when he measured it, substituting his bone-pressed erection length for his non-bone-pressed erection length. Jabbing the ruler into the fat pad above his mons pubis allowed him to pick up an extra half-inch. Like everyone else on the website, Ray hoped one day to possess the "Irish Sword" – a penis measuring eight inches long by six inches around. For girth, Ray "jelqed" – massaged his penis as if he were milking a cow's teat – for half an hour a day, five days a week. His principal length exercise consisted in hanging weights from his penis while he was sitting at his computer. He found this method to be both more effective and less painful than the expensive stretching device he had bought on the internet and now rarely used.

Ray did not work. He and Wanda lived on her small Waldorf salary and his SSI checks. They had bought the house with the two hundred thousand dollar settlement he had received for his motorcycle accident. He woke up every morning at four A.M. and began posting and chatting. In addition to Thunder's Place, Ray frequented an alternative medicine website called CureZone, a Steiner website, eBay, Facebook, Infowars, and Fertile Thoughts. He also played Second Life. His avatar was a blue dragon woman with HHH cup breasts named Raylene.

Every day, when Wanda came home from work at four P.M., the two of them drove fifteen minutes to Duck's Cafe and Bakery together, where they bought their chocolate éclairs. They were crazy about éclairs. Duck's sold gigantic éclairs the size of Triple Whoppers. While they ate their two "Colossal" éclairs apiece, Ray and Wanda each drank a twenty-four ounce cappuccino. At first they went to the trouble of adding spoonful after spoonful of sugar to their giant cappuccinos until they were as sweet as ice cream. Then they discovered that they could ask the employees to add a few shots of vanilla-flavored syrup, which was even sweeter.

They had their own battered plastic gas-station mugs that they would present to the store employees every day to rinse out from the day before and refill with their milky, sugary coffee drinks. The mugs were never washed at home with soap and a thick, sticky, permanent brown film had developed at the bottom.

Ray and Wanda disgusted the Duck's employees. They never stopped touching each other. Their caresses were not those of an adult couple but those of children attempting to draw their mothers into prohibited incestuous contact. Their daily Duck's bill came out to almost twenty dollars. They spent more money on chocolate éclairs and coffee than they did on their utility bills and cars combined. One day Wanda explained to one of the bored, disdainful teenagers who worked there that they had tried to make their own éclairs at home to reduce expenses but they couldn't get the cream filling right. This afternoon snack added over fifteen hundred calories to their daily total and was the principal reason why they were both fat and diabetic.

Ray was nervous but excited. He and Wanda had wanted a child for years. Five years ago they had made a deal with one of the Waldorf parents to let them raise the baby she was pregnant with – her sixth – but once she had the child she couldn't bear to part with it.

Ray frowned when he thought of the money. Where would they get thirty thousand dollars? They had no savings. Ray already knew what Wanda's response would be. She would be willing to do anything to get that baby. Ray frowned again when he thought of the man's voice: menacing, cold, flat. The voice of a killer, possibly working for the FBI. Ray wasn't sure if he believed the man's story about the baby's mother being murdered. He wondered if Trey was the one who had done the murdering. His gut told him that the story was a lie but the offer was legitimate. Chances were that the man had somehow come across the baby and simply wanted to make some money by selling her. What if the man had kidnapped the baby? There was no way to know. Even if he had, chances were that he and Wanda would be better parents than whomever he had kidnapped her from.

A frightening new thought occurred to Ray. What would happen to LaTasha if he and Wanda *didn't* buy her?

He closed the Thunder's Place window on his desktop and looked again at the first photo, the one in which her eyes looked half-open.

An angel.

Ray heard the front door open. Wanda was home. She walked into the living room, settled into her chair, and lit an American Spirit.

"Honey," said Ray, "hold on tight, because I'm about to give you the most exciting news you've had in a long, long time."

Tears of joy streamed down her face as soon as the word "baby" hit her eardrum.

"We're finally going to have a family!" she kept repeating.

"Wanda, where are we going to get that much money?" asked Ray in a gentle voice.

There was a long, pregnant silence. Ray broke it first.

"I...I could sell it."

It was a Salvador Dali lithograph, number 25/300, that Ray's father had acquired when he was in the army during the liberation of Paris in August, 1944. A young, rich, beautiful, eccentric French noblewoman had given it to him as a gift along with a night in her bed as thanks for having expelled the German occupier. It was Ray's most cherished possession. He had barely known his father and this small print possessed a talismanic significance for him. Its value had been appraised at thirty thousand dollars.

Ray gazed at Wanda with his hands clasped under his chin. Their house and everything in it was mortgaged to the gills. Most of Ray and Wanda's paychecks already went to paying off their massive debts. There was no way the two of them could get another loan. The bank didn't know anything about the print. They could sell it without having to give the usurers at Capital One any money. Wanda had begged him to sell it for years. The fact was that they needed the money. Ray always said no. This was his one rule. No matter how bad things got, the print was off-limits.

To part with the print would be to part with the only bit of iron he had. On the other hand, he would not be selling the print to pay for something ephemeral but for a human life. For a daughter!

Wanda stared at her husband. She wanted to scream. How could he hesitate at a moment like this? Her heart slammed against her ribs.

If he doesn't sell it now, I'm going to leave him!

Wanda had been jealous of the Dali ever since Ray had first shown it to her. No...she hated the Dali...despised the Dali! Once, after finding some sexy pictures on Ray's computer that had been sent to him by a woman he had met on the internet, she had gone as far as to light the match with which she intended to burn the print. Weeping, her hands trembling, she moved the match towards the print, only to lose her resolve at the last second and blow it out.

Her husband sighed, shifted in his chair, and looked her in the eyes. His voice was grave and measured when he spoke.

"Sometimes the Goddess moves in mysterious ways. Now I know why I kept that print my whole life. It was in preparation for this moment. We'll sell the Dali."

Wanda stood up and embraced Ray. She had never loved him so much in her entire life. Not only were they going to have a family, but the print that had for so long kept her from being a real woman would be gone!

In an access of transcendental joy, she walked into the center of the room and began doing the Eurhythmy movements that she taught to her kindergarten students.

16

Tyrone woke up at dawn on Tuesday morning. He was too excited to sleep. When he looked in the mirror he realized that he had the exact same nose and indeed the same bone structure as his distant uncle General Butt Naked. He picked up a plastic Light Saber and watched himself slashing downwards with it as if he were beheading an enemy tribesman with his machete.

He bent down and pulled out the secret box of precious stuff that he kept under his bed. These objects had all possessed a certain talismanic value for Tyrone at some point in his life. They included a 1923 silver Peace Dollar, a broken padlock that he had found in a parking lot, a turkey feather, a pencil that he had sharpened down to the eraser, a rubber band ball, and a small, rusted mother-of-pearl handled knife. Tyrone dug through them until he found the snake skull he had scavenged underneath a cypress tree at the edge of Bayou Lacombe. He had boiled the skull to remove the pieces of flesh that still stuck to it. He had not done a very good job of it. There were still little bits of hardened gore wedged in the crevices.

Rummaging deeper, Tyrone found a leather necklace with a turquoise on it that he had bought at the Lacombe Crab Festival from an Indian named Margo for five dollars. He removed the turquoise, strung the leather cord through the snake skull's eye holes, and tied it behind his neck.

Tyrone admired himself in the mirror. He would wear his SR-71 Blackbird T-shirt. The snake skull hung over the cockpit of the plane. He made sure to hide it inside his T-shirt before walking out of his room. His grandmother would consider the snake skull to be Satanic.

Tyrone and Victor met up as usual on their way to P.E. class. Victor glanced at the snake skull and frowned

He opened his mouth to say something, then froze. Richie, Bradley, Carter and Ian, four of the most aggressive nomads at Mandeville High, were standing outside the entrance to the locker room. They all played varsity sports. Richie was the worst. He owned a pickup truck with big wheels that he took mudding every weekend. It was considered prestigious to have as much mud as possible on your pickup truck on Monday morning in the Mandeville High parking lot.

Richie was short, thick and hardboiled pink with thinning blonde hair. He was as strong as a bull and played lineman on the football team. He smiled when he saw Tyrone and Victor approaching.

"What's up, Columbine? Hey, cool necklaces, guys."

The nomads laughed. Richie grasped Victor's medallion with a meaty hand.

"Let me see that." He pulled it roughly over Victor's head. "Whoa. This necklace is sweet. I'm buying it from you, dog. How much you want? Fifty bucks sound good?"

Victor didn't respond. His freckled face had a fishbelly pallor.

Richie screwed up his mouth in an expression of concentration as a he pretended to rummage through his pockets.

"Here, hold this for a second." Richie handed Victor a piece of lint from his pocket with a sincere smile. The nomads laughed when Victor took it.

Tyrone's gaze floated upwards as if it were attached to a balloon. He now watched the action from ten feet above his head. It was like watching news footage from a surveillance camera.

Richie patted his pockets, shrugged, and said, "Looks like I forgot my wallet at home today. I'll pay you tomorrow, how about that? We got a deal, buddy?" With a big smile he held out his hand for Victor to shake. Victor extended his sweaty hand. Richie squeezed it as hard as he could. Victor winced but tried not to show it. The nomad gave a last phalange-crushing squeeze and let go.

He turned to Tyrone and smirked.

"Webster, I'm not even gonna touch whatever the fuck that is around your neck." He turned back to Victor. "See you tomorrow, Columbine!"

They wandered off.

Tyrone and Victor said nothing as they slunk into the locker room to change. Victor went into a toilet stall and threw up. They changed without making eye contact with each other.

Outside, Victor walked up to the top corner of the bleachers and sat staring off into the void. Tyrone wandered onto the basketball court.

There were four basketball games going on. The first game was the mixed nomad/Orc game. Tyrone and Victor referred to the lumpen class of African-American students as Orcs. Most of them had been deemed learning disabled by the St. Tammany Parish public school system. Most of them were from Lacombe. Most of them dealt drugs. All of them had sculpted, muscular physiques with cut, bulging triceps brachii muscles. All of them could dunk. So could some of the taller nomads. The game played at the first goal was rough, loud and fast-paced.

The second goal was for the harlots. They only pretended to play competitively. The real goal of their game was to wiggle their behinds for the nomads.

The third goal was for the normalfags. Their game was a watered-down version of the nomads' game: less violent and athletic but still organized around ideals of aggression, masculinity, and physicality.

The fourth basketball court was for nerds. Their game was not aggressive. They did not attempt layups or muscle past each other towards the goal. They did not dribble or pass. They played "Horse" and didn't speak to each other. This was the game that Tyrone joined.

When class was over, Tyrone and Victor walked back into the locker room. A crowd had gathered around the latrines. Everyone was laughing. Victor's schoolbag had been thrown in a toilet. It was soaked in urine. Some enterprising student had even defecated on it.

The cafeteria was serving chicken nuggets for lunch that day. Tyrone and Victor had to wait in line for ten minutes to get their lunch tickets. Everyone liked chicken nuggets. Tyrone's ticket was free because he was poor. All the other black students got free tickets too. Instead of waiting in line, they shouldered past the whites to demand their handout.

Tyrone and Victor took their trays and sat down at the table occupied by the retarded students and their aides. This was the only table they were allowed to sit at socially. Tyrone and Victor knew the names of all of the members of the "Learning Zone".

Stacy was a stunted, twisted, nineteen-year-old body that wouldn't have measured longer than four feet if it were possible to stretch her out. She was confined to a soiled high-tech wheelchair and couldn't eat or breathe without a Foley tube. Her face looked wrinkled and evil.

Michelle was also confined to a wheelchair. She was capable of breathing and swallowing food but not of speaking or controlling her bladder. Her eyes never stopped rolling back and forth in her head. Her disposition was generally pleasant.

Katie resembled Michelle with her Beatles shag. She was capable of standing, walking, and swallowing food without spilling too much of it. She could not speak, but when she was happy she made a ululating noise like a seal.

One day Katie had a seizure just two feet away from Tyrone. When her head slammed into the tray some of her corn splattered into Tyrone's mashed potatoes. For the next week, he and Victor made a series of drawrings of the incident. They invented superhero costumes for the retarded students and drew them fighting crime.

Today there would be no drawrings at lunch.

"Rats," Victor said in a fake casual voice. "They'll get what's coming to them." He stabbed a chicken nugget into a blob of mayonnaise. "Did I ever tell you my dad's story about rats in Vietnam? One day his unit discovered that if they left a plank against a drum full of cooking grease the rats would just run up it and fall into the bottom of the drum. Every night they would leave the plank up and every morning the drum would be a foot deep with rats squirming around in the grease. They would just drop a match in there and watch them burn. That's how you deal with rats."

Tyrone stared at Victor's pores. He had never noticed them before. There were so many of them. They finished their meal in silence.

There was a pep rally that afternoon. The handful of outcasts who chose to skip it were led into Mrs. Decker's biology classroom by Coach MacGregor. He had been assigned babysitting duty after Coach Clave had gone to jail for having sex with a fourteen-year-old student. He sat behind the desk and opened a copy of Sports Illustrated magazine. The students sat in small groups and chatted in hushed voices. Tyrone, Jessica and Victor sat at the back of class, near the turtle.

Coach MacGregor put the magazine down and stood up.

"I'll be back in a few minutes."

He left.

Jessica turned to Victor. "Hey Victor, what happened to your medallion?"

"I sold it."

"Really? Why? It was cool!"

The corner of Victor's mouth turned up in a bitter smirk.

"Let's just say I got an offer I couldn't refuse." He snorted. "And it wasn't that cool anyway." He stood up brusquely. A few heads turned to look at him. He put on his trench coat and walked to the back of the classroom with his chest thrust out and his hands clasped behind his back. He began marching back and forth like a soldier on patrol. Tyrone stared at the blank piece of paper on his desk. Everyone else gaped at Victor. When he reached the wall he marked a brisk pivot like a Buckingham Palace guard.

"Victor...stop...come here," pleaded Jessica. He continued pacing.

"Dude...what are you *doing*?" asked Jennifer Anderson in a mocking voice. She was a flat-chested redhead with glasses who gossiped nonstop with her gay best friend Clay. He snickered next to her. Victor didn't respond. Jennifer continued.

"No, seriously, man, what the hell do you think you're doing?"

Victor reached into the side pocket of his trench coat and took out a big Rambo knife and a whetstone. He slid the blade across the stone with a theatrical gesture. He continued to stare ahead of him. Clay's mocking laugh had a distinct lisping quality. Jennifer continued.

"Dude, put that away. You think you're all like, tough and Matrix, but you're not. You're just going to get in trouble. No one is afraid of you. Seriously."

Victor ignored her.

"God, give me a break." Jennifer Anderson shrugged and turned back to Clay. The two of them resumed their gossip. Jessica addressed Tyrone.

"Tyrone, what the hell is going on?"

He continued to stare at his paper.

"The warrior is preparing for battle."

"What? What battle? What are you talking about? What's wrong with you two today?"

"Richie stole his medallion and desecrated his property. Looks to me like Victor has taken it as an act of war."

"An *act* of *war*? Oh my god. Poor Victor...that fucking mongoloid Richie...he makes me sick!" Jessica stood up and walked towards Victor.

Clay snickered and motioned with his head for Jennifer to watch. Jessica's loose, confident, devil-may-care gait was that of a woman who believes that she is being watched and desired by every man in the room.

Jessica stopped in Victor's patrol path and put her hands on her hips with blowsy confidence. He went around her. She turned around and followed him.

"Fuck that shithead Richie! Don't give him the pleasure of making you crack up. Listen to me, Victor. Put the knife away, OK? Just come sit down with me." She spoke louder than necessary. Victor didn't respond. Jessica grabbed his arm and spun him around.

"Victor Sanders...if this is what it will take..." She leaned towards him and kissed him on the lips. Clay and Jennifer sniggered viciously at their desks.

Tyrone turned away from Victor and Jessica and looked at Bill, the boy who had gotten the perfect score on the geography test. Bill looked so kind and intelligent. He wasn't laughing at Victor and Jessica, although Tyrone was sure he was embarrassed for them. More than anything in the world at that moment he wanted to go talk to him but there was an absolute barrier between them. Tyrone belonged to a different species. He had never felt such sadness in his life. Turning back towards the stupid, tawdry spectacle his friends were putting on, he felt a desperate revulsion for them both as well as for himself. They were now making out in the back of the room. Tyrone imagined them as two worms or slugs rubbing their mucus holes against each other.

Victor and Jessica stumbled back to their desks holding hands. They were both flushed and beaming. For the rest of the pep rally they cooed, pawed at each other and kissed. Tyrone laid his head on his desk and pretended to sleep. His hands were on his lap and the entire weight of his head was on his forehead. He rolled it back and forth. It was painful because of his numerous forehead pimples. He imagined his round forehead bone as a steamroller and wondered if his pimples would pop if he put all his force into mashing his head against the desk. He tried it. Pain shot through his forehead but none of his hard, deep pimples exploded. He imagined them rupturing under his skin and infecting his bloodstream. He wanted to die.

Jennifer Anderson and Clay dashed out of the room as soon as the bell rang. Within two minutes they had found Coach MacGregor and told him about Victor's knife. Coach MacGregor alerted Kurt, the school policeman, and the two of them rushed back to the classroom.

Kurt loosened his gun in his holster as they approached the room. It was happening. This was why he had joined the police. To protect Americans from terrorists. If this Columbine punk tried anything, he would nail him between the eyes. He had seen the freak around campus before with his black trench coat and always knew that one day he was going to try something.

When he and Coach MacGregor burst into the classroom, there was nobody left but Victor and Jessica. They were making out ferociously in the back row. Jessica's hand was massaging Victor's erection through his jeans. A tiny spot of pre-ejaculate had soaked through the denim. They stopped as soon as they saw the adults.

"Put your hands up and stand up slowly!" barked Kurt. Victor looked bewildered. "Now!" shouted the police officer. Victor did as he was told. His erection was visible through his pants.

"You too, girlie!"

Jessica crossed her arms and didn't move.

"Or what – you'll shoot me, pig?"

"Leave her alone! She didn't do anything!" cried Victor. "It's me you want." He strode to the front of the room with his wrists held out in front of him.

Officer Kurt slammed him face-down on the desk and frisked him.

"Easy, Kurt," said Coach MacGregor.

"Easy, huh? Looks like this little fucker wasn't planning on going easy on anyone with this!" Officer Kurt brandished Victor's Rambo knife. "Were you, punk?"

A few minutes later, Victor was being led away from the school in handcuffs.

Tyrone's ride home seemed to last forever. The schoolbus was hot and smelled like naugahyde and sweat. Most of the students who rode Tyrone's bus were also black: the Orcs from his P.E. class. He tried in vain to read the book on mental disorders that he had discreetly checked out from the school library but couldn't concentrate. Something was wrong with his brain. He had taken off the snake skull and put it in his pocket. What on earth had he been thinking?

Tyrone flipped through his book until he found the chapter on paranoid schizophrenia. There was a picture of a white teenage boy sitting on his bed with his head in his hands. Tyrone began reading. *Psychotic episode... delusions of grandeur... feelings of persecution... language troubles...*

Tyrone put his book away as he neared his stop. Normally this was the scariest moment of the day. He got off at the same stop as Terrell and Clifton. Sometimes they beat him up. With glazed eyes Tyrone stared at the back of their muscular necks.

Let them kill me, he thought. *I don't care.*

But they didn't pay any attention to him, just walked home talking to each other and dribbling a basketball.

When Tyrone walked into his trailer, he saw his grandmother's huge body lying in the middle of the floor like a piece of installation art. She was dead.

PART TWO: THA GAME

17

Trey woke up Tuesday morning to find Shemeta watching *The Price Is Right* on television. He sat up, rubbed his eyes, and hit the blunt on the nightstand. Shemeta yelled out the prices of the consumer products in question along with the contestants. She had no idea how much dish liquid or gold cleaner cost but she was spot-on when it came to electronics. When *The Price Is Right* was over, Trey and Shemeta fucked. This time it was Shemeta who initiated their coupling. When she coyly put her hand on Trey's penis he chuckled and told her once again in a smooth voice that she was a little ho already. Afterwards, he was in such a good mood that he walked across the parking lot to the Waffle House down the strip and brought Shemeta a Pecan Waffle and chili cheese hash browns.

Shemeta was still watching television when he got back. Tamica had taken another dump. The smell infuriated him and ruined his good mood.

"How many fucking times do I have to tell you to change the fucking diaper when she takes a dump? Fuck!"

Shemeta ran to the bathroom and changed the diaper. Trey sat down, took a bite of his Patty Melt, then threw it down in anger.

"It smells like fucking shit in here! I can't even eat my goddamn Patty Melt!"

Shemeta ate her Pecan Waffle like a pizza. With each bite she crammed her mouth so full of food that her cheeks bulged. She hardly chewed at all before swallowing. Syrup dripped from her fingers onto the bed.

Trey shook his head in disgust and opened his laptop. No messages from RayOfLight. Good. Trey was horny and agitated but didn't feel like fucking Shemeta again. He was sick of her. He wanted some white pussy. He slammed his laptop shut.

Like any good general, Trey had planned his attack from multiple angles. It was time to start the ball rolling on Phase B of his game plan. The idea had come to him during the long car ride. He grabbed his LSU cap and pulled it down tight over his eyebrows.

"Don't even think about leaving," he barked at Shemeta. "I'm going for a walk." He slammed the door behind him.

Once outside, the first thing he did was suck down a lungful of fresh air. The motel room had begun to smell like black person. He walked towards the squat, aging strip mall on the other side of the Waffle House. Half of the storefronts were abandoned. The three remaining businesses were a Chinese restaurant called Yang's, a liquor store, and a strip club called Double D's. The windows of Double D's had been painted black from the inside. He put on his dark sunglasses so that no one could see his eyes and pushed open the plate-glass door.

The dark strip club smelled like beer and cigarette smoke. The ceilings were low and made of acoustic tile. Six motherfuckers were seated around the small, circular stage where a fat bitch with dyed blond hair and a tattoo of a spider on her stomach thrashed to the old Four Non-Blondes acoustic-grunge song, *What's Going On*. Two or three other ratchet day strippers walked around the bar talking to the clients. Trey took a seat near the stage and ordered a five-dollar Budweiser.

From behind his dark glasses, he audited the clientele. Three roughnecks were dropping a lot of ones on the fat blonde. The rest of the clients were alone. Two of them were black, one a young, tattooed goon in a fresh white undershirt, the other fat and middle-aged with a mechanic's jumpsuit on. They both smoked cigarettes. The mechanic was a possibility but neither of them was quite what he was looking for.

Then Trey spotted his man. Next to the goon, right by the stage, sat a fat, soft-looking, middle-aged white man with greasy hair, thick, plastic-framed glasses, and bulging, nervous eyes. His pock-marked face was moist with sweat. He looked like a toad. The man wore a short-sleeved white button-up shirt and brown polyester pants. He had sweat stains underneath his armpits. Trey adjusted his chair so that he could observe the man better from behind his dark glasses without drawing attention to himself. He drank what looked like a mixed drink. Every time the stripper came to him, he leaned forward a little and held a dollar bill out with the same wooden gesture, and every time she accepted it the same way, by pulling aside her g-string and letting the man catch a glimpse of her withered-looking meat curtains. She did this for all the men. Occasionally she turned around and let them see her vagina from behind her cellulite-stippled thighs.

The three offshore men kept yelling "*Good...Night!*" as they slapped each other on the back and laughed like chumps.

The next stripper to come up was a chubby black girl with a tattoo that said *DeAngelo* in cursive script across her left ass cheek and a tattoo of a huge marijuana leaf on her right cheek. When she took off her shirt to reveal a pair of flat, sagging breasts, Trey saw that she also had a tattoo of an erect penis spurting cum in the middle of her chest. Underneath the drawing he could make out the words "Seven Licks". His own penis stiffened a little. If he hadn't been so sick of black pussy at the moment he would have been eager to shell out a little cash for a chance to last longer than seven licks with DeAngelo's girl.

Meanwhile, the toad hadn't moved an inch, just continued producing a steady stream of Washingtons for the girls.

Trey ordered a second beer. The first stripper came up to his table and sat down next to him, pressing her legs against his under the table. She wore nothing but her pink g-string, clunky pink high-heels, and a pink sheer top.

"Hey, handsome. What's your name?"

"Don't worry bout my name," said Trey, running his hand up one of the stripper's thighs and flashing her a gold smile. "But you can tell me yours."

“My name is Candy,” said the stripper, pawing at Trey's chest. “I like your sunglasses.” She moved to take them off. Trey grabbed her wrist.

“The glasses stay on...Candy. But that don't stop you from letting me see what you got under there.” Trey hooked a forefinger in her sheer negligee and pulled it down so he could see her breasts. With his other hand he explored her camel toe under the table. She didn’t stop him. His eyes remained glued on the man seated at the stage.

“Why don't we go to the back room, sugar,” said Candy. She caressed his chest. “Let Miss Candy give you a lap dance.”

The goon seated next to the toad got up to leave. Trey pushed Candy’s hand away.

“Save it...Candy.”

He took the goon’s seat and turned to his mark.

“Nice view, huh bruh?”

The man flinched and stole a nervous look at Trey. He gave the slightest of nods before turning his face back towards the “Seven Licks” stripper on stage.

Trey leaned forward and rapped with the stripper.

“Damn, girl, that ass look like two scoops of Haagen-Dazs chocolate!” Trey pulled out the wad of one-dollar bills the cocktail waitress had given him. The stripper turned back, smiled at him, and wobbled her ass in his face. Trey slid a bill in her G-string.

“That ain't no Haagen-Dazs bullshit you got in your face, baby. That's that Ben and Jerry's.”

“Whatever it be, you keep moving it like that, I'ma be tempted to drop some sprinkles on that thang.” The stripper laughed and wobbled harder. Trey smacked her on the booty and threw five ones on the stage. She gathered them up and moved off towards the offshore oilmen. Trey turned back towards the toad.

“Damn, bruh, did you see that ass?” Trey nudged him with his elbow and pointed to the stripper. “Look at that, bruh.”

The man twitched. Trey whistled the cocktail waitress over.

"I'd like another Budweiser and whatever this gentleman would like," said Trey, indicating his neighbor.

"No, no, I'm fine," stammered the man.

"Come on, bruh, it's on me. Anything you want, dog."

"I'll have...a...uh...a Sprite."

"You like that hard stuff, huh bruh?" said Trey, clapping him on the shoulder. He turned to the cocktail waitress and said, "One *Sprite* for Rambo here and another Budweiser for myself." The waitress laughed. He was the mayor of this goddman place already.

Trey raised his glass. "Here's to fine-looking bitches." The man gave a slack toast. "What's your name, bruh?"

"Richard."

"Well, Rick, today is your lucky day. You know why? Because you gonna be excited when you hear what *I* got to tell *you*."

Richard looked desperately around him.

"Let's move somewhere a little quieter, bruh," said Trey. "I got something to show you." Trey grabbed Richard by the arm and marched him over to a corner table away from the stage. Richard resisted at first, then let himself be led. "Now, Rick, the moment I saw you, I knew you and me had the same problem." Trey looked around conspiratorially, leaned in closer and lowered his voice to a near-whisper. "We both love that chocolate pussy, bruh. Like a couple of bloodhounds on a buck. Course, liking pussy ain't nothing to be ashamed of. Like I told you, dog, you ain't gonna regret having met me, not when you see what I'm about to show you. Now, that bitch up there is pretty tight, but I got something a lot better than that for you. Don't ask no questions, dog, just check this out." Trey took out his phone. He scrolled through the pictures of Tamica until he found the video he was looking for. He pushed play and handed the camera to Richard.

Richard's eyes bugged out of his head when he heard Shemeta say that she was twelve years old. Watching the video over Richard's shoulder, Trey thought with satisfaction that his dick looked huge in Shemeta's mouth.

"She's right down the road, bruh. Two hundred bucks gets you half an hour with her. Tightest pussy you ever felt."

"Is this some sort of a trick?" croaked Richard. His face had gone as pale as the belly of a toad.

"No trick, dog. Give me the word and that could be your dick in her mouth in about five minutes."

Richard swallowed, blinked, then swallowed again.

"Okay."

"There you go, dog," said Trey, holding out his fist for Richard to dap. Richard stared at it in incomprehension. Trey smirked and clapped Richard on the shoulder.

"Smartest decision you ever made. You ain't gonna regret it."

Trey drained his Bud and stood up to go. Richard hadn't touched his Sprite. The two men walked back outside into the waning sunlight. Trey could once again hear the sounds from the nearby go-kart track mixed with the cry of seagulls. The air was soft and velvety and smelled clean.

"Follow me," said Trey. The two of them walked in silence for a few minutes until they were behind the dumpster in the empty corner of the Sun Tan Motel's parking lot.

Trey swiveled to Richard. The friendly body language disappeared. His voice was hard when he spoke.

"The money."

Fumbling, Richard took out his wallet, extracted two hundred-dollar bills and handed them nervously to Trey. Before Richard could put the wallet back in his pocket, Trey snatched it from his hands.

"Hey!"

"Richard Hublak, age forty-six, address 558 Palm Court," read Trey with a smirk. He put Richard's driver's license in his pocket and returned the wallet. "Don't worry, Rambo, I just need to make sure you don't do anything stupid with my girl. You get it back when you're done. Course, if anything *does* go wrong, I got a real good memory, specially for names and addresses." Trey stared hard at Richard with these last words. The sweat stains under Richard's arms had doubled in size since they left the club. Trey's features softened and he patted Richard on the arm. "Come on, homeboy, time to rock and roll. You just wait here for a couple minutes while I get her ready. I'll be right back."

Trey found Shemeta watching *Perfect Strangers* again. She was nursing Tamica.

"Turn that shit off for a second, girl. I got something important I need to talk to you about." Trey's face softened into the puppy dog pout he used to bamboozle bitches. "Girl, you know we in a tight spot. Your momma is dead and gone and you with me now. We ain't going back to Lacombe anytime soon. Listen to me. There's a man outside by the name of Richard wants to meet you. I told him how special you were and how beautiful you were and he agreed to help us out. Like I said, Richard's a real generous man. Now, I'ma be straight with you. I didn't want to tell you cause I don't want you to worry, but we flat broke, and that man gonna give us some money. You just gotta spend half an hour with him, be nice to him. I told him bout the two of us, bout how much you mattered to me. Like I said, he wants to help us. But I need your help too. We in this shit together, girl." While speaking, Trey had slowly moved his face closer to hers until their noses were almost touching. He took Shemeta's hands in his. When he kissed her, Shemeta's body went slack in his arms. "Fact is, I love you, girl, and that's the truth of the matter. So you just do this for us and everything gonna be alright, ya heard me?" Shemeta nodded. "Alright, girl," said Trey as he stood up and walked back outside. He had a pained but resigned expression on his face.

Richard was still standing next to the dumpster. Trey's lips curled off his gold teeth in a predatory smile.

"Kickoff time, bruh. Follow me." He opened the door. "Richard, meet Shemeta."

18

As soon as he had fished his tiny penis out of the fly of his briefs, he lurched forward and stabbed himself into Shemeta from behind. His whines increased sharply in volume and he convulsed like a jackrabbit. When he came fifteen seconds later, the noise he made was that of an abandoned infant wailing for its mother.

Richard's frenzied features returned to normal. The switch inside him had been flipped back to its original position. Fear now spread through his body like a paralyzing neurotoxin. What had he just done? What the fuck was he doing here? He jumped off of the girl as if she were burning hot and fell down backwards with a crash. She flipped onto her back and looked at him. He saw mockery in her eyes.

"I-I'm sorry!" stammered Richard in an accusatory tone as he zipped his pants back up. He had only one thought: get the hell out of there as quickly as possible. What had he just done? He felt no remorse, just blind terror at the idea that he might get caught. He almost fell over a second time attempting to put his shoes back on. The girl Shemeta continued to stare at him with her indecipherable facial expression. He wanted to stab her. Pulling his shirt back on, Richard ran to the front door and threw it open. He stopped dead in his tracks when he saw Trey blocking the exit.

"In a hurry, bruh?" said Trey with a big smile on his face. He reached over Richard's shoulder and pulled the door quietly shut.

"Move." Trey grabbed him around the arm and marched him back into the enclosure behind the dumpster. Richard trembled.

"Where you going, dog? You got twenty-four whole minutes left!"

Richard stared at the ground. Trey chuckled.

"You're a pathetic piece of shit, you know that?"

"Shut up! Just give me my driver's license back!"

"Cool off there, bruh, you losing control. Listen, Rick, I been thinking. I think I'm going to have to hold on to your license for a little while. You had such a good time with Shemeta in there that I figured I'd make you a special offer. You come by tomorrow at the same time and I'll give you a full two hours with her for the low, low price of five hundred dollars. Take your time and make the passion last. How's that sound to you?"

"No! I never want to see her again and I never want to see you again either! Let me go!"

"That's unfortunate, bruh. See, Shemeta likes you. She wants to see you again. Wants you to groove with her for real next time. You coming tomorrow, bruh, end of story."

"That's extortion! You can't do that to me!"

Trey casually reached behind his back and pulled out his Glock. He showed it to Richard with a smile.

"Cool off, Rambo. I got something else to show you." Trey took the camera out of his pocket and showed Richard a photo of him eating Shemeta's ass. Her underage face was plainly visible. Richard's stomach turned. What was happening to him?

"See these photos? God bless satellite technology. I already sent them to a buddy of mine. Now, my buddy's a dirty motherfucker, bruh. I bet he's choking his chicken to them right now. Shit, I would be. Course, you can figure the next part out. Anything happens to me, my buddy hits send and you in jail for a long, long, time. Now, I already been down. Jail don't scare me too much. I get respect in jail. I *like* jail. A guy like you, on the other hand" – Trey looked Richard up and down – "I ain't so sure."

Richard was too frightened to move or speak. He realized with sickening certitude the magnitude of the error he had just made. This man would now start bleeding him dry. He would be lucky to escape with his life.

Trey put his hands on Richard's shoulders and turned him around. "Now you go on home and get you some rest. I'll be seeing you tomorrow at six P.M. in the parking lot of Double D's. Remember, bruh, you got a full two hours tomorrow, so take it nice and slow and get your money's worth next time, ya heard me?"

Richard stumbled back to his car in a fog of fear and rage.

Balki put a pot on his head. Shemeta laughed. That man Balki was goofy. The cracker walked in and went straight to the fridge. He liked them cold ones. She turned back to the TV. Larry told Balki to take the pot off. Larry was a little bitch. The cracker nudged her on the shoulder. He had twenty dollars in his hand. He paused, then took out twenty more dollars.

"That's for you, girl. Job well done. That wasn't too hard, was it?"

"For real?"

"For real. You paper stacking, girl."

She took the stacks and smiled. Forty dollars!

"That man a pervert," said Shemeta with a giggle.

"You right about that, girl. But that pervert the man putting food on the table. So we gonna have to get used to Richard coming by now and then."

Shemeta frowned. She didn't want to see Richard again. Richard was straight gross. She looked at her stacks. Her boo needed her help. He loved her. He couldn't do it alone. They was in this shit together.

She smiled. It had been kind of funny. She giggled again as she imagined the pervert smelling her panties. And now she had forty dollars! She could use her stacks to buy extensions at the hairdresser's. Maybe she even had enough paper to get her nails done too. She wanted them long and red with little Tweety Birds on them. She loved Tweety Bird. She and Tamica and the cracker would drive together to Disney World and all them other bitches would be jealous of her white man, her baby, her nails, and her weave.

The white man handed her a blunt. She hit it. This time it didn't make her cough. A feeling that was like...*warm* washed over her. She never had to go to school again. She was paper stacking. She had a baby and a baby daddy. Her momma was dead and gone. She could turn a grown cracker into a slobbering bitch just by taking off her clothes. Shemeta looked down at her breasts and smiled as she thought of what her man had said when he first met her: *you got the nicest titties I ever seen.*

19

Richard Hublak couldn't sleep. He had masturbated four times since leaving the Sun Tan Motel and his lipstick-sized micropenis throbbed with pain. Richard worked as a nurse in a hospital. He struggled with a number of sexual fetishes and perversions. As a nurse he was able to satisfy many of these impulses unnoticed. His penis got hard every time he stuck a syringe in somebody's arm, especially if he saw that they were not comfortable. He spent a lot of time cleaning up feces, and this too excited him sexually. Best of all was when a patient died. Richard felt like God when the patient's eyes glazed over at the exact moment of death.

Once Richard had injected an old and unloved cancer patient with a lethal dose of morphine. The man, whose name was Rodney, stiffened, shot him a terrified look, gave a death rattle, and died.

Richard could not sleep for two reasons. First of all, he was afraid of what was going to happen to him. He had gotten himself into a terrible situation and he saw no way out. Richard had no illusions concerning the man who was extorting him: he was a ruthless killer. The second cause of Richard's agitation was Shemeta. He had never been as sexually excited in his life as he had that afternoon, and Richard was a man for whom nothing mattered in life but sexual excitement. He did not have a single friend and had cut off contact with his family years ago. The other hospital staff avoided him. They could tell that there was something wrong with him. When Richard was not at work he spent all of his time looking at sadomasochistic pornography. The only non-sexualized activity he ever engaged in was collecting Beanie Babies brand stuffed animals, and even this activity was saturated with sexuality for Richard in some obscure way. In the rare lucid moments that followed orgasm, Richard felt hatred for himself and his sickness. But this feeling never lasted long. As he lay in bed squirming, unable to sleep, Richard could not keep the image of Shemeta's asshole out of his head. At this moment, he didn't care about the five hundred dollars or the danger that he was in. He just wanted to have his way with the girl again.

Richard began to stroke his tiny penis for the fifth time that evening.

20

It was five minutes to ten and Trey was amped. The weed had worn off and his mind was as sharp as a samurai sword. He sat in the front seat of his parked car and bopped his head to the T-Bo album, *Dat White Dude*. Trey had left Shemeta in front of the TV with another blunt.

The phone rang at ten P.M. sharp. He turned off the CD and answered on the third ring.

"Good evening, Ray," said Trey in a syrupy drawl.

"I don't know you and I don't trust you, but you've got a deal."

Trey punched the air with his free hand. "There you go. Smart man. LaTasha gonna be real happy with her new daddy. I bet you and the missus done already popped a bottle, am I right?"

"We don't drink alcohol."

"Here's how we gonna do this. You in ATL, right? What kind of car you drive?"

"A yellow 1985 Volvo station wagon."

"Well, you going to be driving that bitch down to Daytona Beach, Florida on Thursday. That's where we meeting. At six P.M., you going to pull into the parking lot of the Waffle House on Highway 27. Now, you just gonna sit there. I'll recognize *you*, ya heard me? When I flash my lights you going to pull out and follow me. Then you going to walk out the car with a paper bag that you going to hand to me. Once I make sure it's all there you get LaTasha and you get the fuck out of there. Come alone."

"That's impossible," said Ray. "I'm coming with my wife."

"Leave her at the Waffle House. Tell her to get a Patty Melt and wait for your ass while you handle your business. We between men. It ain't gonna take long." Trey heard Ray let out a deep breath on the other end of the phone.

"Okay."

"Looks like we good, bruh. See you in two days."

21

On Monday, Inspector Batiste got an unexpected break. Bob Cousin, the man who ran the pawn shop, came down to the station to talk to him. Rhonda Jefferson had come into his pawn shop with a stolen watch not long before being murdered. No watch had been found at the crime scene, which meant that whoever killed her had taken the watch. Inspector Batiste's captain had ordered him to suspend all of his other cases to work on the Lacombe triple homicide.

After getting a precise description of the watch from Bob Cousin – the BALLIN' inscription on the back made it unique – Inspector Batiste sent his men out to comb the different jewelry stores on the Northshore to see if anyone could remember selling such a watch.

Officer Ron Brown was a young recruit to the Slidell PD. He was a muscular young black man of medium darkness with a bright, honest smile. He resembled the football player Reggie Bush and everyone on the department teased him about his good looks, healthy diet, and rigorous workout schedule. Inspector Batiste had high hopes for Ron.

After spending the morning hitting the dingy Gause Boulevard strip in Slidell, Ron struck paydirt at a jewelry store next to the Hammond Square Mall in Tangipahoa Parish. The teenage girl who worked there was a strawberry blonde named Misty. Ron scanned her with his cop-trained eyes: pasty, doughy, trailer-class features, too much eye makeup, large, tubular breasts, a small gut, thin hips, and skinny chicken legs. She snickered bitterly when Ron asked her if she remembered selling the watch.

Misty sure remembered Trey. How could she forget the man who ruined her life? After selling him the watch, she had gone to his trailer in Lacombe and fucked him. He woke her up at seven A.M. the next day, forced her to have anal sex with him, and kicked her out of his trailer in the middle of nowhere, miles from her house in Goodbee. Fuck, her asshole was *still* sore from his huge-ass dick.

After calling all of her friends, none of whom answered the phone, she walked to the Burger Hut and called a cab. There were no cabs in Lacombe and the man on the other end of the line told her she would have to wait half an hour for one.

While she was waiting for the cab, her boyfriend Tony drove by on his way to the Wal-Mart distribution center where he worked. She didn't see him. Later that night when he asked her where she had been the night before, she told him she had stayed home and masturbated twice while thinking of him.

Tony beat her up and broke up with her. That had been a few months ago. Now Tony was engaged to a fat slut named Caitlin who was going to have his baby. That was how Misty knew Trey.

Misty thought Ron, with his crisp uniform, bright smile, brass buttons and bulging muscles, was one of the sexiest males she had ever seen. She loved black men. She decided to break her rule about talking to police.

"Sure I remember. The guy's name was Trey." With a big, flirtatious smile, Misty told Ron the whole story, leaving out most of the details. Her eyes teared up when she told Ron about Tony.

He was the love of her life.

Officer Brown's cop sense tingled as he listened to Misty's story. The name Trey matched the T cut into Rhonda Jefferson's cheek.

"Ma'am, would you be able to give us a description of this Trey?"

"I can do more than that. I can lead you to his trailer. My momma says I have the best memory for directions in Tangipahoa Parish." She gave Ron a flirtatious smile. "But you gotta buy me lunch at Cuco's first. I'm just dying for a big Chimichanga."

Misty ordered a Double Patron Rita with an extra shot of tequila as soon as they sat down. For the next half-hour, Ron ate his enchiladas and listened politely as she told him Tony's life story. When the overweight Mexican waitress dropped off the check, Misty leaned forward and dug her knees into Ron's under the table.

"My tits are nicer than the waitress's. Don't you think?"

"Let's get going, ma'am."

Once they arrived at the trailer, Ron called Inspector Batiste. He showed up with a forensic team ten minutes later.

"Good work, officer." said Inspector Batiste, patting Ron on the shoulder. "Now be a gentleman and escort this lady back home."

Misty invited Ron into her squat brick ranch house for a drink. When he stood up to leave after finishing his coffee, she gave him a raunchy look, dropped to her knees, and unzipped his trousers. Ron tried to protest but his cop resolve was no match for Misty's boss mouth.

As soon as Ron left, Misty ran to the bathroom, spat his semen into her right hand, and plunged it into her chubby meatus. Her vagina was dripping wet and within a few minutes she was fisting herself to get the sperm in as deep as possible. Tears ran down her freckled cheeks. She would show Caitlin and Tony.

Inspector Batiste knocked on the door of Trey's trailer. No answer. He sensed that Trey had absconded. There was nothing in his mailbox. So far he didn't have enough proof to get a search warrant. He got down on his hands and knees and looked under the trailer. An alarm went off when he saw the tip of a black plastic bag emerging from the dirt. He became aware of a faint odor of death.

Fuck.

He crawled under the trailer and tugged on the plastic. Whatever was in there was heavy. He pulled harder. The plastic ripped. Batiste gagged. He put a handkerchief over his mouth and looked inside. The partially decomposed and heavily lacerated face of a pit bull stared back at him. Worms crawled in the eye sockets. There was a huge T branded in the center of its forehead.

Dogfighting was a crime in Louisiana. He had his warrant.

Batiste closed the bag and crawled back out. As he was dusting himself off, an ambulance roared into the trailer park with its sirens blazing. Batiste watched in surprise as two burly EMS men ran into the trailer next to Trey's and came back out a moment later with an enormously fat woman on a stretcher. She was dead. The ambulance drove off. A uniformed cop whom he didn't recognize and a social worker remained at the scene. The social worker was speaking with the young, shy-looking kid that Inspector Batiste pegged for the woman's grandson. He called over the uniform cop.

"What's going on here?"

"Heart attack."

"No foul play?"

"Just too much cholesterol."

Inspector Batiste gave the patrolman a cockeyed look and walked over to where the concerned-looking social worker was speaking in hushed tones with the boy. He interrupted them.

"Excuse me, may I speak to this young man for a few minutes?"

The social worker, a middle-aged white woman with blue eyes and dishwater blonde hair, gave him a stern glare and didn't respond. He smiled and led the boy over by Trey's trailer.

"What's your name, son?"

"Tyrone Washington." His tone was mechanical.

"Tyrone, what can you tell me about the man who lives next door to you?"

The deer in the headlights look that Tyrone gave him told Inspector Batiste that he knew something. The social worker stormed over and interposed herself between Tyrone and Inspector Batiste.

"This boy's grandmother has just died. He is now alone in the world. His mother is a crack addict. He has no money and no family. I refuse to allow you to submit him to a police interrogation right now!"

Tyrone stared at him with an eerie, shell-shocked expression on his face.

"My condolences, son." Under the protective gaze of the case worker, Batiste handed Tyrone a business card with a telephone number on it. "If you remember anything – anything at all – just call this number and ask for Inspector Batiste."

He smiled and tipped his hat to the social worker. She glowered at him with her hands on her hips as he drove away.

22

Nothing happened Wednesday morning. Trey and Shemeta smoked blunts and watched television from eight A.M. until four P.M. There was a *Crocodile Hunter* marathon on the Discovery Channel. Trey loved the Crocodile Hunter. Even though he seemed like a pussy in a lot of ways, Trey had respect for any man who wasn't afraid to dive into a muddy pond and come up to the surface holding a geeked twelve-foot crocodile. He himself had killed gators before, though never with his hands. You put some chicken on a hook, tied it to a tree, and went home. If you were lucky, when you came back later that night there would be a gator on the hook, and all you had to do was shoot it or pop it on the top of the head with a bang stick.

High on blunts, watching the Hunter wrangle croc after croc, Trey began thinking.

The Hunter is a straight baller. He's in the Game too. His game is a little different, but that's not important. He's got that Australia game.

This was a revelation for Trey. He began to pay closer attention to the way Steve Irwin handled his business.

After a few episodes, Trey came to the conclusion that it was all in the swagger. The crocodile was a huge, powerful animal that could kill with a single bite, but Irwin had the swagger that told the crocodile he was boss.

After a few more episodes and another blunt, Trey realized that Irwin had something else in addition to swagger. He had knowledge. Swagger wasn't enough to break a croc. You needed to know what angle to approach it at and where to grab it. All the balls in the world wouldn't help you if you tried to grab a saltwater croc in the wrong place. At the same time, knowing the angles wouldn't do any good if you didn't have the balls to get in the Game and grab the croc in the first place.

Trey's mind was on fire. Now that he was in the Game for real, Trey needed a game plan. *A "Game" plan.* And here it was: knowledge and swagger. These would be the two pillars of his philosophy. *Fear no man. Always know the angles.* Trey got goose bumps when he realized the double meaning of the word "angle": the Crocodile Hunter *literally knew the physical angles.* He thought about how he had handled Rick and RayOfLight and realized that it had all been a question of angles, right down to the physical angle of approach he had taken on Rick in Double

D's. Swagger had never been a problem for Trey, but you could always know more about the angles.

Onscreen, Irwin was preparing to grab a sick crocodile to administer it medicine. He and his dyke wife were knee-deep in mud, circling around the Salty.

"Look at that! Look at the way he approaches the croc...always the same angle! You see that?" Trey gestured energetically at the television with a cigarette.

"That white man crazy," responded Shemeta.

"He got a big pair of testicles is what he got."

Trey's mind drifted towards the future. What would his Game plan be for Rick this afternoon? Trey didn't think Rick would give him too much trouble. He had swaggered his way right into Rick's head. He straight up owned Rick. It was just a question of staying alert and staying one step ahead of him. Trey didn't think that it would be too difficult. RayOfLight was a little more complicated. Then again, he didn't need to make RayOfLight his bitch. He was just trying to conduct a normal business transaction with him. He was sitting pretty.

In addition, his first attempt at true pimping had gone well. He had always wanted to turn a woman out. Pimping was like bow hunting. Any fool could kill a buck with a rifle, but it took real skill to kill one with a bow and arrow. Any fool could make a few dollars selling drugs, but it took a true hustler to turn a woman out, slip into her mind like a water moccasin, and control her. It was hustling in its purest state. Trey saw Shemeta as an opportunity to practice Hustling 101. It was a way for him to amuse himself as he waited it out in the motel. It had almost been too easy. Shemeta didn't have any of the fight or hustle of her mother. He would have enjoyed having to work a little harder to own her.

Trey felt a sudden jolt of paranoia. He couldn't let himself get too comfortable. He had killed two people and the police were looking for him. He couldn't imagine them having any real proof, but it was possible. Lacombe was small, and sooner or later someone would figure out he was missing. Someone would remember that Rhonda bought her pills from him. They would talk to his neighbors. The niggers in Lacombe would be happy to snitch on a white man. Trey cursed to himself when he thought of the little fucker who had seen him through the window.

He told himself to relax. There was a difference between proof and circumstantial evidence. He had learned that from *Law & Order: Special Victims Unit*. No one had a shred of proof against him. The kid bothered him, it was true. But if he talked...well, Trey could just kill him too.

Trey found Richard standing next to an abandoned wig shop a few doors down from Double D's in the strip mall. He looked uncomfortable, which was how Trey wanted him to look. Trey gave him a big grin.

"There he is. Whassup, playboy? You ready to ball out?" Richard didn't respond. Trey dropped his fake smile. "Move. You know where we going."

The two men walked back towards the motel. As before, they stopped in the dumpster enclosure. Trey held out his hand. Richard gave him a murderous look as he put five crisp hundred-dollar bills in his hand. Trey smiled big. Life was easy when you had the swagger and knew the angles. He folded the five bills into his pocket and led Richard to room eighteen. Trey walked to the refrigerator and grabbed three tallboys of Bud.

"I'll see *you* in two hours."

He closed the door behind him.

Richard's heart slammed against his ribs. The girl was lying on the bed just like before. The baby was also in the exact same position. Richard wondered if it was dead. It looked dead. The apartment smelled even more pungent with sex and feces than he had remembered. The odor bypassed Richard's neocortex and acted directly on his endocrine system. He trembled as he approached the bed. The girl glared at him.

He fell squealing on her exactly as he had the day before. This time, Shemeta didn't move or react, just let him use her body.

When it was over, Richard went into the bathroom. What he saw in the mirror disgusted him.

He made a fist and punched himself in the face.

"Cocksucker! Loser! Fucking pedophile loser!"

Richard punched himself again, harder.

"Fat fucking piece of shit!"

He punched himself one more time, took a deep breath, and walked back into the living room.

Shemeta had turned on the television. Richard didn't like that. He felt disgusting, and he needed to be punished.

"Come into the bathroom."

"What for?"

"Just do it!"

Shemeta followed him into the bathroom. Richard got into the tub and lay down. The girl's body was even more exciting to him seen from below, as if she were gigantic and powerful and he were tiny and weak.

"Stand on me."

"What?"

"You heard me...come into the tub and stand on me!"

Shemeta's face screwed up into an involuntary frown of judgment and disgust. She retracted her head in the eternal Jerry Springer gesture of ghetto disbelief. She had heard her momma talking about *how nasty white people was* before. Richard reminded her of a nasty old dead white toad lying on his back in the tub.

Shemeta stepped onto him gingerly, steadying herself against the wall. She now stood on his chest. As soon as she transferred all of her weight onto him he began writhing and moaning.

"Step on my balls!" he gasped. Shemeta's frown of disgust deepened but she didn't say anything. She pressed his hairy testicles with one of her toes.

"Harder!" cried Richard. Shemeta transferred more of her weight onto them.

"Harder!!"

Shemeta now put all of her weight onto his balls. The white man's moaning and writhing grew more intense. His face was red and with one hand he was pinching his nipples. Shemeta wanted to laugh.

"Now jump on me!" gasped Richard.

"*Jump* on you?"

"Yes, jump!"

Shemeta jumped without conviction.

"No! Jump hard!"

After a few leaps from the edge of the tub onto the white man's stomach and balls she began to relax. *Fuck this white man,* she thought. *If he wants me to jump on his stupid ass...*With this thought she began to jump on him with more violence. She took her foot and smashed it into his nose, beginning to enjoy herself.

"Oh, yes! Oh, God!" cried Richard. His little ding-a-ling was getting hard again. Shemeta let herself go, grunting, stamping and jumping now with the intention of hurting the white man. The harder she stomped him, the more excited he seemed to get.

"Now piss on me! Now! On my face! Hurry! Oh God!"

Shemeta hesitated.

"Please! Now! Do it!"

Shemeta squatted down right over Richard's face and straight pissed on him. He stuck his tongue out. With his right hand, he reached down and played with hisself.

She closed her eyes and thought about her new weave.

Trey sat in his car drinking beer and listening to Soulja Slim's 1998 album, *Give It 2 Em Raw*. He bopped his head and occasionally freestyled over the beat.

In the dark, with that chrome, I been known to lurk
Blast yo spine so you jerk like a bitch done twerk
They call me Trey-Deuce, and you know I got them kickers

Drink nothing but Grey Goose, cause this cracker bout his figures

He nodded his head. His rhymes were getting tighter. He closed his eyes and relived the moment he shot Duke.

Them haters always ask me, Trey, what you like most
Pimping, slanging, or killing, I say making them ghosts

The song ended. Trey wasn't sure what to do next. He could let Richard off the hook, which would be safer and easier, or he could try to squeeze him just a little more before leaving town. Trey decided that he ought to squeeze him, just on principle. He thought back to what an ex-Marine turned dope fiend had told him about combat in jail. Never get stuck in a defensive position. Always assault through the objective.

At seven-twenty, Richard walked out the door. Trey got out of his car. The two men walked back to the enclosure.

"Give me my driver's license!" blurted Richard.

"Naw, bruh. I ain't done with it yet. I got one more thing for you and then we square for real."

Richard's eyes bulged out a little bit and his mouth twitched, telegraphing his intentions. When he pulled the knife out of his pocket and lunged, Trey was expecting it. He neatly stepped out of the way, grabbed Richard's wrist with his left hand, and delivered a powerful blow to his jaw with his right hand at the same time as he twisted his arm behind his back. Richard dropped the knife and slammed face-first into the ground like a poleaxed bull. Holding Richard's arm behind him, Trey bent down to whisper in his ear.

"Look, bruh, I ain't even mad at you for trying to take a poke at me. That's how the game works...you just trying to play the game. But see, you didn't take the right angle, and that's why I'm on top of you right now, holding all the cards." Trey lifted his head and looked into the distance in a parody of sober reflection. "I feel your pain, Rick. You broke. You getting blackmailed. You a premature ejaculator. You a motherfucking pervert. But you just gotta accept that there ain't shit that you can do about it, ya heard me? I got you beat, and that's about all there is to it. Am I right or am I right? Or am I right?" Trey nudged Richard to let him know that he expected a formal response. Richard nodded, his eyes bulging with fear, blood trickling out of his mouth into the dust.

"You're right! You're right!"

"Damn straight I am. But you lucky this time, bruh. I'm leaving town. See, I got a vision. I don't *want* to waste my life blackmailing broke-ass chumps behind motherfucking dumpsters. What we doing right now, they call that an opportunity cost, bruh. You know what that is? That's the cost of all the opportunities you miss because you're wasting your time on small-time shit. You lucky I'm so philosophical about this shit, because otherwise I would just stick around and bleed you, and I mean dry as Hillary Clinton's pussy. But like I said, I ain't got time for that. So just one more deal and we done, and I mean that. Now, this deal's gonna be a little different. In fact, we gonna just go ahead and drop the play-acting altogether. Get back down to roots, ya heard me? This time I'm straight jacking you, bruh."

Trey reached into Richard's back pocket and pulled out his wallet. Inside he found almost nothing. There was an ATM card, a work ID card, free entrance passes to a couple of local strip clubs, a few receipts, and twenty-two dollars in cash. All of a sudden Trey was bored. His monologue had satisfied his appetite for blood. He could have forced Richard to withdraw a couple hundred bucks from his ATM but now it seemed like more risk and trouble than it was worth. He didn't even take the cash. Twenty-two freaking dollars...who cares. He just wanted to drink some more beer and watch TV. He stuck Richard's driver's license back in his wallet and stood up. Richard remained on the ground.

"Get up, bruh. I changed my mind. We finished with each other. Now get the fuck out of here before I change my mind again. Don't you ever mention this shit to nobody, and don't you ever come back to this motel. You do that and you done with me for good. And remember, bruh, I still got my insurance policy on you." Trey mimicked taking a photo.

With a grunt, Richard lifted his fat body from the ground. Gravel crunched under his feet. He blinked, then turned around and fled.

Trey chuckled as he watched Richard haul his flabby carcass back to his car and screech off. He dusted himself off and went back to room eighteen for another tallboy of Budweiser.

23

The LACCH database returned forty-four Treys with criminal records in Louisiana. Twenty of them were black. Of the remaining twenty-four, six were currently locked up and ten were too old. That left eight files. Inspector Batiste showed them to Misty. Her finger went straight to the mug shot of the arrogant-looking blond man with notches in his eyebrows.

"That's him. I told you he looked like Vanilla Ice."

His rap sheet was quintessential. Five misdemeanor possession charges, two DWI's, and one felony battery for which he had spent fourteen months in prison. Batiste put out an immediate APB with the photograph. Now all he had to do was establish an evidential link between Trey Barnes the churl and the cold-blooded murderer who had shot three people in Lacombe. As soon as the warrant came through, Batiste, Ron Brown and Eugene the forensic man drove over to Trey's trailer and busted down the door. The scene was stone cold. Other than an expensive-looking cream-colored leather sofa, a huge flat-screen plasma television, and a stack of DVD's, the place was empty.

"So, is it in there?" called out Eugene from the kitchen, where he dusted for fingerprints.

"Hang on, I'm still looking," responded Inspector Batiste. He found it at the bottom of the stack of DVD's.

"Damn! Here it is. Oh well, I should have known better. Why do they all love this movie so much?" Inspector Batiste walked to the kitchen and handed Eugene a twenty-dollar bill. The forensic specialist shook his head in an "I told you so" gesture. He had given Inspector Batiste his standard three-to-one odds that the perp would own either a DVD or a VHS cassette of the movie *Scarface*. He never lost.

Inspector Batiste walked into the bathroom and smiled when he saw the fat drop of blood on the floor right by the shower.

That evening, Inspector Batiste paid a visit to Red, his most reliable informant. Red had only a vague idea of who Trey Barnes was. He had seen him driving around Lacombe in his purple Taurus and had heard that he sold pills, but that was about it. He kept to himself. If he had any friends, Red didn't know who they were. He had arrived in Lacombe about three months ago. No one knew where he had come from. The street had decided that Trey had done the killings. He would be punished if he ever showed his face in Lacombe again. Red told Inspector Batiste that Rhonda Jefferson had been one of Trey's customers. Rhonda Jefferson was everybody's customer, and everybody was her customer too. Red himself had fucked her just two weeks before. He didn't mention that part to Batiste.

Twenty-four hours later, the lab results came back positive. The DNA matched the DNA of the blood found at the crime scene that did not belong to any of the three victims. Rhonda Jefferson's fingerprints were among those collected in Trey Barnes' trailer.

Inspector Batiste had identified his killer. Now he had to find him. It was going to be difficult. There had been no clues in the trailer as to Trey's possible whereabouts. No one seemed to know him, and he had a three-day head start.

24

Trey sat on the hood of his car and smoked a cigarette. He was supposed to meet RayOfLight in an hour and a half. Trey frowned. He had an unpleasant job to do first. There was no way around it. He had been thinking about it for hours and had come to the conclusion that he had no choice in the matter.

Fuck it, he thought. He threw his cigarette to the ground and walked over to the Waffle House. Shemeta had said that chocolate was her favorite flavor of milkshake. Chocolate it would be. There were no customers in the Waffle House and he was back outside within three minutes. From his pocket he removed the Skittles bag and dumped out a handful of Oxy's. He hesitated, then swallowed one. Methodically he began to crush the rest into powder with a beer bottle. He stopped once he had a little pile of powder about the size of a jawbreaker. He opened the top of the chocolate milkshake and carefully poured the powder in. He stirred the chocolate milkshake with a plastic spoon until the milkshake looked normal and put the top back on.

Shemeta put down her third blunt of the day. She felt good. She was holding Tamica and watching an *Alf* rerun on television. Alf was chasing after a cat. Shemeta laughed. She thought Alf was funny. She had the munch. When would her boo be back with her milkshake? They was supposed to go to the hairdresser's in an hour.

Trey opened the door and walked straight to where Shemeta was lying. She looked young. He lit up a blunt tosteady his nerves, then handed her the milkshake.

"Here you go."

Shemeta sucked up a mouthful and frowned.

"It taste funny."

"What are y ou talking about?"

She took another suck. "It taste like *medicine.*"

"That's cause that ain't a milkshake, girl...that's a *smoothie* you drinking."

"A smoothie?" Shemeta's eyes lit up and her lips went eagerly to the straw.

Trey considered telling her to drink it up nice and fast, but he didn't have to. She was sucking it down like a fish. She didn't even pause to breathe.

Her face bore an expression of intense concentration as she noisily sucked the last traces off the bottom of the cup. She set it on the night table and blinked twice, slowly. Her eyelids were already beginning to droop.

"I feel...funny," she said. Her head nodded forward.

Trey took Tamica out of Shemeta's arms and set her on the ground so she wouldn't fall off the bed when Shemeta went limp. Shemeta didn't notice. With trembling hands he lit a cigarette and walked outside.

It wasn't his fault. The situation had forced his hand. He couldn't just take her with him forever. If he let her go, sooner or later she would talk. She was too young and too stupid not to.

Trey shook his head. No, there was no other way.

He walked over to the Go-Kart track and sat on a bench. His eyes idly tracked the Karts as they whirled around the racetrack.

That was how the Game worked, thought Trey with philosophy. The Game had its own logic, and he had no choice but to follow it. In a sense, he hadn't killed Shemeta. The Game had. He had been nothing but a blind instrument of her fate. Like him she had been born into the Game, only her cards hadn't been very good. The Game would kill him too one day, and he hoped he would be able to pass like a man when his time came.

He lit another cigarette. More than ever he knew that he was on the right path. He imagined himself as a little gear in a big machine and suddenly he had a sense of how big the universe really was. It was strange, Trey thought: only by exchanging his freedom to do whatever he wanted for the ruthless logic of the Game did he really begin to feel free.

When he walked back into the motel room, he was able to look at Shemeta without feeling guilty. Instead, he felt regret. He would have preferred not to have to kill her. Of course, he also would have preferred not to have a basehead for a father; would have preferred to grow up in a house instead of a trailer; would have preferred to have a shitload of money. He could prefer anything he wanted, but that didn't mean shit. Things happened the way they had to happen, and that was it. He wasn't going to feel bad for having the courage to make the hard decisions he had to make. He was a survivor, and he was ready to kill if that was what it took to survive.

Trey transferred Shemeta onto her side and moved her into a compact fetal position. She looked smaller dead than alive. Trey walked out to his car and got a bungee cord from the trunk. Back inside, he tied the bungee cord around her in such a way that her knees stayed pressed up against her chest. He took out the box of industrial-strength Glad bags that he had bought the day before and slid one onto Shemeta the way a baker slides a plastic bag over a loaf of cut bread. Fixing it tightly, he put a second bag around the first bag. He continued adding bags until he couldn't fit any more. He wanted to be sure that the bag wouldn't accidentally come open at some point. The multiple bags also dissimulated the shape.

There it was. He was done. Shemeta existed no more. It was as simple as that: surgical and clean. It had only taken him a few minutes to remove her from the world as completely as if she had never existed. It had been as easy as deleting a name from a cell phone. Trey wondered if there was a single human being alive who remembered her. Probably not.

Trey stared at the bag for a few moments, then shrugged his shoulders and turned around. It was time to prepare for his meeting with RayOfLight.

He went into the bathroom and put on the businessman clothes he had bought in Wal-Mart. What he saw in the mirror was a champion Bully Pit. Its eyes were clear and determined, its muscles were firm and taut, its posture was good, and its features were symmetrical. Trey unzipped his Pioneer brand pants and took out his penis. Seeing how long and thick it was never failed to remind him that he was destined for great things. He put it away and walked out of the bathroom. He placed Tamica in the plastic laundry basket he had used to empty his apartment and threw a T-shirt over her so no one would see that he was carrying a baby out to his car. She emitted a weak cry when the T-shirt went over her eyes. Good, she wasn't dead.

It was now five past six. If everything was OK, RayOfLight ought to be squirming and pissing himself in the Waffle House parking lot a quarter of a mile away. Trey turned off the lights and put the DO NOT DISTURB sign the Mexican had gave him on the doorknob.

25

Ray and Wanda's drive from Atlanta to Daytona Beach began in giddy high spirits with a sing-along to the Mamas and the Papas. The closer they got to their destination, the quieter and more pensive they became. They now drove in silence. Occasionally Ray looked over at Wanda, smiled reassuringly, and squeezed her hand.

It took them a long time to get to Daytona because they kept stopping for snacks and bathroom breaks. They couldn't get their éclairs from Duck's that day and had to settle for a series of glazed honey buns, Slim Jims, and six-packs of little powdered donuts bought at various gas stations. Their car was full of trash and crumbs. The back seat was piled with the baby supplies they had bought the night before at Wal-Mart. Every few minutes Ray grumbled.

"I can't help but wonder if this is a trap."

"Don't say that, honey."

"The FBI has been watching my every move for years. The pigs in Langley aren't above a trick like this."

Ray and Wanda got to the Waffle House a full hour before the scheduled rendezvous. They ordered two Pecan Waffles, two orders of hash browns with cheese, onions, ham, and tomatoes, a bowl of Bert's chili, two patty melts, two iced teas, and two chocolate milkshakes. Anxious, not speaking, they crammed the comfort food into their fat faces. At ten to six, Ray squeezed his wife's hand and hobbled out to the car on his prosthesis.

He closed the door, started the engine, and reached under the driver's seat. The touch of the cold steel reassured him. He hadn't mentioned the gun to Wanda. It would have made her hysterical. She hadn't heard the man's voice. FBI, CIA, or street thug, it didn't matter. Trey was dangerous.

He sat bolt upright when the purple Ford Taurus with tinted windows and oversized rims pulled into the parking lot and flashed its lights.

Ray followed the car out into the traffic. Soon they were in a less populated area. The Taurus turned into a gigantic, empty parking lot in the middle of nowhere where a Wal-Mart was being built. The structure was almost done and looked naked without the WAL-MART logo printed on it. Ray followed the Taurus around the back of the Wal-Mart to the loading bays for the eighteen-wheelers. Behind the building was an expanse of high, scrubby grass and plants. No one could see them. The Taurus rolled to a stop next to a dumpster full of construction debris. Ray parked facing him. The tinted windshield was so dark that he could barely make out the driver's silhouette. His hand went down to the gun under his seat.

The door of the Taurus opened. Trey stepped out holding LaTasha. Ray was surprised to see that he was white. He opened the door and stepped out as well.

"You must be RayOfLight. Pleasure to meet you. Let's get this over with and go the fuck home, alright bruh? You got the money?"

Ray handed Trey the brown paper bag of money.

"Open it up," said Trey. "Count it for me."

With shaking hands, Ray began counting the money for Trey on the hood of his car. Every few seconds he glanced up at LaTasha. She was *beautiful.* He wanted to hold her.

"Ninety-eight...ninety-nine...three hundred."

"Count it again." Trey's voice was hard.

"It's all there! You saw me count it."

"I said count it again, Ray."

Ray counted it again. When he got to three hundred, Trey scooped up the money with his free hand.

"Looks like we good, bruh. Here you go." Trey extended LaTasha to Ray. He took her delicately and held her close to his body. She was as light as a kitten. He put his face close to hers. She smelled humid and organic, like she needed a change of diapers. The smell was wonderful. It was the smell of fatherhood. He lost himself in the pools of her dark black eyes.

When he looked up, Trey was gone. He hadn't even heard him drive off. LaTasha had short-circuited his brain. He had completely forgotten to ask any of the questions that he and Wanda had prepared: Was there a birth certificate? What was her exact birthday? What was her mother's name? Where was she born? What time was she born? They needed this information to create her astrological profile. Ray smiled. Such questions meant nothing in the face of the absolute miracle of LaTasha herself.

LaTasha woke up a little. Ray gave her a big smile. She raised one of her little arms to his face. Ray felt like he was going to melt. He had to get back to Wanda. She had to be worried sick. With infinite tenderness, he buckled LaTasha into her brand new car seat and started the car.

Trey gave an old-fashioned Dukes of Hazzard whoop as his tires squealed onto the highway. He slapped the dashboard in glee. He had pulled it off! "Hell *fucking* yes!" he said to himself over and over. He pumped his fist on the *fucking*. Right now Trey needed music, something old-school. He took the C-Murder mixtape he had been listening to out of the stereo, replaced it with a CD of Lynyrd Skynyrd's greatest hits that his father had burned for him, and cranked the volume. After listening to "Sweet Home Alabama" three times in a row, he began to settle down. He couldn't let himself get too carried away. He wasn't out of the woods yet. He still had a dead body to get rid of. Twelve more hours, he told himself, and his new life would begin for real.

Wanda ran out to the car as soon as Ray pulled up. Tears of joy sprang to her eyes when she saw LaTasha. Ray handed the infant to her.

"LaTasha, meet your new mama." His words provoked a fresh wave of sobs. Wanda received LaTasha with lovingkindness. She looked so little and delicate! The vibrations she had been feeling for the last few days intensified. She was now responsible for a human life. Everything she did from this point on would have a new signification. Ray was now crying as well. Neither of them could find their words. Wanda beamed. She was finally a *woman*. No longer would envy eat at her when she greeted the Waldorf mothers. No longer would the practiced way they held their babies against their hip with one arm, the droopy and deflated look their breasts had taken from breastfeeding multiple children, or the hand-sewn West

African papooses they wore cause her to put her head in her hands and weep at her teacher's desk after they left.

She would sew her own papoose.

Wanda sobbed and beamed at Ray when LaTasha smiled at her. This was the moment. With trembling hands, she reached into her pocket and took out a necklace. It was a clear quartz crystal that had been mounted onto a leather cord. Wanda waved the crystal over LaTasha, who did not track it with her eyes. Wanda had trouble speaking through her tears of joy.

"LaTasha, I pledge to do everything I can for you, from now until the day that I die."

Had Tamica's brain not been permanently damaged as a result of Fetal Alcohol Syndrome, the facial mirroring, warm touch, gentle speech, orderly syntax, and love that she was receiving for the first time in her life would have begun raising her IQ and boosting her immune system immediately.

26

There was nothing Trey could do about Shemeta until later. He stashed the thirty grand in the safe in his motel room and cruised to the boardwalk. He was still amped and wanted to celebrate. It felt good to be alone and free again after the last few days of having to keep Shemeta under permanent surveillance. The weather was fine and there were a lot of people walking up and down the strip. Daytona had to be the biker capital of the world. They were everywhere. It seemed like every other motherfucker was wearing either a Harley Davidson or a Dale Earnhardt T-shirt.

The neon lights of the arcades, bars, and pool halls cast a warm glow on the sidewalk. It reminded Trey of Bourbon Street. Old winos with bloodshot eyes, Hawaiian shirts and shaggy mustaches stood outside the bars holding signs advertising "Huge Ass Beers". Trey bought one. The flimsy plastic cup squished a little when he grabbed it.

He strolled behind a group of giggling teenage girls in Daisy Dukes. His heavy bankroll slapped against his thigh with each step. He ought to have about fifteen hundred dollars in his pocket.

Now that he had a cushion, he could afford to do a little shopping. Trey had never been cheap. He knew that you needed to spend paper if you wanted people to take you seriously. You needed people to take you seriously if you wanted to get ahead in the Game.

The burglar bars and bright neon lights of a jewelry store caught Trey's eye. A man of his freshly upgraded status needed an upgrade to his jewelry game. A few scrawny, broke-looking Florida white boys in undershirts were loitering in front of the store with a single older, cracked-out black dude in a dirty, oversized black T-shirt. They tried to lay a hard glare on Trey. He walked past them as if they didn't exist. The fat, sweaty, balding Arab perched on a stool behind a bulletproof glass partition buzzed him in. Trey walked over to where the rings were displayed. His watch game was solid, and his chain game was acceptable – he wore a gold chain that had cost him eight hundred dollars – but he didn't have any rings. He had wanted a pinkie ring for a long time. The camel jockey had some good stuff.

"Let me see that one right there," said Trey, pointing at a heavy, eighteen-karat gold ring engraved with a dollar sign. Diamonds were played out and he avoided wearing them. He liked the rich, deep, heavy look of pure gold with no jewels on it. It looked tougher to Trey, more gutter. The ring fit on his thick right pinkie as if it had been made for him. He reached into his pocket, casually peeled twenty-four Grants from his roll, and tossed them on the counter as he might have discarded a Kleenex. In a flash the Arab had snatched up the bills with his chubby, doll-like hands and slipped them into his pocket, licking his lips.

Back outside he could smell the impotent jealousy and resentment of the chumps who had tried to mean mug him on the way in. Like the Crocodile Hunter, Trey had dominated them without having to say a word. He chuckled inwardly a second time at these haters with no game and no shine. They had given him an idea.

He walked into the first tattoo shop he saw. The girl behind the counter was a chubby, inked-up Goth with huge tits and ugly black plugs in her ears. Trey held out his muscular right forearm and told her that he wanted to get the words ALPHA MALE tattooed there in cursive.

Forty-five minutes later and two hundred dollars lighter, Trey walked back out onto the strip. The Goth chick had done a good job. He admired his new tat in the reflection of a souvenir shop window. On the other side of the plate glass was a box full of shark teeth.

He stared at them. The teeth reminded him of something, but he couldn't remember what. A memory. He walked into the store and grabbed a handful of teeth.

He wasn't a crocodile. *He was a shark*. A crocodile laid low and waited for his prey to approach. A shark never stopped moving. Trey respected the crocodile. But a shark could never be a crocodile. He had just identified the third and fourth pillars of his philosophy. Be what you are. Never stop moving. He imagined having a mouth full of gold shark teeth and ripping into the chubby Gothic tattoo artist's huge, milky breasts.

Trey walked back out onto the strip. He was hungry as hell and wanted to eat a good meal before taking care of business. He went into the beachfront Copeland's and ordered a Courvoisier and the surf n' turf special: lobster and steak. It was the most expensive thing on the menu.

The faggot waiter kissed his ass. Trey liked it. He wolfed down his steak and lobster. It was delicious. He felt like Boss Hogg. All his life he had known that he deserved the best, and now he was getting the best. He finished his meal, paid the check, and left.

Burping and picking at his teeth with a toothpick, he strolled back to the motel full of food and grandiose ideas.

The malignant-looking black trash bag in the corner of the room slammed him back down to earth. He was waist-deep in the shit and he couldn't let himself forget it. The room still smelled like Tamica's dirty diapers. The television was still on Nickelodeon. Trey slammed it off. He couldn't wait to put this scene behind him.

He would have liked to lie down, digest his food, smoke a blunt and fall asleep, but he had work to do. He collected everything in the room that had belonged to either Tamica or Shemeta and dumped it into a Glad bag. He then emptied the motel trash cans into the same Glad bag. They were full of runny, stinking diapers that Shemeta had not bothered to seal properly. This detail made him feel less guilty about killing her. He tied off the bag and set it next to the first bag. He gathered up his own stuff and took it out to the car. He took a scalding shower and double-checked the room. There was no more trace of his houseguests. He set his alarm clock for four A.M. and fell asleep.

27

The first thing Trey did when his alarm went off was to light a cigarette and start brewing a pot of coffee. He opened the front door and scanned the parking lot. It was so silent that he could hear the waves breaking against the beach. The coffee machine percolated behind him. Satisfied that he was alone, he hoisted the heavy black Glad bag and dropped it into his trunk with a thud. Done. The coffee machine beeped. He poured himself a cup and went over the room in detail one last time.

The air was cool and breezy as Trey walked over to the front office. The first Mexican was slumped behind the desk watching TV, exactly as he had been five days before. The cold air and eerie silence put Trey on edge. He had an urge to jump in his car and get the hell out of there without checking out but he knew that it would look suspicious. He doubted that it would make a difference at a place like the Sun Tan Motel, but he didn't want to take any unnecessary chances.

"We outta here, bruh," said Trey to the Mex as he strode in.

"Leaving early, sir? Is there a problem?"

"There sure is...my fucking boss is sick. Gotta be back in ATL by noon."

"How was your stay at the Sun Tan Motel?"

"Fine." Trey's terse response indicated that he did not wish to be asked any more unnecessary questions. The Mexican reached into the cash drawer and refunded Trey fifty-nine dollars in exchange for the key. Trey dapped him and walked back out to the car.

Trey had already decided that a dumpster would be the best and easiest place to get rid of Shemeta. It was dead silent in the Taurus. Too silent. Trey put in Mac's *Shell Shocked* and advanced to the second track. *They got me noid...they got me noid...but I ain't paranoid.* Trey bopped his head to the creepy beat. He knew all about feeling noid. Mac was one of his favorite spitters. Trey freestyled over the beat.

Trunk full of that bullshit
Got to handle this foolishness...

He drove over to the empty beachfront strip and found a narrow alleyway between two seafood restaurants. There were two dumpsters overflowing with garbage. A slimy barrel of used frying oil sat next to the dumpsters and the ground was sticky with a thick coat of food sludge. The alleyway stank. Trey felt exposed as he stepped out of his car. He pulled his LSU cap tight over his eyes in case there were any security cameras. He looked around, then removed a few bags from the dumpster to make a nest for Shemeta.

It was so quiet that the metallic thud of the trunk latch opening echoed in the alleyway and made Trey jump. His steel-cable nerves were beginning to fray. He had trouble hoisting Shemeta's unwieldy dead body over the rim of the dumpster. The bungee cord must have slipped off, because he could feel her body sprawling and shifting like flour inside the loose Glad bag. His skin crawled when he grabbed a random spot on the bag and felt Shemeta's teeth.

He finally got her up and over on his third try. Her head hit the side of the dumpster with a loud bang. Trey was now totally spooked. He began hastily piling the trash bags he had initially removed on top of Shemeta.

"Sir, step away from that dumpster!"

A cop!

It took every drop of Trey's sang-froid not to reach for his Glock and start blasting. He slowly turned around, his hands moving away from his body.

The cop in front of him was ex-military for sure: rigid posture, crew cut, polished boots. Trey blinked and looked at the man's waist. He wasn't wearing a real cop belt or cop badge but reproductions. This was not a police officer but a security guard. Trey exhaled. A pissant security guard was something he could deal with in his sleep.

"Is there a problem, officer?"

The security guard gave Trey a hard stare. Trey could see him looking him up and down, memorizing every detail of his appearance.

"Sir, what is your business in this dumpster?" The guard's tone was brisk and businesslike: the tone of a wannabe patrol cop eager to bust somebody.

Trey scrubbed the gangster from his voice.

"I was just throwing some trash away, officer. Have I done something wrong?" Trey had regained his composure and was beginning to feel angry. He refused to be afraid of some minimum wage security guard.

"Keep talking," barked the guard. "What was in that bag I saw you struggling with?"

Trey paused for a split second before opening his mouth. The guard narrowed his eyes and lowered his hand to his pistol. Trey was surprised at the man's courage. Who the fuck was this clown? Who ever heard of a fucking security guard ready to risk his life for eight bucks an hour? Jesus! One wrong answer and this guard wouldn't hesitate to start shooting. Trey could sense it. There was a crazy, mercenary gleam in his eyes. He had probably been kicked out of the army for being a nut. Trey had known screws like him at Winn State. He was probably as fast with a pistol as he was eager to shoot.

Just Trey's luck to run into this punk and not some old, fat boozer!

"OK, bruh, listen...I'll be honest with you, officer, that was my dog in that bag. He's dead."

The guard's eyes narrowed.

"What kind of dog?"

"APBT, American Pit Bull Terrier, best fighting dog on the planet."

"What's his name?"

"What?"

"You heard me! What was the dog's fucking name?"

"Scarface, sir...like the movie."

"What coloration?"

"White with brown spots."

"Where did you get him?"

"What?"

"You heard me! Answer the fucking question!"

"Razor Wire Kennels in Hammond, Louisiana." Trey was beginning to sweat. How many more questions was this punk going to ask?

"How old was he?"

"Eighteen months."

The guard was beginning to calm down a little.

"And why the hell are you dumping your dead dog in the dumpster behind my boss's restaurant at four-fifteen A.M.?" barked the security guard.

Trey looked down at his feet, hands still up in the air, and shook his head as if he were debating whether or not to say the truth.

"Look...OK, you caught me, sir...see, it ain't exactly my dog...Scarface belongs, uh, belonged to my girlfriend. She asked me to watch him while she was at work. Now..."

"Your girlfriend named her dog Scarface?"

"We named her together, sir."

"Where does your girlfriend work?"

Trey paused and sneered a little.

"She works at Double D's." That ought to stop that line of questioning. Trey was getting tired of this punk. "Look, here's what happened. So I'm sitting at home watching TV and all of a sudden I hear like a screech, ya heard me?"

"What were you watching?"

"I was watching the Weather Channel, bruh...gonna be a real active storm season this year." *Check that, you smart punk,* thought Trey. He could not keep this up much longer. His face was twisting into an angry mask despite himself. It went against every fiber of his being to lick this punk's boots.

"So, like I said, I hear a loud screech outside, like a car's brakes, ya heard me? I run outside just in time to see some homeboys speeding off in a silver Cutlass Supreme. The fucking dog is laying there dead, brains all over the ground. Now, my girl loves this fucking dog, officer. I can't just bury him in the yard, she'll know what happened, you feel me? I was supposed to be watching him. But if I tell her he just ran away she won't be so pissed. You know women...so I scooped him up, his fucking brains and everything, I put him in a garbage bag, got blood all over my fucking pants, put the bag in my trunk...I'm still hosing off the goddamn road when my girl drives up. The fucking bitch makes me walk around the neighborhood with her hollering my fucking head off pretending to look for the damn dog for over an hour. Finally she pops a couple of Ambiens and I drive out here to get rid of the fucking body before she wakes up. I'm real sorry about your boss's goddamn private dumpster, but I've had a shitty fucking night, you feel me? So if you gonna arrest me or whatever the fuck, just go ahead and do it now!" Trey held out his hands as if he wanted the guard to cuff him.

The guard glared at Trey.

"Get the hell out of here. Next time you kill one of your girlfriend's dogs...go dig a goddamn hole somewhere. I don't ever want to see you around here again."

"Yes sir, officer, absolutely," said Trey. "Thank you, officer." It killed Trey not to be able to put his fist in this punk's smart face but he forced himself to walk calmly back to his car.

Ten minutes later, Trey was on I-95 south. It was past time for him to get the fuck out of there, fast, forever. The security guard had just been another test, and he had passed it by thinking quickly. It was as if the Game itself sensed when your defenses were down and sent some new challenge to keep you on your toes.

Trey was in the clear. Not even a nut would go to the trouble of digging through a stinking dumpster to check a story like that. Even if he did find Shemeta, he had nothing but a physical description of Trey to go on. He was glad that he had changed the plates on his car and worn a hat.

He stopped at a gas station outside Titusville. It was still dark outside and the gas station was closed. He parked next to the Dumpster. The first thing to go in was his old clothes. Next went all of his papers. He hesitated, then tossed in the baggie full of Oxycontins. No more slanging.

He opened the trunk. The antlers. He had shot his first deer when he was twelve and his dad had mounted the antlers for him. It was the only nice thing the old man had ever done for him. Andre Barnes had been a crystal meth addict and a thief before Trey found him dead in the front yard one morning. He had gotten fucked up, passed out, fallen into the ditch, and drowned face-down in three inches of septic water.

Trey tossed the antlers into the Dumpster, slammed the trunk shut, and started his Taurus.

Outside, dawn broke over the Atlantic. He reached over to the glove compartment and took out his thirty grand. He smelled it and nestled it in his crotch. Like an incantation, Trey silently mouthed to himself, over and over: *Fuck Daytona, fuck Louisiana, fuck motherfucking Lacombe...fuck the bullshit...I'm going to Miami!*

28

The last rays of the setting sun glinted off of Trey's new pinkie ring as he lifted a glass of Moët Chandon to his lips under the swaying palm trees. He had been in Miami for exactly six hours. It was nine-thirty P.M. and he was eating lobster on the patio of a restaurant called the Lobster Grill on Ocean Drive.

The first thing he had done upon arriving was to book a room at the Delray Hotel. After stashing most of the money in the safe, he went straight to the Lincoln Street mall to freshen his swag. He scored a pair of baggy jean shorts and a couple of striped polo shirts with oversized gold patterns printed over the breast pocket at the Tommy Hilfiger store and a pair of bright white limited edition Nike Air Force Ones at the Foot Locker. He completed his look with a new pair of Ray-Bans and a throwback University of Miami baseball cap which he wore backwards.

Trey finished his lobster, ordered a Hennessy from the bar and lit up a gigantic Cuban cigar that he had bought for fifty dollars. The paper ring around it was embossed in gold. The rich old hag with fake lips and a neck like crumpled newspaper at the next table gave him a sour look. He took a deep puff and exhaled in her direction. He was a Don. If she didn't like it, she could suck his dick. For the first time in as long as he could remember, he had no idea what came next. It was up to him to create a new reality. Until now, his world had been circular in shape. His new life was a line shooting up to the sky like an F-14. He thought of Al Pacino's character in *Scarface*, Tony

Montana. *Scarface* was Trey's favorite movie. Tony started with nothing and turned it into an empire. Trey was as strong and as smart and as ruthless as Tony Montana. There was no reason he couldn't start an empire himself.

Check yourself, thought Trey. He was smarter than Tony. Tony got killed in the end. Trey wouldn't let that happen.

But where would he start? His mind felt cloudy and agitated, like the sky before a big thunderstorm. Monday, he decided. He would give himself until Monday to enjoy himself, wild out a little, have some fun. It was the weekend after all, and if ever anyone had earned some down time after a week of hard work, it was Trey.

He ordered another Hennessy. He was starting to feel drunk. Moet and Hennessy drunk felt cleaner and smoother than Budweiser drunk. He liked it. He liked everything. From where he sat he could see the Friday night parade of stretch Hummers and Lamborghinis cruising up and down A1A Avenue. Almost every limousine that drove by was crowned with women in flimsy, shiny dresses shrieking drunkenly and waving to the passersby. He was tempted to go straight to the beach and serve himself a fresh piece of pussy pie right then and there. The women here! He had never seen anything like it in his life. There were no Mexicans in Louisiana, only whites, blacks, and Creoles. He sprang for these Latin bitches with their standard-issue jumbo asses. As much as he liked big titties, when it came down to it, he was an ass man after all. Everywhere Trey looked, he saw nothing but women and money. Thirty grand was a lot of skrilla for one score but Miami reminded Trey that he still had a long way to go before he could roll like Tony Montana. The thought energized him. He looked down at his right hand and made a fist.

A group of tan, buttery bitches in shimmery club dresses looked at him, then turned and giggled to each other. Trey was familiar with that one. He knew why they were giggling. He turned them on. Trey ignored them.

Whores! There was certainly no shortage of them here. He would find more women later. For the moment he wanted to sip his Henny and think.

When Trey finally finished his drink, it was eleven-thirty P.M. Time to roll out and hit the club. He whistled at the waiter, a faggot with gel in his blonde hair. Trey's check came out to ninety-five dollars. He peeled a hundred-dollar bill off of his thick roll, tossed it down on the table and strolled out onto the strip with his rolling Pimp gait.

Having no idea where to go, and being in no hurry to get there, Trey decided that he would simply follow the stream of limousines until he found a club that looked popping.

His thoughts turned to Shemeta as he walked. He saw her dead body in the Glad bag, smashed up against a bunch of restaurant garbage. He imagined old, rotten mashed potatoes smeared on the outside of the bag and rats nosing around, looking for a way in so they could eat her lips and eyeballs.

Trey shivered. *Get your mind right, dog,* he thought. He needed to wash the memory of the last week out of his body. Rhonda's thighs, Shemeta's hairy ghetto bush, the smell of baby Tamica's shit mixed with the aroma of off-brand baby formula, the puddle of blood that had come out of Rhonda's stomach, the screams...the last week stuck to him like a heavy, decomposing animal. He needed to wash it all off, and there was only one way to do it. He would find himself a piece of clean, white, waxed blonde pussy and wash his dick off inside it. He would fuck the shit out of it and blast everything that had happened over the last week out all over the lucky girl's face.

A stretch Hummer that must have been thirty feet long passed Trey and pulled to a stop outside of a club called Mansion with a gigantic line out front. Trey gave a low whistle and stopped to watch. The first person out of the stretch Hummer was a huge black man with a long, stiff-looking beard, mirrored sunglasses, and a black do-rag, the ghetto pantyhose kind with no ties. Like a bitch dropping puppies, the Hummer began spitting out tan club sluts wearing bright, sparkly dresses so tiny and flimsy that they could probably be rolled up and fit into a plastic Easter egg. Trey whistled. All dimes. Every single one of them would have been the hottest girl in all of Lacombe, hands down.

Trey took a second look at the black man as he helped the eye candy teeter out of the Hummer. He looked like a negro Cro-Magnon. His thick bull neck was dripping in gold and his muscular arms rippled under his white Ecko brand tracksuit. He was one of the biggest bucks that Trey had ever seen. The man must have stood at least six-four and weighed two hundred and fifty pounds. He was obviously some sort of a bodyguard, judging from the alert way he kept his massive frame between the women and the crowd.

Next out of the limousine was a short, stocky white dude with a deep tan, swept-back light brown hair, a goatee, and a big grin on his face. He was wearing a shiny blue shirt underneath a white suit that looked like it cost plenty of cake. His body language said that he was the alpha male of the group: the money man. Trey thought he looked familiar. After him emerged a couple of greasy-looking Miami Latins with expensive clothes whom Trey pegged as the entourage and, finally, another white guy in a T-shirt and shorts holding a video camera.

Once the whole crew was assembled, the black mountain of muscles strode calmly up to the black bouncer and gave him slow dap and a big grin. Something about the way he walked gave the impression not only of coiled power but also of effortless grace. The bouncer opened up the velvet rope and the whole crew entered under the bodyguard's watchful eye. Trey sensed a keen, ruthless intelligence in the bodyguard and knew instinctively that he was not a man to be trifled with.

Trey was intrigued and impressed. This was why he had come to Miami. This was rolling. He had found his club. He would go in and find out who the man in the blue shirt was.

He had no intention of waiting in the long line like a chump. Scanning the crowd, Trey saw a couple of scrawny, pussy-looking dudes near the front of the line. They both had bad posture, sunken chests, hook noses, shiny, expensive-looking clothes, and too much gel in their hair. One of them had a receding hairline. The balding one was talking to a hot, bored-looking blonde who kept looking at her brunette girlfriend, whose arms were resolutely crossed. The girlfriend was slightly chubby and less pretty than the blonde, who had a tight beach body, a cute pouty face, and a tropical tan. The blonde had on a flimsy gold backless dress and the brunette had on a black top with a denim skirt. This group would be his target. Trey had mastered the art of pulling bitches back at Bogalusa Junior High. Time to dust off that old knowledge.

Trey figured that the dudes had met the girls in a bar, convinced them that they had a lot of money, and invited them to the club. Seeing that their dates were not rich or cool enough to bypass the line, the girls were getting bored. He settled on a frontal angle of attack. These boys were no Salties. He walked straight up to the group of four, flashed a gold grin and held out has hand for the less pussy-looking of the two dudes to dap.

"Wassup, bruh," said Trey, positioning his body in such a way that the guy would be forced to give a little ground.

"What's up...*bro.*" The pussy gave Trey ironic dap and shot his buddy a quick "get a load of this guy" look.

Trey smirked. The foolios could suck each other off all they wanted. Trey had just physically established dominance over them and that was all that mattered. He shifted his body again so that he was now at the center of the group and paused. He would be the one who dictated the rhythm of the conversation.

"Y'all looked like you were having so much fun over here that I figured I had to come say hello."

"Hello!" responded the two girls.

"So...how do y'all know each other?" asked Trey.

Trey snickered to himself when the blonde answered, a little too quickly, "Actually, we don't really know these guys...we met in a bar an hour ago."

"Well, Holly and I have known each other for years," added the brunette. "People always think we're sisters." She put her arm around Holly and smiled.

Trey turned so that he was facing the two girls with has back to the two guys, boxing them out completely. They continued to pretend they were part of the conversation.

"Sisters, huh? Let me guess: you're beauty" – he indicated the plain-looking brunette best friend – "and she's brains" – indicating Holly. He avoided eye contact with Holly. She would have to fight to earn his attention. The two girls laughed.

"That's right! That's exactly what everyone says! Isn't it! Isn't it!" The brunette started play-pushing Holly and giggling. Holly fought back in an equally playful way and the two of them almost fell down, which only made them laugh harder.

Holly narrowed her eyes and looked at Trey with a vicious little smile. "So...tell me again...why are you talking to us?"

Trey turned to the first girl with a smirk. "She always like this?" He jerked his thumb in Holly's direction and made a face that said *get real*.

"Oh my god, she is! She never stops! This bitch needs to learn some manners!" More laughter and play-fighting.

The two pussies continued to lurk on the outside of the now-closed triangle.

"Well, since you asked nice, I'll go ahead and answer your question. I'm just a Southern boy looking for a good time here in the big city."

"Aw, he's so *sweet*!" said the brunette. "Oh my god, we love you! You're our new best friend!"

Fifteen minutes later, when Trey and the two girls got to the head of the line, he had an arm around each of their shoulders and their arms were around his waist. The black bouncer waved them in immediately. When the two guys who had initially been with the girls sheepishly made a move to follow them into the club, the bouncer held out his hand in a brisk gesture and shook his head. He didn't need any pussies like these two fouling his dance floor.

Trey whistled when he walked into the club. He had never seen anything like it. The clubs in Slidell and New Orleans had nothing on Mansion. The dance floor was the size of a high school gym. The DJ was suspended in a neon-illuminated cage twenty feet off the ground. Laser beams swept the dance floor from every corner. Trey felt like he was inside a jukebox designed by Louis Vuitton. Loud techno music shook his guts. The entire dance floor was ringed with balconies. The area under the balconies was slightly raised and set off from the dance floor. Here could be found a number of small, low tables surrounded by white leather couches. Everything was lit up from underneath somehow. It looked like the club in the *Project Bitch* video. Mansion was fucking tight.

Trey scanned the room. No sign of the group from the stretch Hummer. They were probably in the VIP area upstairs.

Trey led Holly and the other girl, whose name was Stephanie, to one of the tables in the raised area under the balconies. From here he could keep an eye on the entrance to the club as well as the dance floor. A sexy, bored-looking cocktail waitress in a slinky black dress came by to take their order. Trey ordered a Jack and Coke and the two girls ordered Grey Goose and cranberry juice.

"That'll be sixty dollars."

Trey forced himself to smile as he paid. Sixty dollars!

"So, Southern boy, where are you from, anyway?" asked Stephanie, smiling and leaning in close to be heard over the music.

"I'm from the boot."

"The boot? What is that?"

"Louisiana."

"Oh...I get it." Stephanie gave Holly a little look that said *cheesy*. "Where in Louisiana?"

"New Orleans."

"Oh my God! We love New Orleans! We were there for Mardi Gras last year! Y'all know how to party!"

"It ain't that great."

"You wouldn't say that if you were from Parkland...we drive down to South Beach every Friday night to party!"

Trey kept one eye on the dance floor as the conversation went on. The club was getting more crowded by the minute. He spotted another bouncer in sunglasses standing in front of the staircase leading upstairs. Men came and went from the VIP area with bad bitches on their arms. Most of them looked like professionals.

Stephanie gave a squeal. "Oh my God! Is that Roland Deep?" Trey turned to look. A young, skinny, arrogant-looking black guy with long dreadlocks wearing a fur coat, pink skinny jeans and mirrored sunglasses had just strutted into the club. He was accompanied by four ghetto-looking crew members wearing black "Roland Deep" T-shirts. Everyone held an extra-large double Styrofoam cup full of lean.

"Oh my god, he is soooo hot!" said Stephanie as he walked by.

Trey snorted. "That dude is fake."

Holly and Stephanie looked at him skeptically.

"What do *you* know about fake, *K-Fed*?" said Holly with her same cruel little smirk.

Trey's amiable smile didn't waver but his blue eyes turned to chips of ice.

"Little girl, let me give you a piece of advice. Don't talk about what you don't know about. Real recognize real...fake recognize fake. One look at the chrome and that boy would fold. I ain't hatin' on lil' dude...but why he gotta try to be somebody he ain't? And I ain't even gonna mention them jeans. Who the hell is homeboy, anyway?"

"You've never heard of *Roland Deep*? Where the hell have you been hiding?" said Stephanie. "He's going to be the next Lil' Wayne!"

Trey snorted again as the two girls watched Roland Deep disappear into the VIP area with hungry looks on their faces.

"So, y'all like the brothers, huh?"

The two girls made a sour face.

"Whoa...you're not, like...a *racist*, are you?"

"I ain't racial unless I have to be," said Trey with a little sliding hand gesture.

"What the hell is that supposed to mean?"

"When the world is racial with me, I'll be racial right back, but I ain't no racist," said Trey.

"Ok, whatever, dude," said Stephanie. She gave Holly a look that said *this dude is lame*. After exchanging a long glance, Stephanie squealed, "Oh my God, I love this song! Let's go dance!" The two girls vanished, holding hands, and Trey was left sitting at the table alone. Sixty bucks for a ten-minute conversation with two skanks! In Lacombe you could buy an hour of brain with a redbone for that kind of money.

His ears pricked up. The DJ had just put on Juvenile's *Back That Azz Up*. Finally some real music! He stumbled to the dance floor bopping his head. A group of three white girls were laughing and trying ironically to bounce their asses up and down along with the music the way the black girls in the video did. Their Stairmaster-toned and sushi-fed South Beach asses were too tight and compact for the individual cheeks to slide around lazily in contrary motion, which was necessary for the dance to have its intended hypnotic effect. It took a Magnolia Projects diet of Popeye's, Cheetos, boiled crabs and Big Shot Cream Soda to P-pop correctly.

Trey turned over his shoulder and said, in a loud, confident voice, "Ladies, that is straight up pathetic. I never seen such piss-poor P-popping in my life."

A bleached blonde with big fake breasts responded, "Oh yeah, hotdog? Let's see you try it, then!"

"Yeah, tough guy, back that ass up!" One of the girls slapped Trey's butt and they all laughed some more.

Trey turned to her briskly and warned her, in a mock stern voice, "Hey...hands off the merchandise!"

The girls laughed. Trey turned back to the group.

"Alright, you asked for it. Now watch carefully." He turned around and tried to shake his ass. He lost his balance and fell down. When he stood back up, the girls had already turned their backs to him. The dance circle had closed around them and they exchanged mocking comments about his stupid little routine.

Trey was about to instruct them to suck it when a bright light blinded him. A hand snaked around his waist and grabbed his dick through his pants. He put a hand up to his eyes. The bright light was from a video camera.

Heavily made up sluts now pressed against him from all sides. He grabbed the waist of the girl in front of him and ground his crotch against her proffered ass in rhythm with the music. The ass was round and firm and his dick got hard as soon as it came in contact with it. Through his pants he could feel it nestling in the groove between her ass cheeks like a hot dog sliding into a bun.

Ignoring Trey completely, the girl, a blonde with lots of makeup and vicious eyes, looked back over her shoulder to her friends and announced, "He's got a big dick! I can feel it!"

A hand reached between his legs and jiggered his balls. These girls meant business. Trey turned his head but he couldn't see who it belonged to because of the bright light from the camera. For a second he was afraid that the hand belonged to a man. The blonde who was grinding against Trey's crotch turned and shot him a studied me so horny look: narrowed eyes, mouth suggestively open, upper lip curled back to reveal her sharp, small teeth. The bright light from the video camera reflected off of her sweaty bare back. Trey's body was being jostled as if he were in the lurching Bourbon Street crowd during Mardi Gras. Amid sounds of cruel laughter, Trey felt his hand being guided in between a pair of thighs somewhere behind him. He was now surrounded by women. The hand forced his fingers into a pussy that was completely waxed and dripping wet.

This was no music video they were filming.

The girls swept him across the dance floor and up the stairs. The camera was still on him. It felt like being arrested. He was able to make out four girls: the blonde he had been grinding against, a Chinese chick with long hair, a short, fire brunette with bangs, and a second blonde with a full floral tattoo sleeve. All four looked nasty as hell.

The cortege trundled into a smaller room inside the larger VIP area. This room was long and narrow with a white leather sofa running the entire length of the wall. Television screens mounted on the walls showed the main dance floor. The music was not as loud in here. A miniature disco ball sent sparkly beams from one end of the room to the other. The man in the blue shirt was sitting on the couch. He was naked except for a camouflage hunting cap. A blonde whose miniskirt was hiked up around her waist sucked his dick. With her right hand, she rubbed her clit. A kneeling cameraman documented the action from less than a foot away. The man in the blue shirt also fingered the vagina of the blonde sitting next to him on the sofa.

Trey realized why the man had looked so familiar to him before. He was peeping the MILF Blaster. He now knew exactly where he was: on the "set" of VIPsluts.com. There must have been at least eight women in the little room. They were all either masturbating, having their pussies eaten, eating pussy, sucking dick, or being fucked. Other than Trey and the MILF Blaster, there were four men in the room: two cameramen, a guy with a tattoo of a pit bull on his chest who was analing a blonde, and the bearded black bodyguard, who was standing near the door fully clothed, his massive arms crossed. Visibly his job was to watch everything and make sure nothing went wrong. Trey wondered how he didn't go crazy having to watch all that good pussy without touching it. He could tell that the bodyguard was staring him down from behind his mirror shades. The MILF Blaster spoke.

"What's up, man? Welcome to the VIP! We were short on wood tonight, so the talent decided to go find a replacement. Looks like you're the lucky man...and I do mean that! The all-you-can-fuck buffet begins to your left...help yourself!" The MILF Blaster waved at the room in a gesture of kingly generosity.

Suddenly the black bouncer was standing above Trey in a position of aggression and shoving a clipboard in his face.

"Sign here and you ready to rock out, dog." Trey knew that he should read what he was signing but the alcohol and pussy vapor had short-circuited his higher brain functions. He took the pen attached to the clipboard and scrawled his name. Even before Trey had finished signing, the short brunette from the dance floor had pulled down his boxers.

"Hell yes! We picked the right man tonight! Look at the head on this fucking cock! Oh my God, I love it!" She slapped Trey's penis against her kewpie doll face without breaking eye contact. The greedy, evil look in her eyes sent a fresh surge of blood into Trey's corpora cavernosa. The blonde with the tattoo sleeve kneeled down next to her. The brunette guided Trey's dong into the blonde's mouth.

"Hell yeah, baby! Suck that dick, bitch!" shouted the brunette in the raspy voice of a sixty-year-old smoker. Her hand remained tightly squeezed around the base of Trey's cock. He was so thick that her thumb and forefinger were at least half an inch apart. The brunette took Trey's cock back from the blonde and fellated him vigorously.

Trey suddenly felt noid.

"Where my shorts at?" he asked, looking around. "Where the fuck are they at?"

"Whoa, whoa, be cool," said the MILF Blaster with his perma-grin. "Ferg's got everything on lock." He indicated the bodyguard with his eyes. "Just sit back and enjoy the ride."

Trey relaxed.

Ferg had everything on lock.

Trey now recognized the brunette with his dick in her mouth. He had seen her in a video called *Nerd Hunting* in which she and two other bad bitches drove around Miami looking for nerds to punk. All of the nerds had small dicks that the girls dissed even as they were being fucked. "Is that all you've got? Come on, fuck me like you mean it! Can you believe this fucking loser?" Every time a nerd came on her, the brunette laughed, scooped it up with a McDonald's French fry, and made the nerd eat it.

Trey was no punk. He grabbed the base of his dick and removed it from the blonde bitch's mouth. He would decide how they were going to fuck, not her. With firm hands, he stood the brunette up and turned her around so her back was to him. The skin around her pussy and asshole was several shades darker than the rest of her body. This detail sent his hard-on into overdrive. He gave her a hard slap on the booty and plunged in. Her ass was tight as fuck. The chorus of women around him began shouting.

"Fuck that ass!"

"Yeah, baby!"

"Take it all, Sadie!"

"Fuck that bitch!"

Trey was not finished. With his thick, powerful arms he seized the Chinese bitch and lifted her up into the air. Cupping her buttocks with his strong hands, he held her open legs in front of his face and ate her pussy like Sambo slurping on a big slice of watermelon. She placed her hands on Trey's head to steady herself. Whenever he hit the sweet spot with his tongue, her hands tightened around his hair. Meanwhile he continued vigorously to pump the brunette, whose asshole was loosening up around his thick penis. He was vaguely aware of the shouts and whistles of approbation that he was receiving.

Someone popped open a champagne bottle and sprayed the foam in the humid crevice where Trey and Sadie's bodies were joined.

The Chinese bitch's hips and thighs tightened around his face. She was about to come. It was a good thing, too, because Trey couldn't hold her up much longer. She ground her pussy against his mouth with a rocking intensity that let Trey know that he had just unleashed the peaches and cream. He lowered his trembling arms and set her back on the ground. Once she was down, he pulled out of Sadie and collapsed back on the sofa. He closed his eyes. The room spun around him. He was hammered. His dick felt warm and wet again. He opened his eyes to see that Sadie had climbed on top of him like a monkey and put his penis back inside her. She had loosened up to the point where Trey could sink balls-deep inside her with each thrust. He knew that he had made an impression on her by the way she was looking at him.

"Damn, homie, that's what I'm talking about! My man's got some moves! Put it right here!"

The MILF Blaster extended his fist in a dap gesture. His eyes were red and bloodshot. He was still getting brain from the blonde. Trey grinned and gave the MILF Blaster dap.

When the camera panned up to his flushed, sweaty, face, the MILF Blaster shouted, "Only in the VIP, baby!" and gave a double thumbs up. The camera panned to the bodyguard. He held up his hand in something resembling a West Coast hand signal and said, in a smooth baritone, "Coast to coast baby...you know how we roll."

Half an hour later, every vas deferens in the house was empty and the cameras were back in their cases. Girls rummaged through designer purses and fixed their makeup. The MILF Blaster chopped up fat lines of blow for everybody in the bathroom. One of the cameramen had been dragged into the corner by a Latina who now sucked his dick. Trey followed the MILF Blaster into the main VIP section, where they sat down around a low table upon which the club's party coordinator had put two bottles of Grey Goose vodka and a series of mixers on ice.

The MILF Blaster held his glass up and proposed a toast.

"To pussy!" Everyone laughed and clinked glasses.

The bodyguard had loosened up now that the shoot was over. He was laughing and joking with the two girls who were sitting on either side of him with their arms around him. Every time he smiled, his gold teeth glinted from behind his thick, coarse beard. Trey could tell by the deep, rich, yellow color that they were eighteen karat like his. He nodded in approval. Some of the girls had migrated over to the table that had been commandeered by Roland Deep and his entourage. Others had returned to the main dance floor.

The MILF Blaster extended his hand to Trey.

"Ryan. Pleasure to meet you."

"Trey. I must have choked my chicken to your videos over a hundred times, bruh...I mean...you know what I mean...no homo, dog."

Ryan nodded in comprehension and then turned to the table. "We got a fan here! Hell yes!" Turning back to Trey, he leaned in and added: "Be honest with me, buddy...Sadie's ass feels even better than it looks in Hi-Def, am I right?" He extended his hand for another dap. Trey dapped him back.

Ryan sprawled back on the sofa. "Look at all this." With his hand he indicated the Grey Goose, the girls, the leather couch, the music...the money. "Ten years ago I was a substitute high school teacher. Now I fuck five new girls a week, every week. I drive a BMW and when I get tired of it I think I'll buy a Range Rover. I eat lobster and drink Grey Goose every night. I'm not trying to brag to you, Trey. I like you. I have a good feeling about you. I see the hungry look in your eyes. I saw your moves back there. We got a lot of people coming and going in this industry, and I always need good woodsmen. Most guys can't hack it: can't get it up, can't keep it up, don't have the killer instinct you need to pound pussy on camera day in, day out. Every man thinks he could be a porn actor but most of them can't last ten minutes. It takes a killer instinct...Killer Instinct...like the arcade game, remember that? With Jago and Cinder? Awesome fucking game...man, I haven't thought of that game in years! I used to play that shit at the bowling alley in high school!"

Ryan twitched and looked around manically as he spoke. Trey wondered how much cocaine he had snorted.

"Anyway, we're shooting a pool party video for VIPsluts.com tomorrow, and I need some more male talent. The pay is three hundred bucks. It's not a huge check, but then again, this is not exactly work. I don't know what your hustle is, but whatever it is, it's not as good as this. Basically, your job is to have some drinks, have some fun, splash around in the pool, and fuck the shit out of about ten of the roundest, brownest eighteen-year old asses you've ever seen. What do you say?"

Trey didn't have to think twice. He had been in Miami for less than twenty-four hours and already the world was spreading its legs for him, begging to be fucked and inseminated.

"Hell motherfucking yes, I'll do it," said Trey. "You don't have to ask me twice."

"That's the right answer, my friend," replied Ryan, holding up his drink for Trey to toast.

Trey had known dudes like Ryan before: talkative guys who liked nothing better than sitting around and bullshitting with the boys. The problem with guys like Ryan was that they couldn't inspire fear in anyone. That was probably what Ferg was for.

Ryan continued. "You know how all this started? It's a crazy story, man. Ten years ago, my brother knew this guy named Alvin. Just like the chipmunk!" Ryan grinned like a jack-o-lantern, as if the fact of being named *Alvin* were the funniest thing he had ever heard. Trey was beginning to realize that Ryan only had two facial expressions: the grin and the shit-eating grin. Ryan continued. "*Huge* motherfucking geek. Computers were this guy's life. I mean, he never did anything except fool with his goddamn computer. So anyway, one day, my brother told me that Alvin had bought a house in Silicon Valley. 'Where the hell did he find the money to move to Silicon Valley?' I ask him. Silicon Valley is about the most expensive real estate in the world, no shit. Makes Miami Beach look like Cleveland! I mean, this Alvin guy, he doesn't have any money. He works at fucking *Best Buy*, for fuck's sake. 'Check this out,' my brother tells me. 'Alvin just got a check for two hundred fifty grand.' 'What the fuck are you talking about?' I say. 'What the hell does a creep like that do to get that kind of money?' Now, according to my brother, apparently this Alvin guy had always been known as some sort of fucking joker with his geek buddies. Always playing. Right when the internet comes out, he buys this domain name, slashdot.com. Why? Cause this geek motherfucker just wants to be able to tell people that his e-mail address is 'atdash at slashdot dot com'...but like written out, you see what I mean? So they have to ask him like three times before they get it. Some real hardcore geek shit."

Watching the MILF Blaster's grinning, bobbing, elf-like face, Trey wondered where the hell this story was going. He was tempted to tell him to get to the goddamn point but he didn't want to ruin his new gig. He was already beginning to feel horny again. He had only fucked three girls in the VIP room and wanted to fuck some more while they were still around.

"So anyway, apparently there's this other website called slashdot.net...some sort of tech-industry website or something. But see, everyone always just assumes that URL's end in dot-com and not dot-net...so all these people trying to get to this industry website are ending up on Alvin's empty homepage. All of a sudden his empty homepage is getting a hundred, two hundred thousand unique visitors a day, all people going to the wrong website. Now the people at slashdot dot net are furious. They want this URL! They want their fucking traffic! They try to steal the URL from him but Alvin is like this Jedi fucking geek so that doesn't work, they can't trick him.

Finally they get sick of it and decide to just cut him a check for two hundred and fifty grand. These were the dot-com bubble days when those motherfuckers had more money than they knew what to do with."

The MILF Blaster paused to take a gulp of his Grey Goose and orange juice.

"OK, you're probably wondering what this has to do with the Reality Dogz porn empire. I'm going to tell you. Did you ever see that movie, *American Pie*? You remember that one character, Stiffler, the one with the hot mom? The MILF? Now, before *American Pie*, the word MILF already existed, but that movie really put it on the map. At the time that movie came out, I was just another chump woodsman over at CumTsunami.com. These were the wildcat days, man, when you could still buy sites like Madonna.com for fifty bucks. So anyway, I see *American Pie* and I get an idea. I think of Alvin over there in Silicon Valley with his website and I get a genius fucking idea. I mean, everything you see here" – Ryan once again gestured around the room – "comes from this one motherfucking idea. Now, I saw that this word was taking off. All of a sudden, every fucking teenage boy in America is talking to his buddies on the playground about MILF's."

Trey remembered talking about MILF's with his friend Tyler in junior high school.

"With the internet, it's all about having the right URL. You get a good URL, people will visit your fucking site even if there's nothing on it. Look at sites like BlacksOnBlondes.com or BangBros.com. They just have that ring that makes you remember them. Without that, your site is sunk. So I started thinking. It came to me while I was on the can taking a dump one day. No shit. I knew it was gold as soon as I thought of it: *MilfBlaster.com*."

He grinned.

"The power of the word, my friend. Those eleven letters have made me a wealthy man. Now, I'm proud of my sites, proud of my content. I think we got the hottest bitches on the internet. I mean, look at the scrags they get for some of these other sites." Ryan scanned the room and summoned a starlet from somewhere down the couch. She got up and walked over. Turning her around, he lifted her tiny skirt up so Trey could see her round, smooth, high-perched ass. She was not wearing panties. Trey got hard again immediately.

"Look at this! You will not find a better ass anywhere on the internet." The Blaster turned to the girl. "Thank you, honey. You're the heart and soul of VIPsluts.com." Ryan winked for Trey and slapped her on the ass. The girl rolled her eyes, smoothed her skirt back down, and sat next to Trey.

"But let's be honest: porn is not rocket science. Any fool with a camera and a hard-on can make porn. It's all about the URL, my friend. The power of the word!"

"Hey! Ryan!" It was the black bodyguard. He was grinning and shaking his head in mock disbelief. "Man, leave that boy alone...dude's got one thing on the brain, and it *ain't* the power of the motherfucking URL!" The girls all laughed. They had heard it before. Ryan laughed harder than any of them. He sprang up off the sofa and jogged over to clap Ferg on the back like a game show host.

"This guy...no, seriously...I don't know what we would do without this guy...any chump wants to bust into the VIP and start a swordfight...they take one look at Ferg and they turn the fuck back around! My man!"

Grinning, having fun, Ferg turned to Ryan. "Slash dot motherfucking com...damn! Give that boy a motherfucking break! Let lil' dude enjoy himself!"

At that precise moment, Trey realized that he had never had such a good time in his life. He was...*happy*. He poured himself a glass of Grey Goose and chugged it. It tasted delicious. He felt a hand on his thigh and turned around. It was the girl with the perfect ass. She smiled at him.

"I don't believe we had the pleasure of being properly acquainted back there," she said, indicating the VIP room. "How about it?"

Once again, Trey did not have to be asked twice. The two of them disappeared into the back room, this time with no cameraman.

29

Trey opened his eyes and winced. His head hurt. For a moment he thought he was in Lacombe. He looked over. Sadie slept next to him. Her bangs had fallen aside and Trey could see that her forehead was covered in acne. He had had a terrible dream. He was in the VIP, only instead of Sadie and the blonde with the perfect ass, he was fucking Dolores, Rhonda, and Shemeta. All three of them were dead. Dolores' head was half blown off and Rhonda's stomach was gushing blood everywhere. He lifted up one of Sadie's ass cheeks to get a look at her perfect hot dog bun pussy.

Still tight.

Trey took a shower. When he came back out in the terrycloth hotel robe, Sadie was sitting up in bed and smoking a cigarette with trembling hands. She shot him a vicious look.

"Who the fuck are you again?"

Trey didn't respond. She made a dismissive gesture with her hand and looked at the opposite wall.

"You know what...I don't give a fuck who you are." She turned back to him with a forced, opportunistic smile. "You don't have any crystal, do you?"

"Naw, I don't have no crystal."

Sadie began pulling her party clothes back on. She was trembling and could barely stand up. There was a hardly concealed fury in her gestures. Once she was dressed, Sadie lit another cigarette and took out her phone to make a call.

"Ramon...yeah...it's me, baby...listen...where are you? Yeah? You do? I'll be there in fifteen...no...twenty minutes...sure I will...yeah...bye."

Turning towards Trey, once again making her face hard and mocking, she held out her hand and said, "What the fuck are you looking at? Give me twenty dollars for a cab."

Trey grinned and peeled a fifty off of his roll. He held it up in a "come and get it" gesture. Dealing with women was like dealing with dogs: you always made them jump through some sort of hoop before you gave them any kind of reward.

"What, you want me to walk over there and get it from you? You want a goodbye kiss too?" Sadie stormed across the room towards Trey and snatched the bill out of his hand. "How about this: FUCK YOU!" She spun around and walked out of the room, slamming the door behind her so hard the minibar rattled.

Trey chuckled to himself. *Women.* He got dressed and went downstairs.

The weather was perfect: warm, sunny, and breezy. The palm trees were still there. The beach hotties were still there. The Ferraris were still there. The air still smelled like ocean. He was still in Miami. Miami was still paradise. Trey wanted Mexican food. At a place called Pepper's Grill he bought an oversized California burrito with fajita beef, guacamole and a Dos Equis. He ate it on the patio that overlooked the Atlantic. Already the beach was full of people: Haitian hotties in bikinis, Mexican goons, dudes playing volleyball, rich-looking middle-aged women going jogging.

Ryan had told Trey to be at the pool party at four o'clock. Trey would take a cab there. Driving the Taurus was a bad idea. He had stowed it out of sight on the top floor of a parking garage. As soon as he had a day off he would buy a tarp to cover it.

After killing a few hours on the beach, Trey found a cab and gave him the address. The driver, an old Haitian, listened to French rap on the radio. Trey didn't like it. Ten minutes later, they were driving down a street lined with palm trees and mansions. Trey had never seen anything like it. He felt a stab of jealousy. These wodies knew how to roll. All of a sudden he was impatient. He wanted to live in one of these mansions. He wanted a Range Rover. He wanted to be the one calling the shots, not just some hired cock in a cheap-looking yellow cab.

The cab driver stopped in front of a modern-looking three-story mansion hidden behind palm trees. The entire front of the cubed-out house was made of transparent plate glass. Trey gave the driver a big tip and thumbed the bell.

Ferg opened the door. He wore nothing but his do-rag and a pair of long, bright yellow swim trunks. His biceps were as big as footballs. His beard and black stocking cap made him look like an Orc from *The Lord of the Rings*. He narrowed his eyes and glared at Trey for a second before breaking into a big grin and holding out his fist for dap.

"I recognize you...looked like Chuck Liddell out there last night...come on in, bruh, Ryan's out back...party's just getting started."

Trey found a bathroom and took a leak. When he came out, he was surprised to see Ferg sitting in an armchair reading an orange paperback book.

The party had not quite begun. A couple of girls were laying out by the pool. Trey recognized some of them from the night before. All of them were topless and a few of them were completely naked. Guys wearing sunglasses and swim trunks were sitting around metal outdoor tables drinking mixed drinks and beers.

The pool was at least fifty feet long with a fake rock formation and waterfall at the deep end. The rocks were over ten feet high. The entire back yard was surrounded by a high fence and tropical trees. Trey whistled under his breath in admiration.

Ryan waved to him from the other side of the pool. The apron and chef's hat he was wearing were both emblazoned with the MILF Blaster logo. He was manning a barbecue pit that looked more like an F-14 cockpit than a grill. Ryan appeared to be the center of attention. Girls in bikinis and men with baseball caps turned backwards hovered around him as he flipped burgers and sausages.

"Hey! Trey! Come get yourself a dog!" shouted Ryan enthusiastically.

Trey dapped Ryan and his crew. He grabbed a hot dog and took a big bite. It was delicious. He finished it in three gigantic bites.

"Good, huh? FYI, that's a Thurman's gourmet all-beef dog you're eating. These bad boys don't come cheap. I get them from Costco."

The party heated up. Small clusters of people began fucking here and there: in the Jacuzzi, on the lawn, by the fake waterfall. Women mechanically lubricated their vaginas and anuses off-camera. Grips came and went in the background.

At six o'clock, Sadie showed up with a small, ratty-looking Mexican. She was completely gone on crystal. Her eyes had once again taken on the glazed, sexy, predatory look they had had the night before. She stripped naked and rubbed oil over her breasts and pussy with her fingers. Trey massaged his dick through his shorts. Her frame was off the chain.

When Sadie saw Ferg, she squealed, ran over to him, jumped on his back, and showered his neck with kisses. Even though her legs were wrapped around his muscular torso and her silk snatch was rubbing against his back, Ferg seemed barely to notice. He smiled imperceptibly, gave her a pat, and shrugged her off. Trey nodded in admiration. Homeboy was an iceberg.

Sadie slithered over to Trey, dropped to her knees and started sucking. She gave no indication of remembering who he was. The cameraman from the night before squatted three feet away and filmed. The Mexican stood behind him with his arms crossed and watched.

When Trey came on her face three positions later, she held up her two hands in the AC/DC sign of the devil and exclaimed, "Hell yeah baby!" With each vigorous spurt of cum, she waggled her head from left to right as if she were refreshing herself under a cool waterfall.

The camera panned up to Trey's face. Evidently he was supposed to say something. He looked into the lens, hesitated for a second, then improvised.

"We rock out any spot we hit!"

The MILF Blaster gave him a nod of fatherly approval from the chaise longue where he was being fellated.

Trey was covered in sweat. He pulled on his bathing suit and jumped into the pool. The cold water felt good. He blasted out five quick underwater laps, only coming up once per lap for air.

Sadie now fellated the talent with the pit bull tattoo on his chest. The Mexican watched with a mean frown. He had not let her get more than ten feet away from him since they had arrived. Trey found him straight up pathetic with his skinny arms, little gut, big diamond earrings, and weak eyes. Wherever there was money, wherever there were women, wherever there were drugs, there would be parasites like this Mexican. Trey was already beginning to get a sense for how the porn industry worked: there was a small click of men with bookoo money and power, a bunch of drugged-out whores who were in the business for no more than a few weeks or months, and an even larger parasitic class of pimps, agents, dealers, and other opportunists who attached themselves to the women and vacuumed up the money they made from their shoots. This schema was familiar to Trey, albeit on a larger scale. It was his world, only with hotter bitches, better hot dogs, and deeper stacks.

Trey suspected that the male performers were at the bottom of the power totem pole. Walking dildos. He had gotten lucky: Ryan liked him for some reason. He was probably a faggot. There was definitely something funny about him. Trey's first job would be to find a way to move from the expendable performer class to the more stable and lucrative parasite class, all the while cultivating and privileging his relationship with the inner circle. It would be a challenge but Trey had overcome challenges greater than this. For the time being, his best bet for maintaining his toehold in the Reality Dogz empire was by making himself the best damn woodsman they had.

Things started winding down around sunset. About half of the girls put their clothes on and left. The others hung around, enjoying the delicious barbecue, free drinks, and warm Jacuzzi. Sadie didn't bother putting her clothes back on. No one but her agent seemed to notice or care. He followed her around like a whimpering Chihuahua.

Trey ate a fourth hot dog and wandered over to where Ferg, Ryan and a few other guys were sitting.

"So, Ferg, you ready for tomorrow?" asked Ryan.

"Hell yeah, baby, I'm always ready. I'm ready right now."

"I bet Ronald is lying in his bed right now shitting bricks," chortled a Latin with a checkered shirt, lines shaved into his eyebrows, and big diamond earrings. He punched into the air eagerly as he spoke.

After a few minutes, Trey caught on that in addition to being the muscle for Reality Dogz, Ferg was some sort of bare-knuckle street brawler. He was going to be fighting a guy named Ronald the next day. The fights were videotaped and uploaded to the internet. Apparently Ferg had gained a certain notoriety on YouTube. He was undefeated. Trey was not surprised.

Ryan turned to him. "Hey, Trey, you should come tomorrow, man. It'll be a blast. Ferg usually knocks these suckers out in about thirty seconds. Afterwards we all go get enchiladas and drink Margaritas. How about it?"

"Sounds good," said Trey, nodding.

A scream from the other end of the yard caused everyone at the table to spin around. Sadie was clawing at the face of her agent and shrieking.

"Fuck you, motherfucker! You fucking piece of shit! Fuck you!"

She was in a frenzy. The Mexican put his hands up to protect his face but Sadie was on him like a wolverine. As soon as Ferg saw what was going on, he leaped up and ran over to where the altercation was taking place with linebacker speed. He scooped Sadie up from behind in a powerful bear hug and lifted her off the ground. She continued to kick and froth at the mouth.

The Mexican's face was bleeding where she had raked it with her porn star fingernails. His Yankees cap had fallen off, revealing a bald, lumpy scalp.

As Sadie flailed and screamed in his arms, Ferg calmly walked over to the pool and tossed her in the deep end with a big splash. She tried to swim towards the edge of the pool but Ferg now had the upper hand and could simply push her back in the water whenever she tried to get out.

"That bitch is fucking crazy, man! I'm out of here!" shouted the Mexican. He was shaking in anger. "You can find another agent, you *loca* bitch! You're going to fucking regret this!"

"Fuck you, Ramon! Oh, and by the way, you have the smallest fucking cock I've ever seen! You heard me, you dirty fucking Spic? Fuck you!" She was splashing and thrashing like a shark attack victim.

Ramon grabbed his things and slunk out of the back yard.

"Chill, girl...he's gone...just calm the fuck down...smoke you a cigarette and be cool," said Ferg in a stern, placating voice.

"Somebody *give* me a fucking cigarette then!" spat Sadie as she walked out of the pool, trembling with rage. Ferg handed her one and lit it. She sucked the cigarette down in four gigantic drags, ashing on herself in the process. The ashes stuck to her wet breasts.

Conversations resumed around her. Sadie walked over to her duffel bag, yanked out a skimpy floral dress, and pulled it on. One of her ashy breasts hung out but she didn't seem to care. She walked over to one of the patio tables and took out a little mirror and a baggie of crystal meth. She carelessly dumped it into a pile and snorted.

The other girls began shouting insults at Sadie.

"Fucking strung-out bitch!"

"Get that meth head out of here!"

Ferg calmly walked over to Sadie, picked up the mirror, and flung the powder all over the ground.

"Get that shit out of here...you know the rules. No dope on the grounds. It's time for you to go home."

Ferg grabbed Sadie's arm in an iron grip and marched her towards the house. She tried to bolt free but Ferg was too strong for her. On her way through the house she was able to grab a vase sitting on a table with her free hand and smash it against the wall before Ferg could push her out to her car, a cute yellow Volkswagen Bug convertible.

Sadie peeled out and nearly hit a parked BMW. She raised her middle finger to Ferg and shouted a parting "Fuck You!" as she sped off. Ferg waited a few minutes to make sure she didn't come back, then returned to the backyard and grabbed a beer.

"That girl is trouble," confided Ryan to Trey, shaking his head. "She also happens to be the most popular girl on the site. Man, you fucked her, you saw how she moves. That crazy bitch makes us a lot of money. Once a week it's like that. I'm getting sick of it, but that's the ass game for you. She and Ramon will be back together tomorrow and she will have forgotten everything."

On his way back to the hotel that night, Trey figured that the best thing he could do was wait and see. He would feel out this porn situation for the time being, lay low, gather information, and get a feel for how the Game worked in Miami. The porn shoots would give him living money and time to figure out a real plan. As long as his dick kept working, he was in the clear.

The situation with Sadie intrigued him. He was sure that he could do a better job of controlling her than Ramon did. His experience pimping Shemeta had confirmed what he had always suspected: that he was a born hustler who could turn out anyone, even a bitch as spirited as Sadie. Once he had his teeth in her, he could probably pocket nearly every cent she made from her shoots, plus whatever she got whoring on the side. A bitch like that could bring in a lot of cheddar. Then, if he could assemble a stable of girls to work for him, he would be getting closer to real money. Perhaps he could start with Sadie and make her his bottom bitch. Ramon was weak and he would be able to get rid of him easily.

If he had been in Ramon's place, he would have put his fist in Sadie's face, dragged her back to his apartment by her hair and whipped her raw with a coat hanger. Problem solved.

As for Ryan...he was weak. If a goofy chump like that could make it in the Game...

The character who impressed him was Ferg. Although technically he was only the bouncer, he had a lot of soft power. Anyone could see that. Ferg was a true player: a man who lived for the Game. The Game was like a forest. There were grassy fields, trees, swamps, lowlands, and mountains. Different animals occupied different niches. Miami was special because it contained two types of terrain: land and sea. Trey was a shark. Ferg was a silverback. Two apex predators whose territories didn't overlap. Trey saw no reason they couldn't form an alliance.

He didn't yet know enough about the porn game to make his move. But he would soon. And when he did, Miami was going to say hello to the bad guy.

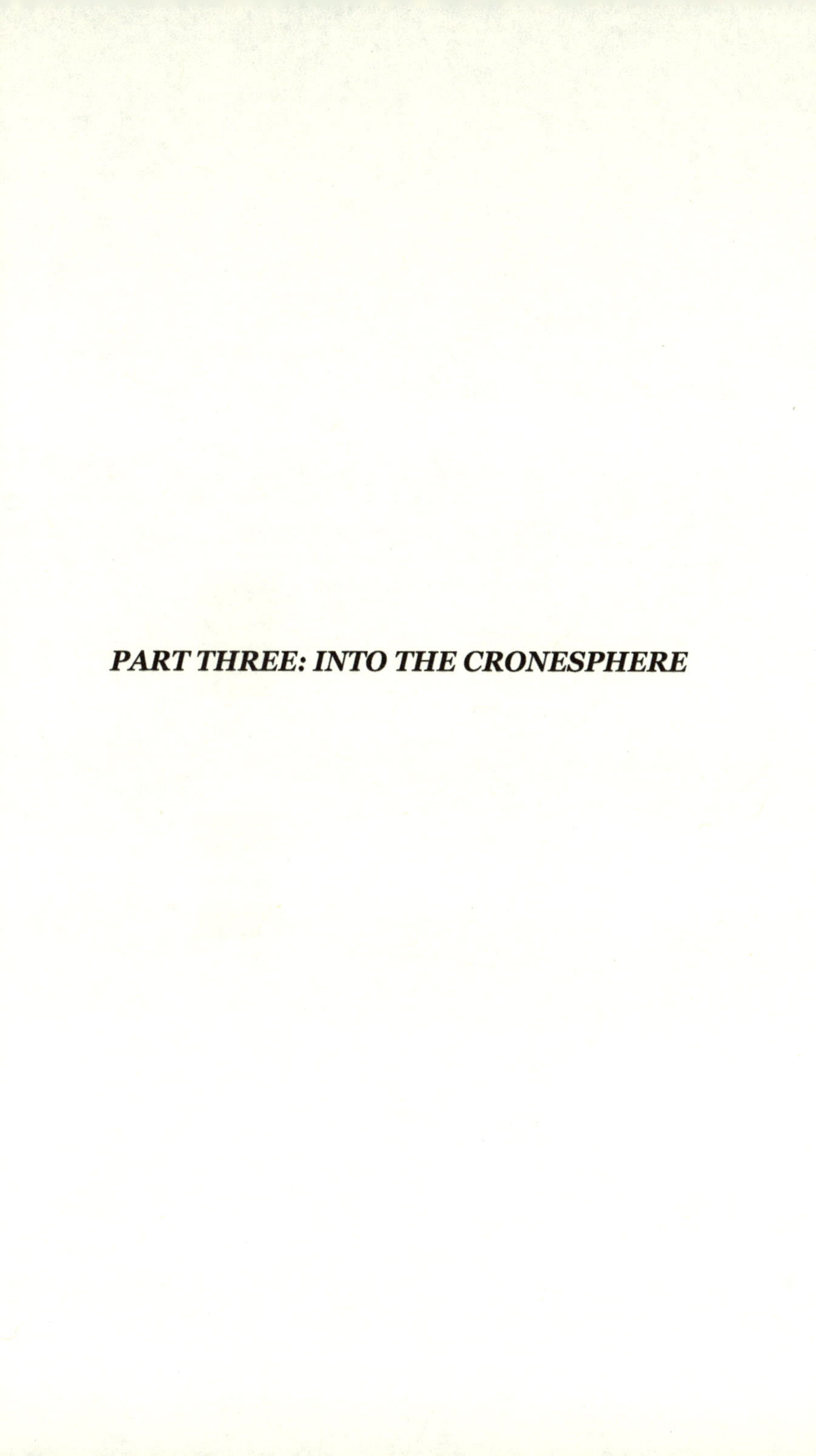

PART THREE: INTO THE CRONESPHERE

30

Gwenn Smith pulled to a stop in front of a sagging white trailer covered in mold stains. It had taken her forty minutes to find Pontchartrain Street. The farther she got from the highway, the crummier the houses became. Eventually Pontchartrain Street turned into a dirt road and the houses turned into trailers. Every yard seemed to come with a stack of crab traps, a rusted washing machine, a pile of beer cans, and a mangy dog. Eventually the dirt road petered out into a clearing with about a dozen skinny 1970's vintage trailers arranged with no rhyme or reason. Half of them looked abandoned.

She grabbed the manila folder marked *Tyrone Washington* and flipped through it. Tyrone had stopped coming to school after the death of his grandmother. As guidance counselor at Mandeville High, it was her job to make sure students like Tyrone didn't fall through the cracks. She had approached each of his teachers and convinced them to pass him even though he had missed all of his final exams.

She stepped out of her SUV. The heat was oppressive. Within seconds she was sweating. Crickets and cicadas buzzed in the tall grass.

She knocked on the front door. There was no answer. She knocked again, harder this time. The door opened. She almost gagged when the sweetish smell of rotting garbage hit her nostrils. Tyrone stared at her from behind the ripped screen door with glazed, unseeing eyes. His cheeks were covered in acne and a scanty mustache sprouted from his upper lip. She forced herself to smile.

"Hello, Tyrone. It's Mrs. Smith from Mandeville High. Do you remember me?"

Tyrone didn't respond. She continued. "I have something for you. It's your high school diploma! You graduated! Congratulations!" She slid his diploma in through the hole in the screen door. Tyrone took it without looking at it.

"I have some good news for you, too," she continued in a bright voice. "You got a 29 on your ACT. That puts you in the 96th percentile among high school students in Louisiana! And since your grade point average is above 3.0, you automatically qualify for the TOPS program. That means you're eligible for free tuition at any public university in Louisiana. The deadline is next week. I tried calling you, but the operator said the line had been cut off. I went to the trouble of filling out an application to Southeastern for you and writing you a letter of recommendation. I hope you don't mind. All you have to do is write a short essay and answer a few questions. As a low-income candidate, you don't have to pay an application fee, and you're practically guaranteed to get free room and board. I even put stamps on the envelope. All you have to do is put it in the mailbox."

She passed a thick brown envelope to Tyrone. "I think this could be really good for you, Tyrone. I know how hard it must be with the death of your grandmother. I am so, so sorry. If there's ever anything else I can do, please call me. I wrote my phone number down in there. Remember, you're not alone."

"Thanks," mumbled Tyrone as he closed the door.

Tyrone walked back to his room and dropped the envelope on the floor. It was strewn with Little Debbie boxes, cellophane wrappers, and two-liter plastic bottles of red drink. The ripped buckle half of the belt that his grandmother had bought him to wear to church lay in the middle of the floor. A few days earlier, Tyrone had tied it around his neck, stood on a chair, tied the belt to the ceiling fan, and kicked the chair away. The cheap pleather ripped immediately and he crashed to the soiled floor like a tarry piece of old feces.

He picked up a half-empty can of Spaghetti-O's and conveyed a spoonful of warm, glistening sauce to his mouth. Tyrone had not brushed his teeth in months and his gums were rimmed with a thick yellow crust. He lay down on his back. The electricity had been cut off and the trailer was as hot and humid as a sauna. Despite the heat, he wore a thick black sweatsuit from which a rancid odor emanated.

A familiar voice exploded in his ear.

"You're not going to college. You're going to die!"

"Shut up," said Tyrone.

The voice laughed at him. Tyrone put his pillow over his ears. The laughter slowly became an unintelligible high-pitched chattering.

"*...polama hando huntala banandata kunalahandi...*" Tyrone moaned. "...NEGOLO HEMANDALALI GONOLIMANDATO..."

The nonsense voice became a chorus of nonsense voices. Tyrone thrashed on his bed. The voices had identified themselves to him months earlier as the Cronobacter Horde. They spoke to him every day.

Tears ran down Tyrone's cheeks. He pulled down his sweatpants and fished out his small penis. It was rock hard. He pulled at it for the sixth time that day. A moment later, he ejaculated.

The voices subsided. Tyrone wiped his semen on the mattress and drifted into sleep.

He was awakened by a loud banging on the door. A second later, it crashed open.

"Tyrone? You in here?"

Tyrone peered into the living room. His mother was sitting on the sofa and sucking on a crack pipe next to a tall, skinny, dark-skinned man he had never seen before. A dirty baby blue cloth that resembled a potholder lay on top of his sweaty head like a doily.

"This Marcus," she said without looking up or removing the crack pipe from her mouth. Her expert lips massaged the glass in an attempt to coax as much crack cocaine as possible from the chamber.

Marcus swiveled his evil, bloodshot eyes to Tyrone and pointed an accusing finger at him.

"So, you the man around the house, huh? Well, you ain't the man no more. I'm the man now, ya heard me?"

A high-pitched buzzing filled his ears. He walked into his room, locked the door, and lay down on the bed.

Men came at all hours. Tyrone could hear them having sex with his mother, who made a big show of shouting and talking dirty. The official price was twenty dollars. Marcus beat her frequently. Tyrone could hear his mother screaming and cursing as Marcus slapped and kicked her. The garbage smell in the trailer was complemented by the acrid odor of crack. Tyrone remained locked in his room all day and often his presence was entirely forgotten. Marcus referred to him as "the runt". Tyrone urinated into a cup and poured it out the window to avoid seeing them. They almost never left the house.

One day, Tyrone woke up to find Marcus and his mother gone. He bolted to the bathroom and defecated for the first time in more than a week.

It was time to put his plan into action. He ran outside and started his grandmother's 1987 Pontiac Bonneville. An hour later, he was walking out of the Wal-Mart parking lot with a heavy bag under his arm. Inside the bag was a $700 black Beretta M9 pistol, paid for in cash. He drove home. Marcus and his mother weren't back yet. He went to his room, read the instruction manual, loaded his pistol, and waited. When they got home he would walk into the living room and shoot Marcus in the head. Then he would shoot his mother in the uterus. Then he would put the pistol in his mouth and blow his brains out.

"Come on, Victor, let's see the tat again!"

Victor, Patrick, and Phil sat in a booth at Ron'z Cocktails on the lakefront in Mandeville. The barmaid, a bottle blonde in her forties with a common face, thick midsection, and acid-washed jeans, set a fresh pitcher down on the table. Thanks to Victor's thinning red hair and coarse-grained freckled skin it never occurred to her that he might be any younger than thirty.

"Bust it out, man!"

Victor grinned and rolled up the sleeve of his work shirt. A wobbly grayscale drawing of Jack Nicholson as Jack Torrance from *The Shining* grinned out from behind Saran wrap and a layer of vaseline.

"Heeeere's...Johnny!" said Patrick. "Fucking right."

Victor smirked and shrugged. "It's alright."

His voice now had a slight Southern accent.

Pat turned to Phil. "So anyway, this dumbass says he wants to use BA13 for his motherfucking slab...no shit...I told him he would be looking at fissures the size of his finger by next summer..."

Victor drifted away from the conversation. Pat and Phil were two Home Depot lifers in their late twenties. They were good guys, but they weren't philosophers like him. He tried all the time to expand their horizons beyond DIY, deer hunting and the Saints, but they weren't interested. When Phil had come over to his house the first time, Victor showed him his collection of Dark Knight graphic novels and even loaned him a copy of BATMAN: ARKHAM ASYLUM, but Phil never even read it. What could he say? They were rednecks. He could speak their language, but they couldn't speak his.

His gaze drifted over to the barmaid. She was bending over the sink to wash pint glasses and he could see down her low-cut top. Her tits were bigger than Jessica's. He grunted. Jessica had gained forty pounds since they moved in together. She no longer wore her choker and had stopped dying her hair. Rage popped in him like a flashbulb. A man with a sexuality as powerful as his was not meant for monogamy. The tame pleasures of domestic life could never satisfy him. He was an adventurer. He was supposed to be in the hold of a ship somewhere, or in the jungles of South America, or fighting rebels in Burma, not tied down by a woman.

"...man, he walked out of there with over forty bags of Quikrete...that deck is going to be huge..."

Patrick and Phil had probably never even heard of

Burma. Both of them were married with young kids at home. Conformists. He stole another glance at the barmaid. It was clear that she liked him. If it weren't for Jessica, she would have been his by now.

His eyes went down to her long pink fingernails. He imagined her torturing his scrotum with them as he lay trussed on the floor. He looked at one of the bar's six television screens. An old episode of *Diff'rent Strokes* was on. The camera zoomed in on Gary Coleman as he twisted his rubbery face into his trademark expression of suspicious incredulity.

"*Whatchoo talkin' about, Willis...*"

Victor chuckled and lit a cigarette. With his frog face and little afro, Arnold Jackson looked just like Tyrone.

Tyrone...He missed Tyrone. He was Victor's only true friend and the only person he had ever met with an intellect approaching his. He hadn't seen him in months. They had drifted apart after Victor's expulsion from Mandeville High and the death of Tyrone's grandmother. At first Victor had tried to stay in touch, but Tyrone rarely answered the phone and never left the house anymore.

Drunk and sentimental, Victor took out his phone and dialed his friend. According to his call log, they hadn't spoken in over three months.

This number has been disconnected or is no longer in service...

"Goddamn it," said Victor. He looked at Pat and Phil. They were talking about WEDI panels again. Pat sold them in the bathroom section of Home Depot. They were cementitious backer boards made in Germany. Top of the line. He never stopped gushing about them. There was no way Victor could talk to an idiot like Pat about his problems with Jessica.

He swigged the rest of his pint and stood up.

"Later, fellas. I've gotta run."

"Where you going, Victor? We ain't even started drinking yet."

"Gotta get back home to the missus."

"Oooh! Pussy whipped!" Phil extended a callused hand for Victor to shake. "Later, dog."

Victor waved at the barmaid as he walked out the door. She didn't wave back.

It was a twenty-minute drive from Ron'z to Tyrone's trailer. When he got there, he was surprised to see that the front door was hanging open.

"Tyrone?"

He gagged as soon as he walked in. The trailer smelled like death. There was old trash and rotten food everywhere. The sofa had been overturned. Victor held his orange Home Depot handkerchief over his nose.

"Tyrone? You in here?"

He pushed open the door to Tyrone's bedroom. Tyrone was lying on his back wearing nothing but a filthy pair of briefs. His skin had a waxy, unnatural sheen. For a moment, Victor thought he was dead. Tyrone slowly turned his head to look at him. His glassy eyes looked evil and paranoid.

"Come on, buddy. We're getting you out of here."

31

Tyrone sucked his eighth Merit cigarette down to the filter, flung it to the ground, extracted another from the pack, and lit it in one smooth movement. It was 10 A.M. He sat in a folding chair in Victor and Jessica's backyard in Slidell. Victor was at Home Depot and Jessica was at the veterinary clinic where she worked as a secretary. Jimmy Buffett's *Margaritaville* filled the hot, humid morning air. When the song came to an end, he leaned over and pressed BACK on the CD player at his feet.

Nibblin' on sponge cake...

Tyrone couldn't explain why he liked *Margaritaville* so much. Victor had said it best when he gave Tyrone the CD: no matter how blue a man felt, Jimmy was always there for him.

On his lap lay a yellow legal pad. Every page was covered in tight, messy handwriting. Tyrone flipped to a blank page, took out a black pen and copied out the lyrics to *Margaritaville* for the fifth time that morning.

The only thing the Cronobacters hated more than Jimmy Buffett was cigarettes. They especially hated it when Tyrone transcribed the lyrics to *Margaritaville*. Now all Tyrone had to do was pick up the pad for them to shut up. Their voices had grown steadily fainter until they hardly spoke to him at all.

Tyrone reached down, pressed *Back* on the CD player, and lit another cigarette.

32

Victor scanned the chrome and porcelain faucet with a practiced gesture. It was nearly closing time. He had worked a double shift and was dead tired.

"That'll be seventy-seven dollars and twenty-six cents," he said in a monotone voice.

The customer, a woman in her seventies with gold rings on every finger, expensive sunglasses, a tight, unsmiling mouth, breast implants, and long, blood red fingernails, spoke up.

"That's not the right price. It was marked $29.99. Scan it again."

Victor scanned it again. The same price came up. He had sold dozens of identical faucets. The price was $69.99. He showed the woman the computer screen.

"It says $69.99."

"Well, the computer is wrong. It was marked $29.99. Change it."

"I can't change it. The price of that faucet is $69.99. That's the second one I've sold today. I could do a price check if you want, but it would be a waste of time."

The woman's collagen-treated lips tightened into a hateful pucker.

"Are you calling me a liar, young man?"

"No, ma'am. The computer..."

"And what if your computer is wrong? Have you ever thought of that, pinhead?"

The old woman's insult caused Victor's penis to stiffen. He looked down at her fingernails and imagined her slicing into his back with them.

"I'd like to speak to your manager."

Victor had shown up half an hour late and Frank had been giving him dirty looks all day. "Ma'am, if you'll show me where you found the faucet, I can go ahead and check the price for you."

"I said I want to talk to your manager!"

Nikkel, the cashier next to him, smiled to herself and shook her head. Victor sighed and called Frank on the intercom. A moment later, a stocky, red-faced man in his forties with a big smile arrived. He shot Victor a baleful look.

"Good afternoon, ma'am. What can I do for you?"

The woman flicked one of her long fingernails at Victor.

"This faucet was marked $29.99. Your cashier is trying to overcharge me."

Frank looked down at the faucet. Victor knew that Frank knew the true price.

"This young man is going to do a price check for you. Victor, will you please assist this lady?"

An explosive hormonal cocktail of anger, sexual arousal, and existential frustration pumped through Victor's veins as he followed the old woman to the bathroom section. She wore high stiletto heels and limped a little. Her withered, anorexic body and huge, bolted-on breast implants excited him. She gloated when they arrived at the faucet aisle.

"Here. You see? $29.99."

On the shelf next to the $69.99 Grohe porcelain faucet the old woman held was a bottom-of-the-barrel Chinese faucet that cost $29.99. Victor indicated it.

"Ma'am, *this* is the $29.99 faucet. The Grohe faucet you're holding costs $69.99." He pointed at the empty space where the box had obviously been. It was immediately above the correct price marker.

The old woman exploded. "That's *your* problem, idiot! You should have put it in the right place! It was right here when I found it!" The woman shoved aside one of the Chinese faucets and jammed the box in. It didn't fit. Victor stared at her fingernails. His penis was painfully hard. Frank had followed them to the faucet aisle and watched the whole scene.

Victor trembled. For months a carbuncle of virile frustration had been abscessing in him. Jessica refused to grow her nails long. They hadn't been intimate in weeks. Tyrone spent all of his time smoking cigarettes in the back yard while he broke his back at Home Depot. Every time Victor tried to talk to him, his eyes wandered off and he could tell that Tyrone wasn't really listening. Pat and Phil had stopped hanging out with him. He made $6.75 an hour. He had a police record and no high school diploma.

A man can only take so much.

"The price is $69.99...you fucking hag!"

The old trout's jaw dropped. Frank turned beet red.

"Victor...you're fired! Get out of here!"

Victor threw his orange apron on the ground and stormed out of the store in a fog of rage. He drove straight to Ron'z and ordered a pitcher of Woodchuck cider. As he drank he fantasized about fabricating a pipe bomb and blowing up Home Depot. He knew how to do it. Gunpowder, pipe, nails. Boom. His fantasy fugue was soon complemented by another scene in which he was tortured and dominated by the old woman. She held a whip and wore nothing but high heels. After a few pints the two fantasies evolved into a composite fantasy in which Frank and Tyrone insulted him as they double-penetrated first Jessica, then the old woman in the faucet aisle.

He stumbled into the house at eleven P.M. Jessica was lying in bed in a nightgown watching *Urotsukidoji: Legend of the Overfiend* and eating wasabi peas. She didn't look at him. He flopped onto the bed and pawed at her genitals. She pushed him away.

"You're drunk."

He tried again.

"Not tonight, Victor."

Victor's flushed face twisted into a vicious snarl.

"So it's true then...once you go black, you never go back!"

Jessica's mouth opened in shock. "Victor Sanders, that's the most disgusting thing I've ever heard!"

"Oh yeah? How about this: fuck you, you fat cunt!"

Victor woke up hung over at three P.M. the next day. Jessica was gone. He had a vague memory of the previous evening. The last thing he recalled was Jessica driving off in the middle of the night. "Fuck you," muttered Victor as he prepared himself a cup of coffee. He shuffled to his closet. Jessica's clothes were gone. He took a deep breath. When he exhaled, his shoulders slumped forward and his stomach sagged. "Fuck you," muttered Victor again.

In the gap left by the retreat of Jessica's wardrobe he espied the old black trenchie. His only true friend. He lifted it off the hanger and donned it.

He didn't need Jessica.

With the sluggish solemnity of a man choosing life, he lowered his bulk onto the sofa, lit a cigarette, grabbed a PlayStation controller, and turned on *WWE: Wrestlemania.*

33

Over the next few months, Victor almost never moved from his position on the sofa. Tyrone paid the rent in cash. The two boys spent all day, every day smoking cigarettes, watching CSI, and playing video games together. Tekken III, SoulCaliber, Final Fantasy, and WrestleMania were their favorites. Tyrone always wrestled as the All-American

John Cena, whereas Victor preferred Kane or the Undertaker. Often Victor would play until five in the morning, pause the game, turn off the television, fall asleep fully clothed in his easy chair, wake up the next day at two in the afternoon, shift his oily, unwashed body, light a cigarette, unpause the game, and begin playing again exactly where he left off. Their conversations remained entirely one-sided, with Victor talking and Tyrone listening. Victor no longer objected to his best friend's new, taciturn personality. These conversations were usually accompanied by a Jimmy Buffett ballad.

One day, Tyrone was playing SoulCalibur alone while Victor was watching videos on YouTube.

"Hey, Tyrone, check this out!"

Victor was always summoning him to the computer to watch the random videos he spent hours trolling for: a man being maimed by a lion, a sleepy kitten, Chechen separatists beheading a kidnapped Russian soldier, or surveillance footage of people being shot during gas station stickups. Tyrone paused the game and walked over to the computer as instructed.

The video was entitled KIMBO VS. DREADS. Victor pressed play. The first shot was of a hulking black man with a gigantic, bushy beard stepping out of a white Hummer in what appeared to be the asphalt back parking lot of a marina. "That's the champ right there," commented an unctuous off-screen voice. Kimbo popped in his mouth guard and began stretching his shoulders out. Cheap electronic music played in the background. Kimbo put his dukes up and approached Dreads, a smaller, less fit-looking black man with long dreadlocks and a dirty undershirt. Dreads looked nervous. Kimbo began stalking him around the parking lot, his massive upper body rippling fluidly left and right in anticipation of the first punch. The two men exchanged tentative jabs, with Kimbo methodically marshaling Dreads backwards. It was clear even to Tyrone that Dreads had no chance at all. In the blink of an eye, Kimbo Slice unleashed a savage uppercut that dropped Dreads to the pavement. His head hit the asphalt with a sickening watermelon sound.

"Yes!" chortled Victor.

Tyrone felt sick to his stomach.

Dreads lay supine with his legs straight like a medieval sarcophagus and his hands over his face. A few men in the crowd walked up to him and shook their heads in disgust, as if examining a dead dog on the side of the road. The cameraman zoomed in on Dreads' fingers gingerly probing his bloody face for serious injuries and commented, in the same unctuous voice, "I don't think he wants any more of that."

"Is that it? It *can't* be over. I was just warming up!" said Kimbo to the camera with a big stage smile as he cracked his knuckles.

Turning to Dreads, still laid out on the asphalt, Kimbo Slice barked, "You wanna finish this?"

"No," mumbled Dreads.

The cameraman followed a strutting Kimbo around for a few moments, then returned to Dreads, who was now lying on a stack of packing crates. Kimbo lifted him into a seated position. Zooming in on his dazed, disoriented, still-bloody face – blood was dripping from one of his eyes like tears, as if he had ruptured something inside his head – the cameraman said, once again in the same unctuous, patronizing voice, "Good sport right here, buddy."

"He all right. Good shit, dog," added Kimbo Slice.

The camera panned to Kimbo's gloating entourage.

"Line 'em up, baby, line 'em up," said a fat black man wearing a "Team Kimbo" T-shirt.

Then Tyrone saw him.

Among the riff-raff celebrating Kimbo Slice's victory was his next-door neighbor.

Tyrone's skin crawled. A sound like radio static crackled in his ears. The camera zoomed in on Trey. He threw up a gang sign and said, to the camera, "Top of the line shit, dog."

"Three-oh-five, baby, that's what I'm talking about. Done deal. It's a wrap," said a black man with dreadlocks and gold teeth. The last shot of the video was of this same man holding his blinged-out watch up to the camera and spinning the oversized face. It was a spinner-rim watch.

"Yes! I love the watch!" chortled Victor, dragging on a cigarette.

Tyrone went wordlessly back to his seat.

Over the next few days, he watched the video in his room over and over. On the fifty-second viewing, he noticed a detail that had escaped his attention until then. One of the men was wearing a T-shirt that read "MilfBlaster.com".

Tyrone typed in the URL. It was a porn site. He clicked through the videos. On the second page he found a video of Trey having sex with a MILF. There were two more on page three. Most of the MILF's looked no older than thirty to Tyrone.

The Nothing.

It verified itself with ever-greater evidence every day. The idea had occurred to him as he lay on his back in Lacombe. The world he lived in *appeared* real. It was full of colors, details, and fabricated conflicts. But it was an illusion. Victor's fantasy women, for example. The never-ending stream of cashiers, barmaids, and television actresses he told Tyrone about did not exist the way he thought they did. There was no point even in responding to anything Victor said. It was all the Nothing. The people in the videos were the Nothing. The hideous penises and porn vaginas were the Nothing. The $30,000 life insurance payment he had received from his grandmother was the Nothing. Kimbo Slice, Trey and the MILF Blaster were the Nothing.

Tyrone found over twenty videos spread out across eight different porn websites in which Trey was the featured actor. All of these websites – RoundBrownAzz.com, VIPsluts.com, MilfBlaster.com –

belonged to a conglomerate called Reality Dogz Inc. based in Miami.

Tyrone was next able to establish a precise chronology of the videos. The most recent one had been uploaded to the internet only a week earlier. It was for a brand-new site called WhiteasaurusRex.com. Trey was the star of the site: Whiteasaurus Rex himself.

Tyrone clicked on one of the "Whiteasaurus Rex" videos. The camera followed Trey as he approached a blonde girl sitting on a bench in a park. He introduced himself. The two of them began chatting about dating. The girl had an accent like Jennifer Dupre. She giggled and told Trey that she only dated black men because only a black man could satisfy her. Trey responded that there were white guys out there with dicks just as big and even bigger than the dicks of black guys. The girl said she didn't believe him. He made a bet with her: he would show her his dick, and if it was bigger than her black boyfriend's, she had to fuck him. If not, he had to "take her on a shopping spree". The whole thing was clearly staged. After a few minutes, the two of them went back to a motel room and had sex. Every time the camera zoomed in on Trey's penis, the girl made an exaggerated "Oh My God!" face.

Ugliness...vulgarity...degradation...ugliness...

As Tyrone watched video after video of his neighbor mugging, posing, penetrating, sodomizing, and ejaculating, puzzle pieces slid together in his brain. Tyrone was a piece of dog shit. That was evident. His transformation had occurred when Trey saw him looking out of his window. The extent of his degradation was too complete for this to have been a coincidence. Trey was somehow responsible for the holocaust of his life. Like King Midas in reverse, everything he touched turned to shit from the moment Trey entered his life.

Tyrone knew what he had to do. The video had been a sign. Clearly it was addressed to him. His destiny was calling. He remembered the scene in *Total Recall* where Arnold Schwarzenegger learns that there is a tracking device implanted in his skull. He has no choice but to pull it out with the help of a scary-looking surgical instrument that must be jammed violently into his nasal cavity. When he finally pulls the golf ball-sized probe out through one of his dilated nostrils, it is red and pulsating. This scene was an image of absolute horror: Schwarzenegger contemplating the living parasite that he has just pulled out of his body. Trey was also a malignant, pulsating beacon, only instead of controlling him from inside of his body, he controlled him from outside. Like Douglas Quaid in *Total Recall*, Tyrone had no choice but surgically to extirpate the beacon from the flesh of the world.

Tyrone shook his head. Finding Trey wasn't enough. He had to kill him. Of course, he would have to kill himself after killing Trey. The thought brought a smile to his face. It wasn't as if he had anything to live for. He would simply find Trey and shoot him with his Beretta. Then he would put the gun in his mouth and project his brains through the roof of his skull.

For the first time in a long time, maybe forever, Tyrone felt excited about the future.

On his last night in Slidell, Tyrone and Victor watched *Pulp Fiction*. It was Victor's favorite movie. He knew all of Samuel L. Jackson's monologues by heart and recited them along with the movie. Afterwards they played *Wrestlemania*.

Victor finally passed out on the sofa at around four AM. His pasty, hairy gut hung out of his T-shirt. It was time to leave. Tyrone carefully laid the short note that he had written on the kitchen counter top. It read:

Dear Victor,

I've left. It is long past time that I take care of unfinished business elsewhere. Please do not worry about me. You will hear about me soon. Thank you for the kindness you have shown me over the last six months. Please take this money as a sign of my eternal gratitude.

Tyrone

He neatly laid ten thousand dollars in cash on the countertop. What remained of the thirty thousand was in his front pocket.

It did not take Tyrone long to pack his car. He had almost nothing: a few oversized WWE T-shirts from K-mart, two pairs of pleated shorts from K-mart, a pack of black cotton socks from K-Mart, a pup tent from K-Mart, his little box of treasures with the snake skull, a photograph of his grandmother, his Beretta, a box of bullets, and Victor's CD of Jimmy Buffett's Greatest Hits. Victor could use some of the ten thousand dollars to buy himself a new one.

Tyrone felt a surge of excitement as he started his grandmother's Pontiac and pulled out of the driveway. This was it. Life. Even if it probably wasn't going to last long, at this moment at least, he felt alive. Life was such a stupid phenomenon. He took the thick roll of money out of his pocket and looked at it. This was almost funnier than anything else. As if he could exchange it for anything but more Nothing. He shoved the money back in his pocket.

It was four-forty A.M. when Tyrone pulled onto I-12 East. The interstate was empty. The sound and texture of the cool, moist air rushing in through the wide-open windows was pregnant with signification. His skin tingled as if he were being caressed with feathers.

Tyrone pulled off at the exit marked *74 – Lacombe.* There was no traffic and it only took him a few minutes to drive to the old trailer park off Pontchartrain St. He had not been there in more than six months. He took a deep breath, then walked into Trey's trailer.

It was empty. There was nothing on the floor but empty bags of Cheetos and empty cans of Busch Light. He walked into Trey's kitchen and looked out the window. It faced his old bedroom.

Tyrone stood immobile and stared for a long time at the black empty square that used to be his life.

He left the trailer and got the can of gasoline from the trunk of his grandmother's car. He doused everything: the mattress, the carpet, the walls. When he was done, Tyrone walked across the muddy clearing to his own trailer. It looked even worse than it had when he had left. His mother had apparently come and gone a few more times. Tyrone went straight to his room. It had been ransacked. He closed his eyes and sloshed gasoline everywhere. He did not want to notice the little shreds of his old life that he would certainly find underneath the waste and the trash if he looked. He stepped through the garbage and across the overturned sofa in the living room until he stood at the threshold of his grandmother's room. He did not want to see what was inside but it was of vital importance to him that this room in particular should burn to the ground completely and leave no trace.

Tyrone paused, then opened the door. A rat scurried out. Marcus and his mother had trashed the room. The naked mattress was covered in stains and the floor was ankle-deep in Styrofoam food containers, empty bottles, cigarette butts, plastic bags, and dirty clothes. Tyrone imagined his mother's ruined body squirting and dripping juice everywhere, poisoning the mattress and staining the walls. He wanted to curl up on the bed, pour the gasoline over his head, and light himself on fire. The window had been left partially open and everything had been soaked in rain and mold. The framed photos that had been on his grandmother's dresser had fallen to the ground and been trampled on.

Tyrone forced his gaze to a blank spot on the wall and emptied the can of gasoline into the disgusting, soiled mattress. He lit a match and threw it. The mattress immediately caught fire with a loud whooshing noise. Within two seconds the flames were licking the ceiling.
Tyrone ran back to his room and tossed a second match. In the time it took him to jog over to Trey's trailer, flames had begun licking the outside of his grandmother's trailer.

He needed to hurry. He lit a match and dropped it onto Trey's carpet. The flames spread so quickly that he barely had time to jump away from them. He turned around and ran back to his car. As Tyrone drove away, he could see the flames beginning to reach into the sky.

34

Tyrone stepped out of his Pontiac and stretched his legs. He was in the parking lot of Waffle House in Pensacola, Florida. It was eight A.M. and already hot. Tyrone was hungry.

The Waffle House was crowded and he had to sit at the counter. Before moving in with Victor, he had never eaten in a sit-down restaurant before. He felt like a character in a movie. They were always sitting at counters and talking with the short-order cooks.

Tyrone ordered a Pecan Waffle with Blueberries. The only waffles he had ever eaten were square Hungry Jack brand frozen waffles with little bits of blueberry inside the waffle. He was surprised when the Pecan Waffle came out circular and with actual blueberries on top.

He took a bite of the Pecan Waffle. It was delicious. There was no comparison with the Hungry Jacks. The Waffle House blueberries tasted nothing like the Hungry Jack blueberries. He finished it in five minutes and washed it down with an ice-cold glass of tap water.

Even the water tasted better in Pensacola. Tyrone went to the bathroom and refilled his water bottle with good Pensacola water for the rest of the trip.

Across the highway from the Waffle House was the beach. Tyrone approached it with fear in his heart. He had never been to the beach before.

The first thing he noticed was the fresh, salty odor. It smelled clean. Why should salt smell clean? He took off his shoes and waded knee-deep into the water. It was clear and he could see shells on the rippled ocean floor. Tyrone had never seen water like this before. All natural water in south Louisiana was muddy and came with venomous snakes and the odor of decomposing marine life. A school of small fish swam around his black legs. They looked happy.

"Get out of the water, nigger!" shouted a man's voice two feet behind him. He spun around. A white family was making a sandcastle together a few hundred yards away. They paid no attention to him. Tyrone hustled out of the water.

He opened his car door, then hesitated. Was he really in so much of a hurry? He liked Pensacola. He had never imagined that the beach could be so nice. Nor had he imagined how good a waffle could be if it were circular and blueberries were added to it.

Too bad I didn't find this place sooner, thought Tyrone with finality. He got back into his car and slammed the door.

Five hours later, Tyrone was eating lunch on a concrete parking bumper in a Citgo parking lot in Tallahassee. The pavement was so hot that he could feel it radiating upwards through the soles of his shoes. Fragrant scalp sweat ran down his forehead. He shoved a handful of Cheetos into his mouth and washed them down with a sip from his 48-ounce fountain red drink. His good mood had vanished. He balled up the empty Cheetos bag and threw it in the trash can. With a bitter smile he reminded himself that he would be putting a bullet in his brain in a few days.

His grandmother's Pontiac had gotten exactly 14.6 miles to the gallon between Lacombe and Tallahassee. It was an ugly number. He pulled out and merged back onto I-10. He was a passive, frightened driver and easily lost his composure in traffic. He was afraid to go over sixty miles per hour on the interstate and clutched the steering wheel with both hands. Every time a big rig blasted by him at eighty miles per hour he imagined his Pontiac mangled in its undercarriage like an aluminum can with a slug inside.

I-10 turned into I-95. The sun began to set to his right. He had been on the road for fourteen hours and his nerves were destroyed. The green exit sign ahead read DAYTONA BEACH. He took it. The service road funneled him onto a two-lane highway that ran along the Atlantic Ocean. Traffic slowed down. Should he turn? He went straight. The road narrowed, then veered onto the sand. Orange cones delimited it.

The spectacle on the beach repulsed Tyrone. Loud people in flashy cars grinned and shouted at each other in a vast collective ritual of mating and dominance. A group of pumped-up, drunk young people hosed each other down with fluorescent green and orange Super Soakers. Everyone had a tattoo and everyone was drunk. Knaves disported themselves on Sea-Doos in the shallow water next to the beach. The loud, whining drone of the jetski engines felt to Tyrone like a drill being shoved into his ears.

The car in front of Tyrone had purple neon ground effects and kept stopping as girls wearing denim shorts, bikini tops and baseball caps came over to say hello to the driver, a tan, muscular, tattooed white man wearing his baseball cap backwards. Loud rap-rock music issued from the oversized speakers in the trunk. Tyrone`s intestines shuddered with the bass.

The car was crawling. Tyrone smoked cigarette after cigarette. He was hot and agitated. Pensacola was Heaven. Daytona Beach was Hell. He drifted off into a reverie in which a sudden acid rainstorm reduced all the Sea-Doo riders to melting skeletons who were then picked clean by red-bellied piranhas.

Lost in dreams, Tyrone did not notice the drunk hedonist approaching his car. His fantasy was interrupted when she jammed her pasty white buttocks into the frame of his window and wobbled them. He jumped in surprise like an electrocuted gerbil and ashed on himself. The girl's friends exploded in idiotic laughter. One of them tried to spray her with his Super Soaker. She jumped out of the way and the water hit Tyrone in the face, wetting his hair and T-shirt.

The dirty blonde poked her flushed, drunk face into the window. Her eyes were bloodshot and glazed.

"Sorry, cutie...aw, you're so sweet with your little afro and your old Pontiac!"

"Pontiac – Poor Old Nigger Thinks It's A Cadillac!" brayed a male voice with a Southern accent behind her.

"Oh, shut up, Randy!" shouted the girl, laughing. She turned back to Tyrone. "Sorry about them. They're so rude. Do you want to see my tits?"

Before Tyrone could respond *NO*, the girl stood up, pulled down her bikini top, and jiggled her floppy, splotchy breasts for Tyrone. Her friends cheered. Randy raised his neon Super Soaker to the sky and chanted, "Double D's! Double D's!" Tyrone fantasized about extinguishing his cigarette on one of her ugly, droopy breasts. She pulled her top back up and the whole group staggered down the line to the next car.

An hour later, Tyrone was back on the road. His ordeal on the beach had reduced his morale to nothing. He had planned on camping on the beach in his pup tent. He no longer had the courage to camp. He drove back to the Wal-Mart he had passed on the service road on the way into town and parked at the back of the lot.

It was still too early to go to sleep so Tyrone wandered around the Wal-Mart for an hour. He bought a twenty-ounce plastic bottle of blue PowerAde, six glazed donuts, and a bag of Spicy Nacho Doritos for dinner. He ate sitting on the bench next to the vending machines at the entrance. No one paid any attention to him.

After dinner, he trudged back to his car, crawled into the back seat, and immediately fell into a deep, unpleasant slumber.

The sun woke him up at seven A.M. He felt disgusting. He was hot and his body was covered in a dusty, sticky film. He went back into the Wal-Mart to use the restroom. On his way out he bought a road map of Florida, another bottle of PowerAde, and six more glazed donuts for breakfast. The parking lot was so vast that he was able to eat two whole donuts before he got back to his car. It was already hot and Tyrone was covered in sweat when he started up the Pontiac. He hadn't wiped the donut glaze off his fingers and his moist hands stuck to the hot vinyl steering wheel. He drove off.

Tyrone got goosebumps when he caught his first glimpse of the Miami skyline from the top of an overpass. The sparkling glass skyscrapers looked like the Crystal Palace from *Conan the Destroyer*. He wished he had a CD of the theme song to *CSI: Miami* to listen to as he entered the city. His grandmother had nothing but gospel music and sermons by Pastor Leonard Lucas.

The car ahead of Tyrone got off at the "Opa Locka" exit. Tyrone followed it. Within five minutes, he was lost in a slum area. There were no trees anywhere, just squat, ugly shacks and apartment complexes with ghetto people loitering and staring at him as he drove by. Everything was made of concrete. It was broiling hot. Most of the men were not wearing shirts and they all had hard, muscular physiques. There was not a palm tree, blue cocktail or Panama hat in sight, just a bleak landscape of grinding poverty and evil, ruined-looking black people.

After driving around a maze of numbered streets for twenty minutes, Tyrone finally pulled over in the parking lot of an abandoned corner store and took out his map. He was in an area called Overtown, miles away from the ocean. He discovered with surprise that Miami and Miami Beach were two different entities separated by a body of water called Biscayne Bay. Miami Beach was a long, narrow island that looked as thin as a hair on his map.

A movement in his peripheral vision caused Tyrone to raise his eyes. A group of shirtless boys his age were walking through an overgrown, litter-filled lot towards his car. They all had muscular physiques and gangster swaggers. They were a block away and getting closer. Tyrone flung his map on the floor, started the Pontiac with trembling, sweaty hands, and sped off just in time. One of the boys gave the car a hard kick as Tyrone squealed past them. They laughed and brandished their guns in his rearview mirror as he drove away.

Tyrone resumed driving in circles. An hour later, he finally escaped into the downtown area. Everything here looked clean, new, and shiny. Tyrone smiled when he drove past the plate-glass building that he recognized from television as CSI headquarters. For a split second he wished Victor were with him.

At last he found the MacArthur Causeway. Biscayne Bay sparkled around him like a sapphire desert. Beyond it lay the magnificent wall of Miami Beach. Tyrone marveled. How could such a thin strip of land hold up so many skyscrapers?

Tyrone parked his car on the corner of Washington Avenue and 14th Street. The weather was hot but not as humid as it was in Louisiana. There was a breeze. It felt good. He was in Miami Beach. It actually existed. A delicious odor wafted out of a restaurant called Pepper's Grill. The exterior facade was painted orange with jalapeno peppers everywhere. Decals bearing the phrase "Savor the Flavor!" were splashed across the plate-glass windows. Tyrone hesitated, then walked inside.

His heart pounded in his chest as he approached the counter. Everyone in the restaurant was fashionable and attractive. He did not belong. He was an impostor.

He closed his eyes and visualized to the box of Remington slugs he had bought from Wal-Mart. One of them would soon shatter his palate and transform his gustatory cortex into a blob of gray jelly running down an Art Deco wall. The thought gave him the courage to order the most extravagant meal of his life: a vegetarian California Burrito with authentic "pico de gallo" salsa and guacamole. Including his red drink, chips, and tax, the tab came out to almost fifteen dollars – the most money Tyrone had ever spent on a single meal. He took his gigantic roll of money out of his pocket and peeled off a hundred-dollar bill. The cashier, a sullen, bored-looking Mexican wearing an orange T-shirt and orange baseball cap, glared at Tyrone's money with undisguised hatred.

Tyrone took his burrito to a small table near the trash cans where no one could watch him eat and sat down. He rounded his narrow shoulders down and around and held his head just inches over the tray, giving him the aspect of a vulture or a turtle. He unwrapped the foil and took a tentative first bite of the gigantic burrito.

It was delicious.

By the time Tyrone finished, he had decided that it was the single best meal he had ever had in his entire life. It was even better than the Pecan Waffle. As he shoveled the mountain of plastic and paper detritus into the trash can, he pondered the fact that it was only now, when his time on Earth was drawing to a close, that he was discovering what a real Burrito tasted like. Would the course of his short, wasted life have been different if he had eaten a California Burrito from Pepper's earlier? Did food always taste better when it was more expensive? A light bulb went off in his head. Expensive things were not just more expensive, *they were better*.

Pepper's was only two blocks from the beach. Tyrone did a double take when he turned onto Ocean Drive. He was standing right in front of the club where most of the VIPsluts videos were filmed. It was closed. The sidewalk was full of people. They all seemed to be eating ice cream or sipping frozen drinks, possibly Mojitos or Margaritas. He had heard about these cocktails on television. Many of these people wore nothing but bathing suits. A fat, old man with a gigantic cigar in his mouth, a baby-blue seersucker jacket, and a slender blonde bimbo on his arm caught his eye. The bimbo had breast implants and looked no older than twenty-one. Her skirt barely covered her buttocks. The man shouldered past Tyrone without looking at him.

Tyrone left the strip and walked towards the ocean. He wanted to take off his shoes and wade in the water. There were sunbathers everywhere, but they had a different look here. They were tawnier and fitter than the people he had seen in Daytona. They looked like television characters.

With no protection from the sun, Tyrone began to sweat. He grabbed the front of the oversized John Cena T-shirt that he had bought from K-Mart and ventilated his torso as he struggled to walk through the thick sand. His black socks and gray Velcro K-Mart shoes were already granulated. He stumbled.

A group of sleek beach women in bikinis looked at him and giggled. He knew they were laughing at him. Everyone was laughing at him. He felt like a giant, sweating black turd. The thick sand was hard to walk in and suddenly it was as if he were slowly sinking into cement. He began to hyperventilate.

Stuck in the sand, broiled by the sun, flayed by the gazes of the beach hardbodies, Tyrone gave up twenty feet from his goal. He turned around and staggered back to the beachfront park, making sure to take a different route across the sand so it wouldn't look like he was fleeing. After weaving his way back through the gauntlet of colorful towels and oiled bodies he sat down underneath a palm tree in the beachfront park. Bushes ensconced him. The good mood he had been nursing ever since passing the CSI building had been pulverized.

Tyrone was protected and invisible under his tree. He felt something cool and wet on his face. Wiping his cheek with his hand, he noted with surprise that fluid was leaking from his eyes.

Tyrone forced his thoughts back to his mission. From where he sat he could see the entrance to the club. It wasn't open yet. He would keep an eye on the South Beach Strip in the hopes of catching the Reality Dogz on their way into one of the clubs. Miami Beach was big. It would be more difficult than he had imagined. A morbid smile crept across his lips. He would have to keep his Beretta on him at all times in case he ran into Trey somewhere. With any luck, he might even have time to blow away a few beachgoers after killing Trey and before killing himself.

Tyrone felt calmer as soon as he recovered his Beretta. He stuck it in the right front pocket of his pleated navy-blue K-Mart shorts along with his map of Miami and walked west. He arrived at a busy street called Dade Boulevard. On the other side of the street was a small, tranquil canal with grassy banks. He sat down on a bench, lit a cigarette, and took out his map. He had walked eight blocks. The canal was called Collins Canal. It led to Biscayne Bay. A hardbody in a kayak paddled by. Two fat brown ducks followed in his wake. They swam up to the edge of the water and quacked at Tyrone. He smiled. Someone had left half of a Twinkie on the ground next to the bench. There were ants on it. He ripped off a piece and tossed it to the ducks. They fought for it. He tossed the rest in. Three more ducks arrived. They all quacked at him. He stood up and walked on.

By the time he got back to Ocean Drive, the sun was low in the sky and most of the bathers had gone home. The outdoor cafes and tapas bars that lined Ocean Drive had filled up. A cool breeze blew in from the ocean and the sun was no longer boiling hot. No one paid attention to him as he walked towards the water. A discarded bottle of Hawaiian Tropic caught his eye. He attempted to imagine the Miami Beach hardbody lifestyle: cocoa butter, tapas, Margaritas, drugs, dissolute sexuality, DJ's, Ferraris, hair gel...an infinite number of concrete permutations of the Nothing.

Tyrone took the Beretta out of his pocket. A middle-aged woman wearing Prada sunglasses and listening to an iPod jogged right past him without noticing that he was holding a gun. He lifted the Beretta and aimed it at her pancreas. The pancreas was shaped like a pipe. All he had to do was pull the trigger and she would die. The woman jogged on. He put the gun back in his pocket. He wanted to go into the water.

This time he was able to make it all the way to the ocean. The surf felt cool and delicious on his sweaty feet. As he waded through the water, his eyes were drawn to the gymnastic apparatus he had noticed earlier. It was a large metal frame like a swingset from which eight long chains with metal rings at the end were suspended. The rings hung about seven feet off the ground and were spaced about eight feet from each other. Tyrone had noticed a group of muscular beach hardbodies showing off earlier. Instead of simply swinging from ring to ring, they leaped and flipped like buff monkeys. The hardbodies had gone home and the rings were empty.

Tyrone walked over to the first ring and stood under it. It looked higher up than it had from the water. He leaped, missed the ring, and fell. Were the hardbodies watching him? He glanced over his shoulder. A Latin couple walked hand in hand down the beach. Had they been watching him? Tyrone caressed his Beretta. Let them watch! He leaped again. This time he was able to grab the ring. A second later, his palm stung and his shoulder felt like it ws going to pop out of its socket. He let go and dropped to the sand with a smack. A shooting pain in his hip caused him to yelp. He had landed on his gun. Pulling up his shorts, he saw that a dark bruise was already forming on his hip against his black skin. He lit a cigarette.

Sport was idiotic.

His stomach rumbled. It was dinnertime. Another California Burrito was out of the question. He had noticed a McDonald's on his way back from Collins Canal. It would do.

It was the biggest, most impressive McDonald's Tyrone had ever seen. There were eight cashiers and an upstairs dining area. He had never seen a two-story McDonald's before. He bought a box of nine chicken nuggets, a Biggie fries, a Coke and a McFlurry.

Upstairs, a group of men were huddled around a row of tables next to the window overlooking Washington Avenue. There were four chess boards set up. Two of the men were having an animated conversation over what appeared to be a finished game. The tables around them were piled with trays, wrappers and Styrofoam cups. Tyrone sat a few tables down from them. As he ate, he stole glances at the chess players. They appeared to range in age from eighteen to eighty. Some of them looked like bums, particularly one older white man with long fingernails, shoulder-length, stringy, thinning hair, and thick plastic-framed glasses. When this man smiled, as he did frequently, Tyrone could see that he was missing half of his teeth. He played against a huge black man with a short beard, a red polo shirt, white sneakers and crisp khaki pants. A couple of other people watched the game and commented on it in hushed voices. There was not a single woman in the group.

Tyrone took out his map of Miami Beach. Ocean Drive began at 15th Street, four blocks away. He would begin his patrol there. From 15th Street to South Pointe Park was 1.6 miles. Like a sentry in the French Foreign Legion he would walk up and down Ocean Drive all night, every night in search of his quarry. This plan pleased him. He looked at his watch. It was ten o'clock. Time to begin his patrol.

An abandoned McFish sandwich on the table next to his gave him an idea. Making sure no one was watching, he carefully wrapped it in a napkin and stuck it in his pocket.

The hardbodies of Ocean Drive now wore black sports jackets and tight cocktail dresses instead of swim trunks and bikinis. Tyrone caught a whiff of perfume from a young woman who resembled the repulsive pop singer Rihanna. The corner of his mouth turned up in a hermetic smile. The principal ingredients of perfume were whale vomit and a fecal paste extracted from the anal gland of the civet cat. The woman didn't know that. Hardbodies were stupid.

The denizens of Miami that he passed on his patrol were a uniformly disgusting collection of water automatons. Tyrone imagined the entire city as one glabrous, tawny surface perforated with orifices and coated in a glistening film of sweat, cocoa butter, and sperm. The people who lived there were nothing more than plastic mannequins with functioning spinal cords and oversized sexual organs.

A peaceful, exalted feeling spread up through his legs as he walked. This was a task that he was capable of carrying out. The more steps he took, the more inert and thinglike his march became. Each step was like a brick added to a monument. The higher the monument grew, the freer Tyrone felt. He began to count his steps. It took him 6,222 steps to walk from 17th Street to South Pointe Park and 6,185 steps to walk back. He identified a tall, illuminated palm tree across from Wet Willie's as the halfway point. Each time he passed it he tapped his forehead twice with his left hand, winked at the tree, and whispered the word *Croatoan.*

Several times Tyrone thought he saw Trey from a distance, but each time it ended up being someone else. There were a lot of people who looked like Trey on South Beach.

After three hours, Tyrone's legs and feet were numb. He had walked more in the last day than in the previous six months combined. He rewarded himself with a thirty-two ounce Mountain Dew and shuffled back to his car. He had one thing left to do before he could conclude his first day in Miami Beach. The numerous parking towers on Ocean Drive had given him an idea. He drove his Pontiac to the seven-story Avalon Hotel garage, the most beautiful on the strip, and followed the arrows up to the nearly empty top floor. From where he was parked he could see the ocean. It was black. He turned off the ignition, crawled into the back seat, and fell asleep.

35

Tyrone woke up with a start as a car peeled out somewhere in the parking garage. His black plastic digital watch read 6:31 A.M. He sat up and rubbed his eyes. His legs ached and his mouth felt slimy and disgusting. He poured the last gulp of warm Mountain Dew into his mouth, swirled it around for a few seconds to melt the morning slime, and then swallowed the Dew. It was the closest he had come to brushing his teeth since he had left

Slidell. He unzipped his fly, inserted his short, thin penis into the rim of the plastic bottle, and emptied his bladder. He held it up to the dawn sunlight. His urine was dark orange. He screwed the cap back on tightly and set it on the ground next to one of his front tires.

He lit a cigarette. After months of heavy cigarette smoking the moment at which he set fire to tobacco still felt artificial and exciting to him. The cigarette tasted good. He contemplated the ocean rendered polychromatic by the auroral sun, then shifted his gaze to the bottle of urine that just minutes before had been filled with Mountain Dew. Tyrone decided that this was a metaphor for his life.

His joints were stiff. Transferring his cigarette to his mouth and extending his arms in front of him, he executed a deep knee bend. His knees cracked with a loud snap. A pleasant warmth spread through his legs. Tyrone decided to take a jog around the perimeter of his section of the nearly-empty parking garage to loosen up his stiff legs.

He lumbered forward. Within twenty seconds he was winded. A brisk walk would do. He turned the corner and stopped dead in his tracks. The cigarette dropped from his lips. He was looking at a purple Ford Taurus with chrome spinner rims and tinted windows.

He ducked behind the nearest car and took the Beretta out of his pocket with shaking hands. For a long moment he couldn't breathe. His heart slammed against his ribs. It was dead silent in the parking garage. There was no one around. He took a deep breath and stood up. Holding the Beretta in front of him, he tiptoed towards the car as if it were a sleeping Bantha.

The car was covered in a thick film of dust. He peered inside. The floor was filled with the usual detritus: Styrofoam cups, receipts, cigarette butts. He hesitated, then slowly reached for the door handle. It was locked. He held his Beretta by the barrel and struck the small vent window just in front of the driver's side window with the butt. It made a loud smacking noise but did not break.

On his fourth try, Tyrone finally broke the glass. It made almost no noise as it shattered. Musky sweat gushed from his underarms. He looked around in a caricature of the criminal caught *in flagrante delicto* and reached in through the small hole.

A car turned a corner somewhere in the parking garage. Tyrone jumped and jerked his arm out of the hole, scratching himself on the broken glass in the process. His heart pounded in his chest. A trickle of blood ran down his forearm. His DNA was on the car now! He could not see any blood or skin, but that meant nothing. He knew that he had left microscopic epithelials on the broken glass and that David Caruso and the Miami forensic team would find them.

He took a deep breath, reached back in, and unlocked the Taurus. He found a plastic bag on the floor and filled it with anything that might be a clue. Every receipt that he found went into the bag. So did the CD sticking out of the stereo. Under the driver's seat, Tyrone found a quarter, a nickel, and an unmarked white pill. Under the passenger side seat Tyrone found a plastic colored ball hair twisty. The glove box was empty.

He ran back to his Pontiac and slouched down in the driver's seat. One by one he examined the articles closely.

He had an idea. He took out his yellow legal pad, turned to a blank page, and wrote the word FACTS. Underneath this word, he drew up a list.

FACTS

Plastic colored ball twisty

Four receipts predating murder

Three receipts postdating murder:

May 3rd, 2007, 5:12 PM, Wal-Mart, Gulf Shores, Alabama, $125.65 (Beef Jerky, Clothes, Twizzlers, Jewelry, Diapers, Baby Formula, Bottle)

May 3rd, 2007, 11:18 PM, $413 (Unmarked) RAYOFLIGHT written in pen on back.

May 5th, 2007, 2:20 PM, Texaco, Daytona Beach, Florida, $40.00 (Gas)

May 8th, 2007, 11:45 AM, McDonald's, Daytona Beach, Florida, $13.08 (No detail)

White Pill

Thirty Cents

Knife wound on back

Black girl in passenger seat

Murder occurs at noon on May 3rd

Kimbo Slice video uploaded May 11th

Tyrone next wrote the word STORY.

STORY

Trey kills three people.

Trey drives home with girl.

I see Trey.

Trey drives to Wal-Mart.

Trey buys baby supplies.

Trey drives to Daytona sometime between May 3rd and May 5th

Trey stays in Daytona until at least May 8th

Trey eats McDonald's in Daytona

Trey arrives in Miami before May 11th

He put down the yellow legal pad. His stomach tingled uncomfortably. He lit a cigarette and forced himself to continue.

QUESTIONS

Who is the girl?

What is RAYOFLIGHT?

What cost $413 on May 3rd?

Does Trey have a baby?

Did Trey know Kimbo Slice before arriving in Miami?

HYPOTHESES:

Here Tyrone drew a blank. His head hurt. He set the legal pad on the passenger seat. He had gone far enough for the day. It was too early to find Trey. The hunt was supposed to build slowly to a grand, dramatic conclusion. He double-knotted the bag of clues and put it in his glove compartment. It was not even eight o'clock yet. The list exercise had given him a painful erection. He pulled his shorts down and stroked his penis. He had not masturbated in days. His unfocused eyes rested on the odometer as he stimulated himself.

Thirty seconds later, he ejaculated on his stomach. Most of the sperm dribbled onto the black John Cena T-shirt that he had been wearing since he left Slidell. The largest dollop landed on one of John Cena's muscular forearms. There was a long, shiny streak underneath the silkscreened image.

Tyrone smiled. An idea occurred to him.

Fuck the Miami hardbodies! I'll wear my useless seed for all to see! They can keep their coitus a tergo *and their Latinas. I've got this black John Cena T-shirt!*

There was a greasy white stain on his shorts as well. Tyrone bent over and lifted the loose fabric to his nose. It smelled like mayonnaise. A smile broke across his face. He reached into his pocket and extracted the McFish sandwich from the night before. He had forgotten all about it. It was a perfect way to start the day. He stuck it back in his gun pocket and strolled out of the parking garage.

Collins Canal was quiet and peaceful. The sun was still low in the sky and it wasn't too hot yet. Tyrone sat on his bench, set the McFish sandwich next to him, and lit a cigarette. A few minutes later, the two ducks from the day before swam up and quacked. Tyrone smiled, tore off a piece of bun, and threw it to the bigger duck, whom he had already named Richie. Carter, the smaller duck, got the next piece. Soon they were joined by Bradley, Ian and

Blake. They gobbled up the industrially farmed tilapia and quacked for more.

"Sorry, I'm all out," said Tyrone. "No more McFish." The ducks quacked for a few more minutes, then swam on. Tyrone stood up. It was time for his morning wade.

As he walked from Collins Canal to the beach, he reflected with pleasure on the fact that he still had the whole day ahead of him to do whatever he wanted. He decided then and there that he would celebrate his trove by eating lunch at Pepper's Grill. The morning air was cool and breezy and the ache in his legs felt healthy. Someone had left a cardboard box marked FREE on the corner of 19th Street and Meridian Avenue. He stopped and looked inside. It was full of books.

Most of the free books were romance novels. At the bottom of the box, Tyrone found a copy of *The Da Vinci Code*. This one he had heard of. He remembered Jessica reading it. He picked it up and took it with him.

Other than a few joggers, the beach was mostly empty. Tyrone walked to the water's edge, took off his socks and shoes, and waded in. He closed his eye and hummed the melody to *Margaritaville*.

Suddenly it hit him. *He was in Margaritaville*. He was *living the song*. Margaritaville *was a real place*. There was a connection between the steel drums and the cool morning air that someone who had never waded in the Atlantic Ocean could not understand. Tyrone became aware the cool breeze, the salty odor, and the warmth of the sun on his cheeks. All of these sensory details *completed* Jimmy's music. Tyrone, paused, then grinned. Not only that, but *Jimmy's music completed the beach*. Jimmy Buffett *was* the beach and the beach *was* Jimmy Buffett. At the same time, the beach was nothing but the beach and Jimmy Buffett was nothing but Jimmy Buffett.

The hair on his forearms stood up. A seagull glided over his head. A cruise ship plied the sea. It wasn't just Jimmy Buffett and the beach. *Everything* in his field of vision was connected. An unbroken chain of atoms stretched from Tyrone to the the sand to the water to the cruise ship to the air to the bird to the air again and back to Tyrone.

He imagined himself as a neutrino. Neutrinos were tiny particles that raced through the universe at 99.9999999% the speed of light. They were so small that they simply passed through the empty spaces between atoms. Earth was as insubstantial to a neutrino as a cast net was to a grain of sand. From a neutrino's point of view, there was no line of separation between him and the seagull. At that very moment, millions of neutrinos were shooting through his body as if it were Swiss cheese. He looked at the palm of his hand. It was made out of Swiss cheese. There was nothing but Swiss cheese. Was Swiss cheese empty or full? It was both, and it was neither. Empty space wasn't empty at all. It was just another word for full space. Fullness and emptiness *were the same thing*.

The thought gave Tyrone fresh double goosebumps. In the distance, a white hardbody performed pushups on the sand. His handsome face bore an expression of solemn concentration as he pistoned up and down. The early morning sunlight glistened off of his well-defined intercostal muscles. He wore earbuds. Tyrone smiled and addressed him telepathically.

Hey hardbody...I am you, and you are me.

The hardbody sprang up and jogged off.

Tyrone looked at his watch. It was a quarter to nine. He still had three hours to kill before going to Pepper's for his Burrito. He walked back to the Croatoan palm and opened *The Da Vinci Code.*

Renowned curator Jacques Saunière staggered through the vaulted archway of the museum's Grand Gallery...

He closed the book. His back ached and his stomach gurgled with hunger. He looked at his watch. It was two P.M. He had been reading for five hours! Time to go to

Pepper's. He held the book in front of him to read even as he walked, looking up only to avoid other pedestrians and navigate crosswalks. Every page was more exciting than the previous one. The chapters flew by. He couldn't stop. Dan Brown was a genius.

His reading was interrupted by a peal of cruel female laughter. He looked up to see a group of Hispanic teenage girls staring at him. They wore short skirts, large hoop earrings, and lots of makeup. They looked at each other and cracked up when he made eye contact with them.

Let the harlots laugh, thought Tyrone. *They know nothing of the Sacred Feminine.* He descended back into the adventures of Sophie Neveu, Silas, and Robert Langdon.

At Pepper's, Tyrone pretended to study the menu, even though he knew exactly what he wanted. He was relieved to see a different Mexican working behind the counter this time. This new Mexican had a friendlier face.

His second California Burrito was even better than the first. He read *The Da Vinci Code* as he swallowed his Tex-Mex lunch, pushing the tray away without looking at it as he chewed his last mouthful of Burrito.

When Tyrone resurfaced, it was past four P.M. He was the only customer left in Pepper's Grill. All of the Mexicans behind the counter stared idly in his direction like meerkats. Tyrone slunk out.

Next door was a Tower Records. It was a sign. He walked in.

"Can I help you?" asked the cashier, an older white man with glasses and an intelligent face. He glanced down at Tyrone's T-shirt.

"Do you have any Jimmy Buffett CD's?"

"A Parrothead, huh? Right over here."

There were five Jimmy Buffett CD's in the rack: Last Mango in Paris, Coconut Telegraph, Floridays, Riddles in the Sand, and License to Chill. Tyrone went straight for Riddles in the Sand. The cover featured a photograph of Jimmy standing on the beach wearing a sombrero and holding a guitar. He walked back to where the man was shelving CD's.

"Find what you were looking for?" said the man with a wry smile.

"Yes. Do you have a CD of the CSI music?"

The man winced.

"Young man...what you call 'the CSI music' is known to the rest of the world as The Who. You know, the greatest rock band of all time?" He led Tyrone to the ROCK AND ROLL section and handed him a CD of The Who's greatest hits.

"You've got all three of them on there...'Who Are You', 'Baba O'Riley', and 'Won't Get Fooled Again'...known to your generation as 'CSI: Las Vegas', 'CSI: New York', and 'CSI: Miami'".

Tyrone paid for the CD's and walked four blocks to his tree. He was almost halfway done with his book.

The problem with *The Da Vinci Code* was that each chapter ended with a cliffhanger. How could he stop reading when he knew that the solution to the cliffhanger could be found on the next page? There was no way to stop reading!

Tyrone finally shut the book at six PM. His eyelids were too heavy to keep plowing ahead. He had reached page 381.

He slept for an hour and a half. When he woke up, the sun was almost down. He was hungry again. He decided to eat at McDonald's a second time. As he had done the day before, Tyrone bought nine Chicken McNuggets, a Biggie Fries, a Coke and a McFlurry. He walked back upstairs and sat in the same seat he had sat in the day before. The first thing he did was wrap three of the McNuggets in a napkin for the nomads. He was happy to see that the chess players were still there. The giant black man was playing against a Chinese teenager this time and the stringy-haired white bum with the long fingernails was playing a handicapped middle-aged white man. Tyrone stared at the man. Where two normal arms should have been, the man had short, misshapen flippers. Tyrone smiled. He knew the name for this condition: *phocomelia*. The man bent over and moved a chess piece with a melted-looking flipper. Tyrone turned away from the phocomelus and sank back into *The Da Vinci Code*.

At ten-thirty, Tyrone forced himself to shut his book even though he was getting close to finishing it. It was time for his patrol. The chess players had all gone home. How was it possible for a book to be so engrossing as to block out everything happening around him? *The Da Vinci Code* was the best book he had ever read. Why hadn't Jessica recommended it more enthusiastically?

Tyrone began his patrol exactly as he had begun it the night before, counting his steps and winking at the palm tree. He imagined himself as a little mouse exploring an infinite Swiss cheese cavern. With satisfaction he recognized some of the faces from the night before. The fat cigar smoker and his bimbo were eating lobster on the patio of an expensive-looking restaurant called Palazzo. The man gesticulated aggressively at the waiter as the bimbo pouted with her arms crossed over her silicone chest. They were gone by the time Tyrone made his second pass.

Tyrone's mind wandered to strange and pleasant places as he walked. He imagined owning a falcon, which he would name Cutrus. Cutrus would keep him company on his walks. If anyone bothered him, Tyrone would loose Cutrus, who would dive-bomb them and rake their eyeballs with his talons and razor beak. He could bring Cutrus to the beach and teach him how to swoop down and steal things from the hardbodies. He would buy Nachos from Pepper's and feed Cutrus as he walked.

By one-thirty A.M., Tyrone felt too tired to continue walking. He had done his three hours and it was time to sleep. He imagined himself punching a time clock like a character in a movie. When he lay down on the back seat of his car, something hard jabbed him in the thigh. His CD's! He had forgotten all about them. He turned the key in the ignition, put *The Who's Greatest Hits* into the player, and advanced to Track 7. The familiar psychedelic organ music gave him goose bumps. He reclined the driver's seat as far as it would go and closed his eyes. He visualized David Caruso racing a fan boat through the Everglades.

By the time the song ended, he had decided that it had been the greatest day of his entire life.

36

Tyrone finished *The Da Vinci Code* in Pepper's as he ate his third Burrito in as many days. He closed the book and shook his head in amazement. Somehow Dan Brown had written a book about *him*. He was Robert Langdon, unraveling the secret code that until then had determined the entire structure of a world that he had previously taken for granted as simply existing without following any sort of logic. At the same time he was the albino monk Silas, a man who had been perverted and corrupted, his mind and soul raped exactly as his had been.

Tyrone's body yearned for more words with atavistic force. He set off for the "Free Books" box. It was once again hot and sunny. The new cum stain that Tyrone had aimed at John Cena's silkscreened head stood out sharply against the dark black T-shirt. A few hardbodies took furtive second glances at his T-shirt as he walked past them, clearly wondering, *is that...?*

You're damn right it is...motherfuckers!

The box was still there, but most of the books had been taken. There was nothing left but a handful of romance novels, the autobiography of a man named Lee Iacocca, and *Sahara* by Clive Cussler. There was a bright gold and blue embossed picture of an Egyptian sarcophagus on the cover of *Sahara*. Tyrone grabbed it along with the Lee Iacocca autobiography.

On the way to his tree, Tyrone stopped in Walgreen's to buy a PowerAde. At the rack right before the checkout counter, he saw that they sold Croakies. Croakies was the brand name for the wide, form-fitting elastic straps that athletes attached to their glasses to keep them from falling off their heads as they balled. A pair cost $5.99. Tyrone bought one.

He attached the Croakies to his welfare glasses as soon as he got outside. He looked at his reflection in a plate glass window. The Croakies gave his face an attractive aerodynamic aspect. He looked like Kareem Abdul-Jabar or Geordi La Forge from *Star Trek: The Next Generation.* He liked it.

Sahara turned out to be almost as good as *The Da Vinci Code.* The main character, Dirk Pitt, was a cross between James Bond and Indiana Jones. Tyrone liked his sidekick, a short, resourceful Italian named Al Giordino. The two men were treasure hunters and kept getting into scrape after scrape from which they always found a way out.

After what he decided would become his customary nap, Tyrone walked back to McDonald's. How long would he be able to maintain his new daily routine? He remembered being seven years old and lying in bed counting as high as he could go. It was a dead serious enterprise. The higher he got, the more his lower stomach tingled. Every night he went a little higher and every night it got a little more painful and frightening. After weeks of incremental gains, Tyrone seized his courage with both hands. He would keep counting no matter how painful it got. He opened the window next to his bed, took a deep breath, and began counting. He made it to a thousand with no difficulty. The tingling started around two thousand. He concentrated on the moon outside. Three thousand. He crossed his legs tightly and kept counting. Four thousand. He had just beaten his previous record. Five thousand. The tingling spread to his entire body and he began to shake. Six thousand. He gave a thrash and stopped. The final count was six thousand, one hundred.

The itchy electric tingle that Tyrone now felt was identical to the old sensation. How long would he be able to maintain this new routine before he would be forced to pull the plug? He massaged the Beretta through his pocket. *I could take this gun out right now and put a bullet through my brain. It would take me less than two seconds.* With this thrilling thought, he pushed open the doors to McDonald's.

As he had done the two previous nights, Tyrone bought nine Chicken McNuggets, a Biggie Fries, a Coke and a McFlurry. He didn't want the McFlurry but he bought it anyway. Everything had to be the same. He sat at the same table. The cashier had flung his dinner on the tray with no concern for trim. He frowned and put the loose fries back in the box. He would have to establish a standardized tray algorithm that he could apply to his future McDonald's dinners. As he manipulated the six discrete elements of his meal, he imagined that he was constructing an electrical circuit. His food was cold by the time he found a satisfactory arrangement: the McFlurry and the Coke lined up against the left edge of the tray, the closed Chicken McNuggets box directly in the center, the two little tubs of Barbecue sauce directly underneath the McNuggets, and the Biggie Fries against the right edge of the tray. Tyrone made sure that all the fries were neatly arranged in the mouth of the box. He breathed a sigh of relief, conveyed a limp fry into his mouth, and plunged back into *Sahara*.

The hand on his shoulder made Tyrone jump as if he had been tasered.

"Whoa! I didn't mean to startle you. I couldn't help but notice that you're reading *Sahara*. We've got a couple of Cussler fanatics over there. I thought I would come say hello."

It was the gigantic black chess player. Tyrone stared at him. Why was this man talking to him? The man with stringy hair also gazed at Tyrone.

"Why don't you come join us? I bet you know how to play chess. We could always use another player. My name is Don. It's a pleasure." Don extended a massive hand. "What's your name?"

"Tyrone."

"Come on, let me introduce you to the gang." Don led Tyrone over to the chess table.

"Eddie, Mr. Wong, Brett, Louis, Carlos, Gil...meet Tyrone."

The man with the long, thin, stringy hair extended a bony, papery hand in Tyrone's direction. Tyrone took it in his own limp, moist grip. The man's long, yellow fingernails raked against his flesh.

"Gil here is our president and fearless leader. Don't let appearances fool you. Gil is the third-ranked chess player in Florida and among the top forty players in the U.S. He has an Elo rating of...what is it these days...about twenty-three fifty?"

The whole table laughed conspiratorially. They all turned toward Gil, who shook his head regretfully. He began speaking. His voice had a heavy Brooklyn accent.

"You see this devil right here? Five years ago, at the Fort Lauderdale tournament, I find myself up against this devil in the first round. Don O'Brien, seventeen seventy-five."

"Seventeen *fifty*-five," replied Don with a big grin. He resembled an African Santa Claus: big, black, jolly, and powerful.

"Seventeen fifty-five." Gil's eyes darted across the floor as if tracking an invisible mouse. "Three weeks before the Fort Lauderdale tournament, I beat Arkady Schulpansky in New York to go over twenty-four hundred for the first time in my life. I was just a few controls away from my International Master title."

"There are only three thousand International Masters in the world and five hundred Grandmasters, two of whom live in Florida, and Gil's beaten them both," interrupted Mr. Wong with a proud smile.

Gil looked like he was going to cry. "So I walk over to the board and I see this barrel-chested negro—"

"Gil, we haven't been called Negroes for about thirty years now. It's African-American these days. Don't you read the newspapers?" Don, his eyes crinkling in amusement, winked at Tyrone, who immediately looked at the floor.

"So I try out a new opening..."

"The Dutch Stonewall," added Don crisply.

"The Dutch Stonewall. I'm barely paying attention. My mind is on Charnov in the next round. All of a sudden...pow!"

Gil shuddered as if he had just received an electric shock. He appeared to be reliving some deep trauma. Tyrone looked around at the other chess club members. They seemed to find Gil's disarray amusing.

"This devil captures my king pawn with his queen bishop! Next thing I know I lose the exchange and he's up three points, the pawn plus his rook to my bishop. And then, suddenly, I realize that it's over, I'm screwed! I lose! My rating dropped thirty points that day. I never got up over twenty-four hundred again. Meanwhile, this guy goes on to win the tournament." Gil's body went limp.

"Don's up to twenty-one eighty now, Gil," teased Mr Wong.

"Twenty-one eighty...he's only twenty points away from his Master title. I'll never see twenty-four hundred again and I know it. I keep telling this joker if he ever gets to Master he needs to put a little note on the certificate thanking Gil Weintraub!"

Gil shook his head disconsolately and threw up his hands in resignation. "I need another coffee!" He stood up and limped off towards the counter. Tyrone looked down at his feet. He wore filthy white socks with Wal-Mart house slippers that were at least two sizes too big. A plastic shopping bag bulging with what looked like paper trash dangled from one of his eczematous claws.

"Gil has never forgiven Don for that," confided Carlos with a big grin.

Don turned to Tyrone.

"Say, why don't you try Eddie on for size?" He indicated a shy-looking Asian teenager with lots of acne and thick glasses. After exchanging brief, uncomfortable glances, Tyrone sat down across from Eddie, who set up the board without making eye contact. They played three quick matches. Tyrone lost all three, succumbing to fool's mate on the third. To Tyrone's relief, Eddie made no attempt to talk to him. After the third game, Don came over to watch.

"Mind if I comment on the next match?"

Since Tyrone was playing white, it was his turn to move first. He advanced a rook pawn two spaces.

"OK, let me stop you right there. You see these squares right here in the center of the board? Those are the squares that you want to control. That's prime real estate. That's the South Beach of the chess board. Now, the easiest way to control South Beach is by parking a few pawns up there. Think of them as sentries with their guns trained on those center squares. If you don't do it, I know Eddie sure will. Why don't you move the pawn in front of your king up two spots instead of that rook pawn?"

Tyrone did as Don suggested.

"I would even go as far as to suggest that that should always be your first move, at least until you get a little more strategy under your belt."

Eddie moved his own king pawn up two spots.

"OK, now Eddie's mirroring you. He's not going to let you have South Beach without a fight."

Don went on to explain the basics of the game to Tyrone, walking him through his next two matches with Eddie. He occasionally gave counsel to Eddie as well.

With a few judicious pieces of advice from Don, Tyrone managed to win the fourth match. As Don was explaining to Eddie and Tyrone what they had done right and what they had done wrong in the match, Gil walked over to the table.

"Time for our match," he said to Don, with a broad, psychotic smile.

As Gil and Don set up the pieces, Eddie explained to Tyrone that the two of them finished up with a blitz match against each other every night. They had been keeping track of these matches for months. Gil and Don were by far the best players there. No one present had ever beaten either of them. Gil could still beat Don seven times out of eight with a normal time limit but when each of them had only five minutes on his time clock – blitz chess – they were almost evenly matched. His voice breathless with awe, Eddie told Tyrone that Gil was up forty-three matches to thirty-eight but that Don had won three in a row.

"Don is like...the Kimbo Slice of chess!" concluded Eddie.

The two gladiators sat down across from each other, shook hands, and began playing. Tyrone was amazed at how fast the two of them moved their pieces, hitting the clock briskly in machine-gun rhythm for the first ten moves on either side. Within thirty seconds they were in the middle of a pitched battle. Don's merry face had gone dead serious and suddenly he looked like what he was: a huge, powerful man with a sharp, trained mind. Gil had stopped fidgeting and gibbering. His face now looked presidential.

The game moved too fast for Tyrone to follow. The other club members occasionally gave each other appreciative nods after a particularly effective feint or thrust on Don or Gil's part.

Gil's time was running out faster than Don's. Here was Don's relative advantage. Eddie whispered in Tyrone's ear. "Gil has a hard time committing to a move without thinking it through. He wastes time in the midgame and ends up hurried in the endgame. That's where Don makes him pay!"

The crowd *oohed* when Don forced an unexpected exchange: his two rooks for Gil's queen. Carlos explained breathlessly to Tyrone that two rooks were considered slightly more valuable than an opponent's queen, but that at Don and Gil's level of play, such a simplistic system of judging the value of a given exchange was useless.

"Audacious and stylish...no safety net...that's how Don plays," whispered Carlos with admiration.

With only thirty seconds left on his clock, Gil went up a point, exchanging one of his knights for one of Don's rooks. Don shook his head in disgust. Six moves later, Gil checkmated him with a rook and a bishop.

Gil turned to Tyrone with a smile. "Looks like you brought me luck. I was beginning to think that this joker had my number for good! I sure hope you come back tomorrow night!" The club members laughed politely at Gil's pleasantry.

As they packed up their boards, Don took Tyrone aside.

"Hey, Tyrone, I'd like to give you something. It's in my car. Will you wait for me right here?"

Was Don trying to humiliate him?

The big man walked downstairs and jogged back up three minutes later holding a book and a travel chess set.

"This book will tell you everything you need to know about basic strategy. You can practice on this travel set. It's magnetic. You can keep the book, but I need the set back in two days. Is that okay?"

"Okay."

"Great! Well, I'll see you Friday then. Most of us are here every night from seven to ten. I'll be gone tomorrow but Gil and Eddie and most of the other guys will be here. Is that a deal?"

Don extended a massive hand. Tyrone had no choice but to shake it. As soon as everyone left, he ran to the corner of Ocean Drive and 15th Street. He was late.

Tyrone's gait was slack as he patrolled. He couldn't concentrate. The fragile machine that he had been carefully assembling for the past few days had been smashed. He wasn't supposed to talk to anybody! Don had ruined everything. It made him furious. Instead of faces he saw only featureless pink and brown blurs. After only two passes he shambled back to his car in defeat.

Had he been looking up, he would have noticed Sadie Vixen and Tabitha St. James drinking Mai Tais on the patio of the Starlight Hotel Bar.

37

Tyrone forced himself to spend the next morning and afternoon exactly as he had spent the day before, but something wasn't right. He waited over an hour for his nomads but they never showed up. He tossed their cold Nuggets to the grass disconsolately. The original Mexican was back at work at Pepper's and he glared at Tyrone again. The burrito didn't taste right. The Mexican had probably put rat poison in it. Tyrone forced himself to throw up in a bush on Washington Avenue.

He couldn't concentrate on *Sahara*.

Dinnertime arrived. Tyrone didn't want to go back to McDonald's. His routine had been disrupted. He would go back the next night to return Don's book and chess set and then never go back.

There was a Burger King on 12th St. Tyrone went in. Instead of McNuggets and a Coke he got a Chicken Sandwich and a Pepsi. They didn't fit on the tray. The fries were too crispy. Most of the tables were occupied by shady-looking blacks and Hispanics. There wasn't even a second story.

He finished his meal in five minutes. Reluctantly he took out Don's chess book and opened it. He skipped Chapter One, which explained the rules of chess, and went straight to Chapter Two. There were three basic techniques for taking a piece: forks, skewers, and pins.

Fucks, sewers, and penises! cackled a high-pitched Cronobacter voice.

"Shut up!" hissed Tyrone. The Mexican girls at the next table glanced at him.

He took out the travel chess set and tried out a few maneuvers. The principle behind forks, skewers, and pins was the same: attack two pieces simultaneously so the opponent has no choice but to lose one.

Chapter Three dealt with some common endgame scenarios: how to checkmate with a rook and a king, a pawn and a king, or two bishops and a king. Tyrone practiced these maneuvers as well.

Chapter Four analyzed the most common openings and their best variations. The most complex of the basic openings described in the book was something called the "Sicilian Dragon".

Tyrone decided on the spot that he would make the Sicilian Dragon his signature opening. He didn't need to work his way up to it. He was smart enough to skip the boring Two Knights and Ruy Lopez openings.

Tyrone felt like he was back in World Geography class. There were plenty of archaic-sounding names and techniques for him to memorize by rote. There were mini-biographies of a handful of the best chess players in history: Paul Morphy, Alexander Alekhine, Jose Capablanca, Tigran Petrosian, Bobby Fischer. Tyrone memorized their names and the order in which they had become world champions.

Sitting alone in the Burger King, memorizing the birthplaces of chess champions of the nineteenth century, Tyrone fantasized about becoming a grandmaster himself one day. He decided, with a vague sense of betrayal, that it couldn't hurt to go back to McDonald's the next night after all.

38

Tyrone entered the Cronesphere.

The short walk from McDonald's to Ocean Drive became a nightly metamorphosis. This stretch of Collins Avenue was a cosmic wormhole that connected two parallel dimensions. They resembled each other as a 9,999/10,000th scale model resembled the original. In that missing 1/10,000th lay what Tyrone had come, over the last few weeks, to consider the secret of existence. He could not say where exactly the Overworld ended and the Cronesphere began. It took him one cigarette and six hundred steps to walk from McDonald's to Ocean Drive. Which of those steps took him across the threshold? He didn't know, and it bothered him. One morning, as he sat on the Overworld beach watching crabs scuttle across the wet sand, a forgotten word imposed itself on his consciousness. That word was *littoral.* He had learned it in Coach MacGregor's class and never understood it. A littoral was neither land nor sea. It was both, and it was neither. Its borders were mobile and porous but no less real for being so. The stretch of Collins Avenue that connected McDonald's to Ocean Drive was a littoral. It was impossible to say *which* of the six hundred steps took him across the threshold. As he smoked and watched the crab crawl across the sand, he finally understood why. He couldn't identify the threshold was because *the threshold itself* didn't know where it began.

A sense of triumph overcame him.

Every night, Tyrone discovered something new about the Cronesphere. Events that occurred there also occurred in the Overworld. However, they possessed a different valence in each dimension. This was due to the fact that the Overworld was infinite and meaningless, whereas the Cronesphere was a tiny, fortified island in a sea of lava.

Tyrone's nightly passage into the Cronesphere was accompanied by a number of physical transformations. In two blocks his spine curved and he developed a crabwalk limp. His breathing deepened and his pulse slowed down.

Tyrone passed the Croatoan palm. Its long leaves shivered in the ocean breeze. In the Everglades, there was a tree called a Mangrove that grew nowhere else in the United States. He had read about the Mangrove trees of Florida in his new Almanac. The United States was the fourth-largest country in the world. Its surface area was 3.8 million square miles. Of those 3.8 million square miles, only eight hundred were in the Everglades. Yet it was only in the Everglades that the Florida Mangrove grew. It was a tiny, insignificant parcel of land at the very tip of the country. Yet it existed. It was connected to the rest of the country, yet it was separate. 3.8 million divided by 800 was exactly 4,750. The non-Everglades made up 4,749/4750ths of the United States. No Mangroves grew there.

The Mangrove was a halophyte. It planted its roots at the frontier of saltwater and freshwater. It provided a habitat for crabs, oysters, and sponges. The rich mangal mud trapped waterborne colloidal heavy metal particles. The Mangrove was a machine for creating something from nothing. What it created was a littoral.

39

Eddie slammed his knight down on b6 with a wicked grin.

"Checkmate!"

Tyrone grunted. His record against Eddie was now 2-24.

The Sicilian Dragon was beginning to show results. At one point, Tyrone had been up three points – one pawn plus the exchange – but Eddie had found a way to sneak his knight behind Tyrone's front line and fork him for a rook. Once the rook had been taken, Tyrone's defense crumbled, and he was mated within five moves.

Tyrone's opponent rolled up his mat and put it in his bag. It was time to go. It was almost ten and half of the club had already left.

"See you tomorrow, Tyrone," said Mr. Wong. "That dragon is going to start roaring soon...I can feel it."

Tyrone responded with a polite smile and walked downstairs. The first thing he did when he stepped out onto 17th Street was reach into his pocket and caress his Beretta. The touch of the cold steel sent a current of electricity from his fingers to the tips of his toes.

Hardly had he entered the Cronesphere when a purple stretch Hummer slid to a stop in front of him.

The door opened. For a split second, Tyrone thought the huge, bearded black man who stepped out was Don. A murmur of excitement went through the crowd.

The Atlantic Ocean began to boil. A red tidal wave appeared in the distance. It grew larger as it approached the shore. A loud rumbling filled Tyrone's ears. Cutrus screamed and flew off of his shoulder. The blood tsunami smashed into the delicate Mangroves of the Everglades. One by one the dead, ripped-up Mangroves sank to the bottom of the ocean until there was nothing on the horizon but still, glassy red water.

Tyrone blinked and looked around. The Cronesphere was gone. He was back in Miami-Dade County. Here the Nothing ruled. As he stared at the gold teeth sparkling through Kimbo Slice's beard, he understood that nothing had ever changed, ever, in the history of the universe, and nothing ever would.

It was time. He eased the gun out of his pocket. Next out of the Hummer was a cameraman wearing a white undershirt. He took up a position facing the vehicle and started filming. Soon the harlots started pouring out. They all steadied themselves on Kimbo Slice's hand or shoulder as they teetered down from the high-riding Hummer.

"So, you girls ready to get loose?"

Tyrone recognized the unctuous off-screen voice from the Kimbo Slice fights and the porn videos.

A short white man with a sandy goatee popped his head through the hatch and paused before leaping out with a big grin on his face.

"Ta-da!" he exclaimed as he landed in front of the camera with a caper.

Tyrone recognized the MILF Blaster.

The heavy gun began to slip from his sweaty palms. He wiped them on his shorts.

A black girl emerged. She wore no underwear. He caught a glimpse of her glossy labia. Two more male hardbodies stepped out. Kimbo Slice closed the door.

Tyrone scanned the Reality Dogz crew feverishly. Where was Trey?

He snuck closer to the crowd. Kimbo Slice was only ten feet away from him. He lifted the gun to waist level like Jack Ruby. The barrel pointed at Kimbo's stomach. No one noticed him.

He released the safety with his thumb. The cruel brute represented everything he hated: the eternal reign of the strong over the weak. He deserved to die.

He hesitated, then swiveled the gun over to the MILF Blaster. He was a sleazy pimp like Marcus: a man with no soul who lived only for pleasure. He deserved to die.

The two porn actresses next to him brayed in laughter. They were brainless, soulless whores who admired men like Trey, Kimbo and the MILF Blaster for their strength, their money, their cruelty and their ruthlessness, and rewarded them with their bodies. They deserved to die.

A drunk hardbody lurched in front of Tyrone. He put his hands to his mouth and bleated, "Kimboooo!" Tyrone pressed the barrel lightly against the back of the hardbody's belt. All he had to do was pull the trigger and the hardbody's pelvis would shatter into ten pieces. His life consisted of passively consuming the spectacle of cruelty, brutality, and domination that the Reality Dogz provided. He deserved to die.

Tyrone's hand trembled. He removed the Beretta from the hardbody's belt and held it to his own testicles. The

Cronobacters cheered. The person who most deserved to die, of course, was *he*: the useless supernumerary feature that added nothing to the world but one more pain-feeling node.

Tyrone wished he could magically freeze time and slowly walk among the frozen statues, putting a bullet in each one of their brains. He imagined owning a gun with an infinite number of bullets and walking up and down every street in Miami, shooting every single human being in his path. After cleaning Miami, he would walk from one end of the United States to the other like Johnny Appleseed, planting bullets in the brains of every last man, woman and child in existence.

The cortege began to move. Kimbo Slice dapped and hugged the bouncer, exactly as he always did in the videos. The girls giggled and posed for the camera, exactly as they always did in the videos. Everything happened in slow-motion.

They disappeared inside. The crowd dispersed, leaving Tyrone alone on the sidewalk. He had a sudden vision of a gigantic snake, fat and ancient, slithering and churning underground, radiating evil upwards from the bowels of the earth, an evil that infected and perverted Miami, transforming its residents into disgusting, degraded zombies, poisoning the soil and turning the vegetation black. The snake would not rest until the surface of the earth was as smooth and lifeless as the Moon. Tyrone's head throbbed in pain. A man wearing a hierophant's white robe and carrying a crooked dagger approached the snake in his underground Fortress of Suffering. It was Trey. He genuflected before the snake. Slowly the snake began to take human form. Arms and legs sprouted from a trunk as thick as an oak tree. His dark green skin turned brown and a coarse beard grew around his mouth.

The snake was DON.

40

It was hot in the car and the air smelled like stale semen. Tyrone's body was slick with perspiration. He could feel the droplets rolling down his chest and stomach but made no effort to wipe them.

He had been sitting in the driver's seat of his Pontiac for at least four days now. On the floor at his feet lay three PowerAde bottles full of urine. He blinked slowly.

It had been Don all along. Trey had never been anything but a messenger. The snake had sent him to Lacombe to bring Tyrone to Miami. "Don" was the terrestrial form the snake had taken to seduce him. It all made sense. Final Fantasy VII had been a coded message addressed to him all along. He was Cloud. Trey was Jenova-SYNTHESIS. Don was Sephiroth. The snake was looking for him at that very moment. It was up to him to redeem humanity.

"Kill the nigger!" shouted the familiar high-pitched voice.

With a dull, heavy movement, Tyrone unzipped his shorts and began stroking his penis.

Thirty seconds later, he winced as a feeble drop of clear ejaculate streaked with red emerged from the tip of his small penis and dribbled onto his T-shirt. He pulled his shorts back up. The Cronobacters chattered in his ears. Wiping his sweaty palm on his shorts, Tyrone lifted his Beretta and put the barrel in his mouth. The steel was hot. He fantasized about biting down on the gun barrel. He could imagine the crunch his teeth would make as they shattered into pieces and transformed his mouth into a jagged, bleeding cavity.

Tyrone lowered the gun back to his lap and looked out the window. Nothing ever moved on the top level of the parking garage. He wondered how much hotter it was inside the car than it was outside. It was probably over a hundred degrees inside the car. He didn't move to open the window.

41

Don knocked his king over in and shook his head in dismay.

"That makes six in a row!" exulted Gil.

Don grunted. "It looks like you've finally got my number for good."

Don shook Gil's hand and stood up to get a last coffee for the road. He was distracted. Tyrone's disappearance had affected his ability to concentrate. Every morning he woke up and scoured the newspapers to see if any bodies matching Tyrone's description had been found. Don knew what the bulge in Tyrone's pocket concealed and for whom it was intended. He had tried several times to find out where Tyrone lived, but even the most obliquely formulated question about his personal life spooked him. Was Tyrone homeless? He knew what the bulge in his other pocket was, too. Tyrone made no attempt to dissimulate the huge roll of hundred-dollar bills that he carried around. There were a lot of people in Miami who wouldn't think twice about committing murder for a bankroll like that.

He sat back down and sipped his McCafe White Chocolate Mocha. For the last week, he had racked his brains for a way to help Tyrone. He had no illusions about the boy. It would be a miracle if he made it to Christmas. Don finished his coffee and put away his chessboard and clock. The rest of the club members had gone home.

With no warning, the hairs on the back of his neck stood up. The first time this had happened, he nearly got his head blown off by a Viet Cong sniper. Something was wrong. He glanced over his shoulder.

Tyrone was sitting at the table behind him staring at him. His hollow gaze made Don's skin crawl. He looked like a corpse. He was skinny and haggard and his dark black skin had a waxy, grayish pallor.

Don forced himself to smile.

"Just the man I was looking for." He tried to sound casual. "Eddie's been missing his nightly dose of the Dragon."

Tyrone continue to stare through him with glazed, bloodshot eyes. A movement in Don's peripheral vision caused his gaze to flick down. Tyrone's hand was sliding into his pocket. Don hurriedly continued.

"I've got something for you. Now, I like Cussler as much as anybody else, but I have a feeling you might like this one even better."

Tyrone's hand froze. He made eye contact with Don for the first time. Don smiled, reached into his bag and extracted the biography of Bobby Fischer that he had bought for Tyrone a week earlier.

"Here. This is for you."

Tyrone blinked and stared at the book as if he had never seen such an object before.

"Go on. Take it."

Tyrone reached out and took the book with a wooden gesture.

"Thanks," he mumbled.

He stared at the book for a moment, then stood up and walked out of the McDonald's.

42

Tyrone staggered down Ocean Drive clutching his new book. It was almost midnight. On the other side of the palm trees the beach glowed white in the moonlight. He walked towards the water. A group of young people laughed at him in the distance. He stopped between two scrubby dunes and collapsed to the ground. The sand underneath the bush was humid. He took the gun out of his pocket and dropped it with loathing. It landed next to a gold Magnum condom wrapper. He wept.

As tears drained from his batrachian eyes and commingled with the sperm of well-hung hardbodies, an ancient memory surfaced. He was seven years old. His grandmother had bought him an old Atari 2600 game system at Goodwill. It had come with five games: Frogger, Indiana Jones, E.T., Vanguard, and Midnight Magic. Midnight Magic was his favorite. It was a pinball simulator. Every time the player reached a certain score, the color scheme changed. The first level was purple. The second level was blue. The third level was green. He never got past the green level. He had always believed that there was some cosmic logic behind the sequence of colors. Every time he advanced a level, he approached the answer to this sacred mystery.

Tyrone turned over so he was laying on his back. A few stars were visible through the orange skyglow of South Beach. He pulled down his shorts and began masturbating. He closed his eyes and fantasized that he was a Mangrove tree shooting roots down into the sand. He imagined that instead of sperm, his penis shot out propagules that would float in the air like dandelion seeds. If they landed on a hardbody, they would burn into his flesh like hot magnesium. But if they landed in a brackish tidepool, a Mangrove would sprout.

PART FOUR: BALLS DEEP

43

"Come on, dog. One more. One more. Give it to me. Come on."

Trey closed his eyes, exhaled, and pushed the 225-pound barbell up for the tenth and final rep of his superset. Kimbo guided the bar into the slots.

"Fuck yeah, dog. Good shit. You getting there."

Trey sat up and caught his breath. He looked at himself in Ryan's wall-length mirror. His chest and shoulders glistened with sweat. He had gained twenty pounds of lean muscle since arriving in Miami. He flexed one of his pectoral muscles. It twitched on his chest like a horse's rump. DMX's *X Gonna Give It To Ya* played on the CD player. He picked up the hand mirror that Ryan had left on the butterfly bench and snorted a line of cocaine.

Trey, Ryan and Kimbo Slice were all shirtless. Ferg and Trey both wore do-rags. All three men wore identical heavy gold chains around their necks. Underneath the words REALITY DOGZ, a naked woman who resembled Sadie lay face down with her ass in the air. A gigantic, snarling Bully Pit mounted her from behind. The woman's face bore an expression of sexual delight. Trey had designed the medallions himself.

Trey stood up and flexed his biceps in the mirror. He was shredded. Ryan stared at his torso from the butterfly machine.

"Damn, Trey, that V is incredible. You got the physique of Michael Phelps."

"Who the fuck is Michael Phelps?"

"You know...the Olympic swimmer."

Trey grunted and sat back down. "Play the song again."

"Damn, this nigga under your skin for real," said Kimbo.

"Just play it."

Ferg shook his head, changed the CD, and pressed play. A frown of visceral hatred creased Trey's face when he heard Roland Deep's syrupy voice rapping over the sluggish, repetitive beat.

I sell that dope out my house
I was watching Mickey Mouse I nearly burned down my house
Smoke dope in my house
Bitches smoke my weed they put my dick in they mouth
I sell dope and fuck bitches
I love to fuck bitches
You niggas all bitches
Gun in my hand I'm smoking dope with these bitches

Who be that
I be that
Nigga be that like bitch on my set

Who be that
I be that
Nigga be that we like all on deck

Bitch wanna smoke
Gun breathing smoke
Never be broke
Somebody call that bitch I said I we never be broke
Bitch smoke on my weed
I said bitch get that weed
Drinking on lean that bitch love drinkin lean

Kimbo Slice turned the CD player off and shook his head.

"Lil' short bus ass nigga can't even rhyme. There ain't even a hook. That's some Hickory Dickory Dock bullshit right there."

Trey snorted another line of cocaine, stood up and angrily freestyled.

Hickory Dickory Dock
That clock about to stop
Cause I'm a get my Glock
And bitch you gone get dropped!

Ferg grinned. "That's what I'm talking about, nigga. That old-school shit. Miami needs you, dog. This city went soft the day they banned Pits. Niggas still reeling from that shit...fighting with motherfucking Dogo Argentinos...fucking Tosa Inus...it's embarrassing, dog. Now we got this nigga...his ass liable to do a drive-by on a skateboard."

Ryan snorted a line. "We're gonna bam that pussy so hard he won't know what hit him! You just wait. *Balls Deep* is going to be banging from every trunk in Miami soon!"

Trey looked at his reflection and tuned Ryan out. He had played his cards right in Miami. On Ryan's recommendation, he invested Ray's money in a flipper condo in Homestead. Within three months he had doubled his principal. Sadie and his three other bitches brought in big-time cheddar escorting for him. Everything was arranged over the internet and the money was paid into his bank account via direct deposit. The clients were all Japanese. It had been Ryan's idea. He never even touched cash anymore. It all went straight to real estate. The number on his bank statement got bigger every month. He drove an Escalade and lived in a luxury apartment on Collins Drive. He had a white bearskin rug. His mixtape, *Deep In Tha Streetz*, was due to drop in two weeks. The lead single, *Balls Deep*, was a brutal dis of Roland Deep. Ryan had invested bookoo cash in the project. He bought fifteen beats from the legendary DJ Kutthroat, a producer out the Melph projects in New Orleans who had worked with Soulja Slim, Mr. Serv-On, and C-Murder in the No Limit/Cash Money heyday. Ferg recruited a few up-and-coming young spitters from Hialeah and even rapped with him on one track. Ryan had lined up a regional distribution deal for forty thousand albums. Everything was coming together for *Deep In Tha Streetz* to blow up.

But something didn't feel right. He couldn't put his finger on what it was. All he knew was that the longer he stayed in Miami, the worse it got. This Roland Deep shit, for example. Back home he would have run up on Roland Deep by now. In Miami he did nothing. Everyone and everything around him was water whipped. DJ Kutthroat had sold out that old New Orleans murder sound in favor of the new Miami sound. The codeine sound. The new rap sounded like someone had poured sticky syrup all over it. Trey hated it. No matter how hard he tried, he couldn't rap right over these slow-ass new beats. It was as if someone had poured sticky syrup all over him too. He was tired of fucking porn girls. Even the inside of their pussies felt the same. On his last Whiteasaurus Rex shoot, he had to close his eyes and fantasize about Rhonda's nasty old cunt before he could pop. He glanced at himself in the mirror again. He looked like a fag with his gym muscles and his tan. Miami had made him soft. He wiped off his forehead and threw the towel down in anger.

"Where I come from, when you bam somebody, he stay bammed, ya heard me?"

Ferg did a leg press and shook his head in the gesture of a ghetto sage. "Slow your roll, dog. I feel you, Trey...but them hood rules good for two things, getting a nigga locked up and getting a nigga killed."

"What the fuck, Ferg? Didn't I just hear you say that Miami was soft? Didn't those words just come out your damn mouth?"

"Those were them old days. They call 'em old for a reason."

"Motherfucker, *you* old."

"Excuse me, gentlemen," chuckled the MILF Blaster. "If I may interrupt your discussion of the finer points of the G-Code...It just so happens that I had a conversation with my cousin Joshua today about our little beef with Roland Deep. He gave me a very interesting history lesson. Do either of you remember what happened between Vanilla Ice and Suge Knight?"

Kimbo Slice laughed. "That crazy nigga hung old boy out the window by his ankles til he signed his rights over to Death Row."

"Bingo. So check this out. What's keeping us from doing the same thing?"

Kimbo chuckled and shook his head. Ryan continued.

"No, seriously! We got the muscle. We got the money. We got the brains. Joshua graduated from fucking Stanford. He's half Jewish and half Greek. For a lawyer that's like being half Tupac and half Vladimir Putin. I asked him if he could draw up a contract similar to Suge's. He just laughed. He said he could write it in about ten minutes. All he does all day is write fucking contracts to trick people a lot richer and a lot smarter than Roland Deep out of their money. Interesting, huh?"

Trey nodded his head vigorously. "Let's do it. Fuck that bitch-ass bitch. I'm tired of sitting around."

Kimbo shook his head. "Do what, dog? Hang him by his ankles out the window?"

"Just scare the motherfucker...tie him up, show him the chrome."

"I don't know," said Kimbo. "Sounds risky to me. Can't the bitch nigga just turn around and sue us?"

Ryan grinned and shook his head. "Joshua swears he won't be able to. Don't ask me how. He funnels the money through Panama or something. This is why Telly Friedman keeps him on retainer. He knows what he's doing. It's foolproof. We just have to scare Roland into signing a few papers and we're talking six figures, maybe seven. That fool sells a lot of records."

Kimbo shook his head. "It still sounds risky to me."

"Let me remind you of the first rule of investment. Reward is proportional to risk. Think about it. Once the street hears how the Reality Dogz clowned this punk, *Deep In Tha Streetz* is going to sell a hundred thousand copies in a week!"

"Yeah? And what if the lil nigga decides to ride?"

Trey jabbed his finger into the air. "That pussy won't do shit."

"How you know?"

Trey stared at Kimbo Slice. "I looked into his eyes. That boy is softer than soap powder."

"Maybe so...but what about his cousins? What about his dawgs? You looked in their eyes too?" Kimbo grunted and did another leg press.

"And what about his granny and his fucking goldfish? Come on, Ferg, you know the rules! We ride on beef! Fuck!"

Trey flung a ten-pound weight to the floor in frustration and snorted a line. Ryan grabbed the mirror and snorted another line as well.

"You know what your problem is, Ferg?" said Ryan. "You don't do enough blow."

Ferg grinned. "You right about that. You Caucasians feeling some type of way tonight." He grunted and did another leg press. "I'm just fucking with y'all. Let's pay the nigga a visit." He took out his phone and dialed a number. "Hey Christelle...what's up, baby girl...listen, baby, I need some intel...that's right, baby...I need to know if the nigga Roland Deep getting his grill cleaned anytime soon down by your spot...alright, get me back."

Kimbo hung up. "That's my girl Christelle. She work at the dentist's office where our boy gets his grill tightened. She checking the schedule right now."

The phone rang. Ferg answered.

"What's up...is that right....good work, baby girl...hell yeah I'ma holla at you...stay sexy, boo."

A grin broke across Ferg's face. "We serve the lil' nigga Thursday morning at eleven."

44

Scott Karpis, the Smoothie King manager, watched with exasperation as Tyrone prepared a Grape

Expectations smoothie for a customer. Two weeks had passed and Tyrone had still not memorized the routine. *Turbinado,* thought Scott with frustration as he watched Tyrone hesitating over the little tubs of smoothie powder. *How fucking hard is it to remember the turbinado?* Scott cursed under his breath when Tyrone gingerly put down the half-finished smoothie and double-checked the laminated ingredient list that hung by a string from the counter. Scott would have fired Tyrone after three hours if he hadn't been a friend of Don's. He was that slow. He could not seem to understand that when there were a lot of customers it was necessary to move quickly. No matter how many people were waiting in line, Tyrone could not help himself from slowly measuring each spoonful instead of just eyeballing it. If the proportions were not perfect, he became visibly anxious. But Scott owed Don about ten thousand favors so he let Tyrone stay.

Next to Tyrone, Jimmy prepared a Peanut Power without a single wasted gesture. Scott nodded. Jimmy was a baller. He had been working at Smoothie King for a year. When Jimmy was moving fast, he did not bother to look at the dozens of little tubs of powders and extracts. His muscle memory guided his hand to the spoons and he flung the ingredients in without measuring. The amounts were almost always correct and the customers couldn't tell the difference anyway.

Jimmy shook his head when he saw that Tyrone had been wrong-footed by a Grape Expectations for the second time that morning. *Come on, dog. Turbinado. Hustle, homie!* Tyrone never hustled. It bothered Jimmy. He stole an incredulous glance at Tyrone's sneakers. He was fascinated and horrified by the dirty gray Velcro K-Mart kicks Tyrone wore. How was it even physically possible for a young black man to wear shoes that ugly? Jimmy couldn't bend his mind around it. He always had a fresh pair of J's on his feet. It was like...a law. He had over fifty pairs of Nikes at home in Hialeah.

The door jingled open. It was his girl Breanne. Jimmy smiled. He felt naked without his grill but Mr. Karpis wouldn't let him wear it at work. Breanne always came in looking tight and today was no exception. She wore Prada sunglasses and a red dress that hugged her dump truck ass and huge fake tits. Her caramel skin was the exact same color as the turbinado powder. As always, she was accompanied by her boyfriend Chaz, a jacked Cuban with a pencil beard and an Escalade. They smiled when they saw him.

"Good morning, Jimmy," purred Breanne.

"One Angel Food for my angel and one Chocolate Hulk with Yohimbe Extract for my big dawg, coming up."

Jimmy whipped up their smoothies in record time. Chaz dapped him and tossed two dollars into the tip jar.

Jimmy nudged Tyrone and pointed to Breanne's ass as it wobbled out of the store.

"You see that ass, Tyrone? Every time she come in I put a little extra ice cream in her Angel Food...that ass is just going to get bigger and bigger. It's like...my *project*, dog. I'ma wait till it's just a little juicier and then I'ma make my move. Chaz always be hitting that Yohimbe. Breanne must be a freak between them sheets. Lucky motherfucker. You know why we carry Yohimbe, don't you? Cause of Samuel L. Jackson. No shit. He used to come in here and special request it. Now they sell it in all six hundred locations." Jimmy chuckled. "All so Samuel L. Jackson can get it up."

The couple got into Chaz's Escalade. Sunlight glinted off the hood ornament as they pulled out of the parking lot. Jimmy shook his head in admiration. "Peep the Escalade. Chaz be rolling. It's all about the paper, dog, all about the paper." He nodded with philosophy. "Man, I got McDonald's on the brain." He loped over to the protein bars and idly rifled through them. "Yo, Tyrone, you *can't* tell me you didn't notice my new sneakers, dog! Got them yesterday. Set me back a bill and a half. Take a look at that yellow piping. Ain't that beautiful?" He bent over and theatrically dusted off his new LeBrons. "Ain't it? Come on, negro, admit it! I know you secretly wish you had a pair of kicks like these!"

Tyrone did not respond. What on earth was he supposed to say to something like that? The door opened and a group of three men walked in. Jimmy did a double take.

"That's Kimbo Slice, dog!" he hissed.

Tyrone could barely hear him over the rioting Cronobacters. He wasn't looking at Kimbo Slice. Instinctively he reached into his pocket. His Beretta wasn't there. He had left it on the beach.

Trey wore a Miami Hurricanes baseball cap with a black do-rag underneath. He had a new tattoo of a fifty-dollar bill on the side of his muscular neck. Tyrone had never seen him up close and his features looked even more handsome and evil than they did from a distance. He blinked. Before he knew what was happening, Trey was standing right in front of him.

The bad guy opened his mouth to speak. His gold teeth sparkled under the fluorescent light.

"Gimme a vanilla Hulk, dog. Forty ounce. And toss a shot of Yohimbe in there, ya heard me?"

The chattering and cackling of the Cronobacters became a roar. Tyrone closed his eyes and gripped the counter. From far away, faintly at first, then more insistently, like thunder rolling over the horizon, a new voice began to speak. It was deep, mellifluous, and familiar.

"Leave...that...boy...alone!"

The sudden silence of the Cronobacters was deafening. At that instant, Tyrone realized that they had never gone completely quiet since Trey killed him the first time. It was as if he had been sitting in a room with the vacuum cleaner on for so long that he no longer noticed it. The familiar voice continued against the new background of silence. He still couldn't place it

"That's better. Tyrone, come talk to me for a minute. I'm in the stockroom. Tell your customer you need to refill the Yohimbe."

"I need to refill the Yohimbe."

"Good. Now come rap with a brother."

Tyrone walked to the stockroom in a trance. Sitting on the ice cream freezer was Samuel L. Jackson. He was dressed as Jules from Pulp Fiction.

"Young man, I'll make this quick. Do you know what Yohimbe extract is?"

"It's a bark. They get it from a West African tree called the Yohimbe tree. It dilates the blood vessels in the penis, making erections harder and longer-lasting."

"Smart young man. They get it from Liberia to be precise. Only place in the world it grows. I have Liberian origins too, you know. Krahn tribe. Our people been gnawing on that bark for millennia. As far as you or I know, we owe our existence to that nasty motherfucking bark. Let me give you a speculative history lesson. Great-great-great-grandpappy Augustus probably stopped and had himself a chew when he was on his way to bang Grandma Ooga-Booga. Remember, old Augustus owned the biggest sugar plantation in the country. His ass even had a daguerreotype camera. Augustus was *balling*. Those hot to trot Liberian bitches were on a brother's dick like flies on shit. Right?"

"Right."

"You're damn right I'm right. Now riddle me this. What if it so happened that Gus already stopped in to see Grandma Ethel and Grandma Mae that afternoon? You dig me, son? Without a little all-natural dilation, old Augustus can't get it up and *you* don't get born."

"But I'm not really related to Augustus Washington. That was a paranoid delusion."

Samuel L. Jackson nodded his head.

"You're a smart young man. That's correct. I'm a hallucination myself. But I'm here to help you. I got a story for your ass. It happened right here on South Beach. One day, I fucked up and got two of my bitches confused. Melita and Melinda. I scheduled dates with both of them on the same day. Now, Melita and Melinda are not your ordinary ladies. I call Melita 'The Octopus' and Melinda 'The Shop Vac'. You feel me, young man? You got a date with either one of these women, you going home five pounds lighter and with nuts like frozen acorns. So I figure all I have to do is double my daily dose of Yohimbe and I'm straight. Only my philandering ass fucks up. I meant to increase my dose from twenty milligrams to forty milligrams. Only somehow I end up taking four hundred milligrams of that shit."

"Hey youngblood...you get lost back there?" called Trey from the front of the store.

"Don't worry," continued Samuel L. Jackson. "He doesn't recognize you. Shaving your dome was a smart move. That motherfucking glasses strap, on the other hand..." Samuel L. Jackson chuckled. "I'll make this fast. That shit made me impotent. It fried my jimmy. The only way I can fuck now is if I inject little Samuel with Alpostradil. Me, Samuel L. Jackson, the Guinness highest-grossing film star of all time...impotent." He shook his head in dismay. "Thousands of bitches out there begging for it and I can't fuck any of them. So, here's what you're going to do. You're going to put two full grams of Yohimbe powder in that motherfucker's smoothie. His ass is going to stroll out of here feeling like Tyrannosaurus Rex and tomorrow he's going to be feeling like Dink the Little Dinosaur. Now dap a brother and handle your business, young man."

Samuel L. Jackson smiled and held out his fist. Tyrone dapped him. He disappeared. Tyrone spooned two grams of Yohimbe extract into Trey's cup and walked back out. Jimmy was trying desperately to appear cool as he prepared Kimbo Slice's Strawberry Hulk at the other blender.

Tyrone mixed all the ingredients and poured the thick, off-white Hulk from the blender into the Styrofoam cup.

Trey took it and squinted at him. "You sure you put all my protein in there, youngblood?"

Tyrone maintained eye contact with Trey. His fear was gone. The hallucination of Samuel L. Jackson was right. He didn't recognize him. Tyrone took a deep breath and spoke. His words rang like the bells of St. Peter's in the Cronobacter-free silence.

"Sir, there's enough protein in there to create two or three new species in a petri dish." .

Jimmy shot him a shocked, pop-eyed underlook from the other register.

For a split second, incomprehension flickered over Trey's handsome, cruel features. One of his blue eyes squinted a little bit as he scrutinized Tyrone's face. His mouth softened into a casual smirk. "You alright, youngblood...stay in school."

He tossed a five-dollar bill into Tyrone's tip basket and walked out of the store with his toaster-sized Smoothie.

Tyrone picked up one of the flyers the MILF Blaster had left on the counter.

Reality Dogz Entertainment Inc. presents
Trey-Deuce AKA The Whi-T-Rex
DEEP IN THA STREETZ
FEATURING special guests Kimbo Slice, Fat Ron, and the MILF Blaster

The photo on the flyer was of Trey grimacing and aiming a pistol at the viewer. Underneath him was a fuzzy screen cap of the brutal uppercut from the KIMBO VS. DREADS fight as well as a smaller photo of a sweaty and flushed MILF Blaster giving a double thumbs-up to the camera as he sodomized a faceless blonde. There was a star pasted over the pornographic part of the image. Tickets were twenty-five dollars.

The three men disappeared out the front door of the Smoothie King and got into a black SUV.

"Peep the Hummer!" said Jimmy in awe. He picked up a flyer. "Damn, dog, you *know* I'ma be at *that* concert!"

45

As Trey sipped his Smoothie and gazed at Biscayne Bay through the window of the Hummer, he finally realized what was wrong with Miami.

He had no enemies.

He had no enemies!

He had only friends. Before coming to Miami, he had never had a friend in his life. Friends were bullshit. Friends meant compromises. DJ Kutthroat with his syrupy beats. Ryan with his investments. Even Ferg with his Sun Tzu and his bullshit street wisdom. If he wasn't careful, he would end up being fucking friends with Roland Deep.

Ferg was right about one thing. Miami died the day they banned Pits. No wonder Trey had to snort so much cocaine. Just living in Miami was like being slowed down on codeine. He thought back to Scarface. His life had changed forever the moment he released Scarface in the ring for the first time. The Pit shot out from behind the scratch line and sank his teeth into his opponent's throat with no hesitation. It was beautiful. For forty minutes the two dogs tore at each other until they were both too exhausted and ripped up to move. Trey drove home that night a new man. He had never respected another living being as much as he respected Scarface. That was the only way for a man to live. What the fuck was he doing in a city where it was illegal to own a Pit Bull?

The fact was that Trey felt old. Miami had aged him. Even at this very moment, when he and his boys were about to run up on Roland Deep, he felt bored and tired. He took another sip of his smoothie. It didn't taste right. Fuck, nothing tasted right anymore.

The parking lot of the dentist's office was in the back. Kimbo cruised in next to Roland Deep's Escalade. He pointed at the chrome SpongeBob Squarepants hood ornament and nodded. “Our boy’s here.”

“Ski masks on,” said Ryan. He was grinning like a Cub Scout with a dick in his mouth. Trey’s heart pounded in his chest. It felt good. He couldn’t remember the last time his pulse rate had cracked sixty beats per minute. He snorted a quick line off the dashboard and pulled on his mask.

The back door opened and Roland Deep emerged. He wore black skinny jeans, leopard print sneakers, fluorescent green sunglasses, and a black Rick Owens T-shirt that hung to his knees. An extra-large double Styrofoam cup completed the ensemble. He looked tiny next to the huge, fat bodyguard in a white T-shirt that walked behind him.

Trey and Kimbo burst out of the black truck with their guns drawn.

“In the car! Get in the fucking car!”

The cup of lean dropped to the pavement. Ten seconds later, Roland Deep and the bodyguard were handcuffed in the back of the Hummer with black hoods over their heads.

Their guns and phones went in Biscayne Bay.

By the time they arrived at the abandoned warehouse in Overtown that Ferg had scouted, Trey’s shirt was soaked in sweat and he felt like his heart was going to explode.

Something was fucking wrong.

Kimbo sat the bodyguard against the wall. His big white eyes bugged out against the dark black of his skin. Sweat beads rolled down his bald head. The small warehouse was illuminated by a single naked bulb hanging from the ceiling. It hurt Try’s eyes. He winced. What the fuck was wrong with him? *Hold your shit together, dog*, he willed himself.

He marched Roland Deep to a folding chair in the center of the room and removed his hood.

Up close, Roland Deep was an ugly motherfucker. His left cheek was covered in a tattoo of SpongeBob Squarepants holding a pistol. His chin was tiny and his evasive frog eyes looked like two wet marbles. As Trey stared at him, Roland Deep's face began to blur at the edges. Trey shifted his gaze to the aluminum baseball bat he had brought to scare Roland Deep into signing the papers. The holographic DON MATTINGLY logo sparkled under the naked light bulb. It was fascinating. His whole body throbbed. He closed his eyes.

He was back in Bogalusa. The pungent smell of dog blood, cigarette smoke, and sawdust mounted to his nostrils. His ears rang with the sound of snarling Pits, cheering dogmen, and tearing flesh.

"Turn!" shouted the referee.

Trey dragged Scarface back to the scratch line for the twentieth time. Blood poured out of dozen of lacerations in his neck, muzzle, and chest. One of his front legs was broken and he could barely stand up. Yet still he scratched. Corner. Trey rubbed Vaseline all over Scarface's head. Through a tear in his lip he could see a single white, pin-sharp tooth. Light glittered off of it.

A soft, arrogant voice caused him to open his eyes. It was Roland Deep.

"You drunk, motherfucker?"

"Trey, you alright, dog?" barked Kimbo. He stared at Trey with hard, alert eyes.

"*Dog* is right," said Trey, nodding his head.

"Ryan, show this boy the contract," ordered Kimbo Slice. "Let's get this shit over with." His eyes remained on Trey.

Ryan grinned and handed Roland a sheaf of papers. The young rapper snorted.

"What the fuck is that?"

"That's the piece of paper you're going to sign. It cedes all rights from..."

Trey wandered away from Roland, slumped down Indian-style on the floor and held his head in his hands. Everyone stared at him. The momentarily forgotten contract hovered in midair between Ryan and Roland Deep.

"Trey...what's going on, bro? Let's do this!" said Ryan.

Trey's voice was slurred when he spoke.

"Roland...you thought you was top dog in the Game...but the Game don't work that way. The Game is like a forest. Some motherfuckers be up in them trees...other motherfuckers down there on that ground..." Trey stopped and frowned. His face bore an expression of perplexity. "I mean...up in that water..."

Roland Deep addressed Kimbo Slice with a smirk. "What the *fuck* is your boy talking about? He can't even stand up straight. Y'all some Pop Warner motherfuckers. I'm out this bitch. Untie me, fool."

Trey lurched to his feet, then froze. Something appeared to sag inside him. His bulging, unfocused eyes stared into the void. The bat dangled from one of his hands.

"Trey, you alright?" said Ryan.

"This boy done lost his balls on y'all," said Roland Deep. "Untie me."

"Be cool, Trey!" shouted Kimbo Slice.

Roland Deep pressed. "Your boy rocking that fishbelly hue. Better luck next time. Now untie me before I get salty for real, nigga."

Trey spun around and slammed the Don Mattingly bat into Roland Deep's mouth with a loud crunch. Gold- and diamond-encrusted teeth scattered across the ground like Jolly Ranchers exploding from a pinata. Roland Deep slumped forward. Blood poured from his wrecked mouth.

"What are you doing, Trey?" shouted Ryan in a panicked, high-pitched voice. "You weren't supposed to hit him! He hasn't signed the papers yet! You fucking killed him!"

Trey turned to Ryan. His eyes were bright red with burst blood vessels.

"Stop...fucking...smiling!" he bellowed.

"What the fuck are you talking about? Trey, chill out, bro!"

Trey brought the baseball bat down on Ryan's skull as hard as he could. It dimpled like a hard-boiled egg under a thumb. The MILF Blaster collapsed to the ground still clutching Joshua's contract.

"What the fuck!" shouted Roland Deep's bodyguard.

Kimbo Slice lifted his pistol half a second too late. Trey had just enough time to swivel around and club him on the wrist with the Don Mattingly bat. The gun clattered to the ground. Kimbo's left shoulder came up. Trey had attended enough of Ferg's training sessions with the Dutch mixed martial artist Bas Rutten to know that the raised left shoulder indicated that an anvil-like right uppercut was coming. He juked left as Kimbo's fist swooshed up into the void, missing his jaw by less than an inch. Try swung the bat and caught Kimbo on the shoulder with a glancing, off-balance blow. The big man turned around. Hatred burned in his black eyes. He charged. Trey thought back to Mike Tyson's Punch-Out. To thwart the Bald Bull bum rush, you had to press the punch button at the precise moment Bull was about to cream you. Trey swung the bat over his head in an arc. It came down on Kimbo's iron dome like a Scud missile. The brawler fell forward to the ground, tried to get up, and fell down again. His bell was fucking rung.

Trey flung the bat to the concrete and pounded his chest with his fist. "You're down, boy! Where's your break stick now?" Kimbo moaned. Trey took the Glock from his pants. The big man crawled forward on wobbly arms.

Everything suddenly made sense.

"Don't shoot!" screamed the bodyguard.

Trey leaned over and roared in his friend's ear, "Bitch, this pit ALWAYS gone scratch!"

He put the gun to the back of the do-rag and pulled the trigger. Kimbo Slice's brains blew through his forehead and onto the floor like a MILF Blaster nut.

THE END

www.ingramcontent.com/pod-product-compliance
Lightning Source LLC
LaVergne TN
LVHW091129080826
845145LV00008B/2098

* 9 7 8 0 9 8 9 5 0 7 4 0 0 *